THE SCANDALOUS LYDIA WICKHAM

ELIZA AUSTIN

B

Boldwood

First published in 2014 as *Lydia Wickham's Journal*. This edition published in Great Britain in 2024 by Boldwood Books Ltd.

Copyright © Eliza Austin, 2014

Cover Design by Colin Thomas

Cover Photography: Colin Thomas

A CIP catalogue record for this book is available from the British Library.

Paperback ISBN 978-1-83603-305-9

Large Print ISBN 978-1-83603-306-6

Hardback ISBN 978-1-83603-304-2

Ebook ISBN 978-1-83603-307-3

Kindle ISBN 978-1-83603-308-0

Audio CD ISBN 978-1-83603-299-1

MP3 CD ISBN 978-1-83603-300-4

Digital audio download ISBN 978-1-83603-302-8

Boldwood Books Ltd
23 Bowerdean Street
London SW6 3TN
www.boldwoodbooks.com

1

_____

Elizabeth Darcy stood beneath Pemberley's portico with her husband, waving until the departing carriages disappeared from view.

'At last I have you to myself again,' Will said as he took his wife's elbow and guided her back into the house. 'Not that I don't enjoy entertaining—'

Lizzy choked on a laugh. 'You are the most taciturn person on God's earth and you hate putting yourself to the trouble.'

'There might once have been some truth to that accusation.' Will bestowed an adoring look upon Lizzy. 'But since marrying you, I am a changed character.'

'That assertion might soon be put to the test.' Lizzy nodded towards the small sitting room where her sister Lydia sat beside the window, staring vacantly into space. 'Poor Lydia! She probably feels awkward now that the rest of my family have left. We should join her and try to cheer her up a little.'

'And so we shall... shortly.'

Will took Lizzy's hand and headed for the stairs, compelling Lizzy to suppress a smile as she willingly went along with him. They bypassed the sumptuous bedchambers and headed for the nursery floor above, where their eighteen-month-old son Marcus was banging a spoon and bouncing on his seat as Nanny Pocock read aloud from a book featuring lurid pictures of farmyard animals. Lizzy and Will shared an indulgent smile as Marcus pointed to a picture of a sheep and made a loud baaa-ing sound. Then he giggled wildly and repeated the process.

'He's very advanced,' Will said, his voice laced with paternal pride.

Lizzy flexed a brow. 'Because he thinks he's a sheep?'

'Because he can recognise one.'

This time Lizzy's smile defied her best efforts to contain it.

'As your aunt didn't tire of reminding us right up until her departure half an hour ago, her own grandchild, when it arrives in a few months, will excel at everything.'

'Undoubtedly.' Will smiled as he watched Marcus poring over the pictures of the animals and gesticulating with his spoon. 'But you must agree that Lady Catherine is less austere since Sir Marius came back into her life and she permitted her daughter to marry Asquith.'

'No one could be happier for them than me, although I do feel for poor Charlotte. Mr Collins did not approve of the alliance and advised Lady Catherine against permitting Anne to marry Asquith.'

Will snorted. 'And now he must make peace with a man whom he dislikes but who will one day be the master of Rosings.'

'Papa!'

Marcus tottered over to them on chubby legs, waving arms and spoon. Will swooped his son from the floor and tossed him in the air. Marcus squealed with laughter and demanded more. Fearful of his breakfast making a reappearance, Lizzy advised caution.

'We had best do as Mama tells us,' Will said in a theatrical whisper.

When Marcus realised no further tossing would be forthcoming, he reached out his arms to Lizzy. She took him from Will and balanced him on her hip.

'How have you occupied your time this morning?' Lizzy asked, breathing in his sweet, baby aroma as she pushed a downy curl away from her son's eyes.

'Baaa,' Marcus replied with great enthusiasm.

'We have been revisiting our favourite book, ma'am,' Nanny Pocock informed them. 'Master Marcus never tires of it.'

'Moo,' Marcus said in agreement.

'Are the twins asleep?' Lizzy asked, grinning at the farmyard impressions.

'Yes, ma'am.'

Lizzy passed Marcus back to Nanny and she and Will crept into the adjoining room. A second nurse sat in a chair, supervising the two sleeping infants. When she saw them, she put her sewing aside, stood up and bobbed a curtsey. The proud parents peered at the babies, Arabella and Spencer, indistinguishable but for the colour of their layettes. Lizzy sensed Will's fierce pride and gently touched his hand. His responding smile was one of molten tenderness, reinforcing Lizzy's opinion that his growing family had rewarded him with the peace of mind that had eluded him since assuming responsibility for Pemberley.

Satisfied that all was order and contentment in the nursery, but for a lively toddler with aspirations of becoming a sheep, Will and Lizzy made their way back downstairs.

'You seem very content with your family,' Lizzy said, giving voice to her earlier thought.

'I would be more content if you would have the goodness to produce our children without frightening me half to death.'

'It was hardly my fault if Marcus decided to give as much trouble as possible.'

'As always, Mrs Darcy, you are given to understatement. Marcus almost cost you your life, and then... twins.' Will shook his head, struggling to articulate his feelings. 'I was terrified for you once Sanford detected two heartbeats.'

'And yet birthing them was perfectly straightforward.'

'Perhaps it was, but no one will ever convince me that I didn't age ten years on the night they were born.'

'Ask Dominic if you doubt my word.'

'Since marrying my sister, Sanford has forgotten all about us.'

'If you're implying that he's neglecting his patients just because Georgie is herself increasing, I refuse to believe it. He is the most dedicated medical man of my acquaintance.'

'Even so, his first concern is now for Georgiana. I should have something to say on the matter if I thought it was otherwise.'

When they reached the small salon, Lydia was no longer in occupation of it.

'Where can she have got to?' Lizzy asked.

'Stop worrying about Lydia.' Will touched Lizzy's face and cupped her cheek in his palm. 'She will recover her spirit now that she doesn't have your mother fussing over her, constantly bemoaning the loss of her favourite son-in-law. She merely needs time.'

Lizzy spread her hands. 'I never imagined I would have cause to regret Lydia's *good* behaviour. When I consider how she used to conduct herself...'

'She has grown up.'

'Is it to be wondered at? Married to a man of Wickham's ilk, then losing a baby and being widowed when she is still only eighteen.' Lizzy exhaled a frustrated breath. 'But my point is that Wickham died over a year ago now. She has been fussed over and cossetted by Mama, pitied and indulged, ever since. With only Mary still at Longbourn, I had hoped she would realise that her widowed state will afford her more latitude than that of an unmarried daughter.'

'What a very pragmatic view, Mrs Darcy.'

Lizzy pursed her lips. 'I know my sister. Or thought I did.'

'We all deal with grief differently. Just because society dictates a period of one year's mourning and that time is now up for Lydia, it doesn't mean she will simply shake off her loss and return to the way she once was.'

'You're right, of course.'

'I am?' Will elevated a brow. 'You're not usually so compliant.'

Lizzy smiled. 'That's because you enjoy it when I take issue with you. Not many people have ever dared.'

Lizzy thought of Miss Bingley. In spite of the trouble she had tried to cause between Will and Lizzy two years previously, she still hung on Will's every word whenever they met.

'I don't need to concern myself about your candour, or lack thereof,' Will said with a wry smile.

'I think Lydia feels guilty because she told me not long before Wickham was killed that she had finally come to see him for what he really was,' Lizzy mused. 'Perhaps a small part of her is glad to be rid of him, but she isn't ready to face up to the fact yet.'

'Your father told me that Mary is very outgoing and assertive nowadays.'

Lizzy nodded. 'You cannot have avoided hearing about the new curate in Meryton. Mama spoke endlessly of her expectation of their soon marrying.'

Will smiled. 'Your mother excels at matchmaking.'

'From what Papa told me, the match will suit both parties. I gather Mr Peterson is a younger version of Mr Collins; very pompous and self-assured. And Mary was the only one of us who saw anything to admire in Mr Collins.'

'She seemed awfully keen to leave here this morning; Mary, that is.' Will smiled. 'Perhaps now I understand why.'

'And Lydia asked to stay. I shall encourage her out of her introspective state, you just see if I do not.'

'I don't in the least doubt it. But be aware, Lizzy, she is a very different person to the shameless flirt I first met in Hertfordshire three years ago. There is some depth to her thinking nowadays and I doubt whether her only consideration is to remarry.'

'I am not my mother and won't try to introduce her to every single young gentleman of my acquaintance. As far as I'm concerned, she can stay at Pemberley indefinitely. Good society will be beneficial for her. She has Jane just ten miles away and Kitty and her major are also close by.'

'Her married sisters are occupied with their families, or, in Kitty's case, looking forward to the arrival of their first addition.'

'Yes, that must be hard for Lydia. Georgie and Anne Asquith, as I must learn to think of your cousin, are in similar situations. Celia Fitzwilliam also.' Lizzy laughed. 'We are certainly a fertile lot. Do you imagine all this talk of babies has made Lydia regret the loss of her child?'

'It probably hasn't helped,' Will replied, wincing.

Lizzy shook her head. 'I should have noticed Lydia's preoccupation when she arrived and spent more time with her.'

'You have barely had a moment to yourself.'

'That's hardly an excuse.' She rested her head against Will's shoulder. 'You shall not mind having Lydia with us?'

'Not in the least. Georgiana and Kitty have moved away and your sister is more than welcome to make her home with us.'

Lizzy smiled up at her husband. 'I don't deserve you.'

'But you're stuck with me, so we shall just have to make the best of it.'

'Such hardships.' Lizzy tutted. 'I have no idea how I shall manage.'

'I could make a few suggestions.'

'Ha, your suggestions have resulted in three children after less than three years of marriage.'

Will's eyes flashed with satisfaction. 'You see, I can be creative when I try.'

'A little too creative, perhaps,' Lizzy teased.

'Then you shall not hear another word from me on the subject of procreation.' He caressed her with eyes brimming with mirth. 'I was merely trying to be helpful.'

'How very obliging of you.'

Will strolled towards the window and stared out of it, hands clasped behind his back. 'Did I mention that I received a letter from Patrick Shannon a few days ago?'

'I don't believe I have heard you mention his name before.' Lizzy searched her memory and came up blank. 'Is he a local gentleman?'

'His family established itself as a force to be reckoned with here in Derbyshire several generations ago. It's all rather curious. I haven't thought about that family for years.' Will turned away from the window, rubbing his chin in thoughtful contemplation. 'Shannon introduced one of the first water-driven mills to Derbyshire.'

'Does the mill still operate?'

'No, it went out of business.'

'What happened?'

'That's what I find so odd. Shannon's father died when I was away at university. Shannon is a few years younger than I and was due to go up to Cambridge at the start of the new school year. He's an only child and his mother pre-deceased his father by several years. But the strange thing was that within weeks of burying his father, he closed up the house and disappeared, leaving his father's lawyer to deal with his affairs.'

'Where did Mr Shannon disappear to? Presumably he had relations somewhere who took him in, if he was not of age.'

'No one knows to this day what happened to him. As far as I'm aware he hasn't set foot in Derbyshire since quitting the county.'

'It sounds as though his circumstances are similar to Dominic Sanford's.'

'Sanford went to live with his uncle in Scotland when his parents were killed and we all knew where he was, even if he didn't choose to return until recently.'

'And sweep your sister off her feet,' Lizzy added with a grin. 'Where is Mr Shannon's property?'

'It's a modest manor house halfway between Lambton and Kympton. But the size of the property doesn't adequately represent how well thought of the Shannons were in the locality. They did a great deal to ease the lot of the disadvantaged.'

'You do that.'

'As master of Pemberley, the principal estate in the area, it's my duty to do so. People of Shannon's standing need not concern themselves with the fate of the poor if they prefer not to. My own father thought highly of Shannon. He employed women with handlooms to weave for him in their own homes.'

'Before he introduced the water mill, I imagine.'

'Yes, but he kept them on afterwards. He also took a lot of children from the orphanage in Newcastle, housed, fed and educated them and trained them to work in the silk industry. But unlike many of his fellow mill owners, he paid them a fair wage and didn't overwork them. Consequently he created a willing labour force that was undyingly loyal.'

'But the son turned his back on all of that?'

Will shrugged. 'Apparently so.'

'I think I know the house you refer to. Is it that rather neglected place set back from the road? I have often wondered who owns it.'

'That's the one. I have absolutely no idea where Shannon has been all these years, why he's coming back and what he wants of me. I asked Sanford about it but he has no idea either. No one has seen him anywhere around and the house doesn't appear to be occupied. His letter was posted from London, so perhaps he's not yet back.' Lizzy could see that Will was curious and a little concerned about Mr Shannon's odd behaviour. 'I'll admit that it has me intrigued.'

'You're thinking of all those livelihoods that depended upon Shannon's mill, I would imagine, and wondering what became of them all.'

Will sent her a tender smile. 'How well you know me.'

'Don't think too badly about the young man until you know the full particulars. He had not reached his majority, remember; and anyway, you said the mill went out of business at about the time his father died. It was probably outside of the current Mr Shannon's control.'

'Actually, now that I think about it, it all happened at about the same time. One minute Shannon was alive and running the mill, the next he was dead and a competitor – Gunther, I think it was – had unilateral control of the silk industry in this area.'

'Perhaps Mr Shannon did not expect his father to die when he was still young and wasn't ready to assume his responsibilities. So he took himself off to do whatever young men of fortune and leisure do to amuse themselves.'

'Possibly.' Will resumed rubbing his chin. 'Anyway, he intends to call upon me tomorrow afternoon and so we shall soon know.'

'Now you have made me curious and I should like to meet him.' Lizzy glanced out of the window. 'Oh, there's Lydia, strolling in the garden. I ought to go and join her. It's time we had an uninterrupted conversation.'

'Which I shall take as my cue to catch up with the affairs that I have neglected these past two weeks.' Will leaned over and bestowed a lingering kiss upon Lizzy's lips. 'Until later, my love.'

2

Lydia wandered aimlessly around Pemberley's rose garden, breathing in the heady scent of a dozen different varieties in full bloom. But the tranquillity of her surroundings did little to soothe her, which did not augur well. If she couldn't live with her conscience in this lovely oasis, where every luxury was at her fingertips and she could pass her days in idleness if she so chose, then she truly was a lost cause.

She sat down in a secluded arbour close to the lake and watched a family of ducks swim in a disorderly line from one side of it to the other, envying them the simplicity of their existence. If only her own situation could be as straightforward – instinct over society's expectations. Her lips quirked at the thought of how shocked her relations would be if they knew the truth. Wickham was dead, everyone thought she was prostrate with grief and no one knew quite what to say or do to make her feel better.

The fact of the matter was there was nothing they *could* say. She was not sorry, more relieved, that he was gone from her life, and she didn't know how to live with the guilt such wicked feelings engendered. It simply wasn't normal – she wasn't normal – and didn't deserve all the condolences that had been heaped upon her.

She recalled how desperately she had loved Wickham just three short years ago and how beside herself with joy she had been when she so carelessly eloped with him, not stopping to consider the devastation that decision would cause to the rest of her family. In her own defence, she had genuinely believed her feelings were reciprocated and that they would be married just as soon as it could be arranged. But Wickham hadn't had the least intention of marrying her and had to be coerced into so doing. Perhaps her animosity had been slowly festering since the blinkers had been removed and she was forced to acknowledge that unpalatable truth. A glimmer of justification broke through her sullen mood when she recalled just how difficult their life together had been due to his disinclination for honest work.

Wickham had been a womaniser, a gamester, idle and dissolute – qualities that did not make for a constant husband. He had spent the short years of their marriage continuously bemoaning the fact that he had been badly treated – cheated, even – by Lizzy's husband. At first, Lydia had believed every word and took his side. Why would Wickham lie to her, and how could Lydia persuade Lizzy to help her find justice for him?

Lydia's eyes had been opened to his true character shortly after he left the army and they were thrown into one another's company more regularly. Only then did she realise what a terrible mistake she had made, committing herself to a lifetime with such a man. He most definitely didn't love her and were it not for Mr Darcy... well, she was overjoyed that he happened to fall in love with Lizzy. Had he not, the entire family's reputation would have been destroyed, all thanks to her careless disregard for anyone's pleasures other than her own.

She plucked a rose from the rambling array sweeping above her head and held it to her nose, closing her eyes as she inhaled its fragrant perfume. Lydia sighed as unsettling feelings of guilty discontent continued to plague her. She had never been much of a thinker; now she seldom occupied her time any other way, trying to decide what to do with her future. She had been assured she could live here, or with Jane or Kitty. She did not deserve her sisters' kindness; nor did she want to be regarded as the poor relation – a charity case to be passed around like an inconvenient parcel. Rather like Caroline Bingley, who divided her time between her brother and sister – although of course she wasn't precisely poor, just unmarried.

Things had all seemed straightforward when the five of them were still at Longbourn. They all aspired to be married – some admittedly more eager to embrace that institution than others. Everyone now assumed Lydia would marry again, but having delighted in being the first to wed, she was equally determined not to make the same mistake twice.

'May I join you?'

Lydia was jolted out of her introspective state, not having heard Lizzy approaching.

'It's your garden.'

Lizzy's expression displayed curiosity rather than offence at Lydia's incivility. 'And yours, too, Lydia, if you would like it to be.'

Lydia sighed. 'I'm sorry, Lizzy. I shouldn't have snapped at you.'

'I suspect you have wanted to snap at someone for a long time,' Lizzy replied, seating herself beside Lydia. 'Snap away. I'm glad you still feel you can speak your mind.'

'Because you are mistress of all this and so I ought not to be rude to you?' Lydia flashed a rueful grin. 'You know me better than that.'

'I'm not sure I know you at all any more. You have had a lot to put up with these past three years.'

'Which is no one's fault but my own. You tried to warn me but I wasn't ready to listen.'

'Wickham *was* very handsome,' Lizzy said, grinning.

'Which was the only circumstance I troubled myself with.' Lydia shook her head. 'I didn't stop to consider how we would live or... or anything else.'

'It wasn't entirely your fault.'

'Then whose was it? I don't believe I was treated any differently from the rest of you. But all of you attended to your lessons and acquired accomplishments, whereas I...' Lydia spread her hands and allowed her words to trail off.

'You were our mother's favourite, your personality was naturally lively and your wilder behaviour wasn't checked. It was not your fault that someone as suave and experienced as Wickham talked you into eloping.'

'You make it all sound so simple,' Lydia said, twisting the rosebud through her fingers.

'I will confess I could have cheerfully throttled you for your thoughtlessness at the time, but all that's in the past now.' Lizzy squeezed Lydia's hand. 'You are quite forgiven.'

Lydia flashed a smile. 'I thought when I went back to Longbourn that I would be able to hide myself away and contemplate my future. But everything is so different there now.'

'Well, it would be. Jane, Kitty and I are no longer there.'

'It isn't just that. Mary is so full of herself, and not in an attractive way.' Lydia lifted her shoulders. 'Not that I am in a position to cast aspersions, as Mary never tired of reminding me. She is very withdrawn when she comes to Pemberley but that's because she is overawed by what she once described to me as an ostentatious display of wealth.'

Lizzy laughed. 'You used to have a happy knack of not hearing one word in ten that Mary spoke.'

'When we all lived at Longbourn she was easy to ignore. She was so much quieter in those days. Now she fashions herself as "Miss Bennet"...'

'Well, she is the only Miss Bennet left. We must allow her that distinction.'

Lydia rolled her eyes. 'Mary and her precious Mr Peterson are so sanctimonious they made me want to say something to really shock them.' Lydia turned to fully face Lizzy. 'The wretched man told me that if I opened my heart to God, He would forgive my sins and I would find peace.'

'Oh dear!' Lizzy covered her mouth with her hand.

'It's not funny, Lizzy.' But Lydia couldn't help smiling as well. 'Mary obviously told him how Wickham and I came to be married, which she had no right to do, and he now looks upon me as a fallen woman.'

'No wonder you didn't want to stay in Hertfordshire. In your position I should not have been able to help telling Mr Peterson to mind his own business.' Lizzy took the rosebud from Lydia's fingers and tucked it behind her sister's ear. 'That poor flower has done nothing to deserve such a violent death.'

Lydia glanced at her lap, which was littered with rose petals. 'It wasn't the curate so much as Mama who made me decide against going back to Hertfordshire with them this morning. Before my marriage, I had not realised just how... Well, the truth is, Mama can be tactless.'

'Let me guess. She took you about our neighbours, portraying you as the tragic widow and enjoying every minute of the drama?'

'Precisely.' Lydia scowled. 'I must sound ungrateful, especially after all the trouble I caused, but she would keep on and on about Wickham and how unfair it was that I should be deprived of my husband at such a young age. Truly, I was ready to tear my hair out, and Papa did nothing to stay her tongue.'

Lizzy sighed. 'Papa never does. He finds her indiscretions diverting.'

'I didn't know how to make her understand, which added to my guilt. I wasn't grieving in the prescribed fashion, not in my heart, but I couldn't tell Mama the truth about Wickham's character; she would not have understood. It all became so trying that I remained in my room just to escape Mama.'

'Which made her think you really were grieving.'

'Quite. And as for our neighbours, you know how much talk and speculation there was about my hasty marriage to Wickham and the reasons for it. Well, of course you do. You had to bear the brunt of the scandal while I barely spared you all a thought. I was so very selfish. However, now that Wickham's dead, I'm perfectly respectable again; an object of pity.'

'No one in Derbyshire knows the particulars of your marriage,' Lizzy said briskly. 'And so you may enter society or not, while you are here. You will get no pressure from me to do anything you would prefer not to.'

'It will surprise you to learn that I have no great yearning for parties and balls nowadays.'

'No, my dear, that comes as no shock. You've been through a lot and need time to recover.'

'What I need is something useful to do.'

Lizzy appeared surprised. 'Whatever do you mean?'

'What I say. I cannot imagine myself ever marrying again...'

'Lydia, you're nineteen! Still younger than I was when I married Will.'

Lydia flashed a sardonic smile. 'And probably a lot wiser.'

Lizzy conceded the point with the elevation of one brow. 'What is it that you wish to do?'

'That's just the point.' Lydia scowled at the lake. 'I am not qualified to do anything. I was too busy chasing officers to take the time to acquire accomplishments. You play and sing, Kitty draws, Jane is absolutely perfect at everything and even Mary tries to be a scholar. Whereas I... Well, I can sew and I enjoyed looking after the goods in our uncle's warehouse when Wickham was employed there, but that is no occupation for a woman.'

'You're plagued by guilt because your reaction to Wickham's death is not that which society expects of you, but you pretend that it is. It's sapping your character and robbing me of my vibrant sister's company.' Lizzy tucked one of Lydia's wayward curls behind her ear and offered her a reassuring smile. 'My suggestion, for what it's worth, is that you write your feelings down in a journal. It might help you to make better sense of them.'

Lydia stared blankly at her sister. 'Why? What will that achieve?'

Lizzy shrugged. 'We shall not know until you try.'

'I wouldn't know where to begin.'

'Start at the beginning. Write down your earliest memories from Longbourn. Be absolutely honest about your feelings since no one but you need read the journal.' Lizzy smiled. 'Perhaps you have long-hidden resentments that need to be aired.'

Lydia shook her head. 'Hardly.'

'Then you have nothing to fear from your honest recollections. The exercise can do no harm and might very well help. All I see at the moment is a shadow of the sister who so vexed and sometimes delighted me.' Lizzy squeezed Lydia's hand. 'I want that sister back. You have had no time to properly grieve because of Mama.'

'But I'm not really grieving.' Lydia turned tear-filled eyes towards her sister. 'Is that so terrible?'

'Not in the least. In fact, I am glad you can admit your feelings to me. Wickham was a charlatan and you're better off without him. He was a permanent thorn in my husband's side and neither of us is sorry to see the end of him either.' Lizzy bit her lower lip but a grin still escaped. 'Although, it would probably be better if we kept those sentiments to ourselves.'

'He was obsessed with Pemberley, convinced he had been badly treated.'

Lizzy tossed her head. 'He was treated far better than he deserved to be.'

'One day you must tell me what drove a wedge between Mr Darcy and Wickham.'

'One day perhaps I will, but in the meantime, what do you say to my suggestion of keeping a journal? It might help you to make better sense of what's happened to you and give you a better idea of what you would like to do with yourself.'

'I shall try it, but there is little that a woman *can* do for herself. It's not as though I can adopt a career.' Lydia suppressed a smile. 'Only imagine what Lady Catherine would have to say on the subject. She already thinks badly enough of me.'

'Then you and I are in the same boat. She merely tolerates me because she doesn't want to be on bad terms with Will.'

'I think she has a sneaking respect for you because you don't allow her to bully you.'

'Perhaps. However, it was your situation we were discussing. I dare say all the talk of babies, born and to be born, this past fortnight wore on your nerves and I'm sorry about that. It must make you think about the baby you lost.'

'Of course I'm sorry about my baby, but I don't mind seeing the rest of you surrounded by your families. I enjoy being an aunt. I was not ready to embrace motherhood; not when Wickham was such an unreliable provider. Not that I wished my baby dead though, and I shall always blame myself for that.'

'Lydia!'

'No, Lizzy, I do. It's God's punishment for my past conduct.'

'Well, my dear, I shall not waste my breath telling you you're wrong.' Lizzy smiled. 'Instead, I suggest shopping for some gowns this week. You have no need to restrict yourself to grey now that you're out of half-mourning.'

'I'm perfectly happy with my wardrobe.'

'Lydia!' Lizzy gaped at her sister. 'At last you've said something to truly shock me. I never expected to hear those words pass your lips.'

Lydia flashed a brittle smile. 'You see how much I've changed.'

'Stop blaming yourself.' Lizzy gave Lydia's shoulders a squeeze. 'Wickham brought his misfortunes upon himself.'

Lydia widened her eyes. 'I expected a scolding for being so hard-hearted.'

'From me? Whatever can I have done to make you imagine I've become so straitlaced?'

'Well, since you put it like that, Mr Darcy is a different person to the austere gentleman who so frightened us all in Hertfordshire. You must take the credit for the changes in him.'

'Thank you, I shall.' Lizzy and Lydia stood and walked towards the house arm in arm. 'But as to your situation, not only do I understand, but I also share your sentiments.' Lizzy bit her lip. 'And if that's an unchristian notion, I really don't have the energy to care.'

3

One of Patrick Shannon's first actions when returning to English soil was to purchase himself a decent gelding at Tattersall's. He then sent Gladiator up to Derbyshire ahead of him while he attended to his business affairs in London. That had been over three weeks ago and now, finally, he stepped off the coach at Derby and found Gladiator in the posting inn's mews, anxious to stretch his legs.

It was good to be back amongst the majestic Derbyshire peaks, Patrick thought as he rode along the country road that would lead him directly to Lambton. He breathed clean air deeply into his lungs as he took in a rugged view that had changed little over the centuries. Steep hillsides dotted with grazing sheep, clear streams trickling through the valleys and trees in full leaf, stirred by a soft breeze, the entire vista bathed in summer sunshine. Derbyshire was putting on a show to welcome him home, Patrick decided whimsically as he trotted Gladiator along at a leisurely pace. A strange sort of contentment gripped him as he absorbed his surroundings, knocking aside the anger and determination that had fuelled his ambition for the past decade.

He had come home in all senses of the word.

He had left Derbyshire as a mere youth, distraught with grief at the sudden passing of his beloved father. Confused by the tangled business affairs the pater had left behind him, Patrick had been exploited by those who were supposed to have his best interests at heart. He was returning a grown man with questions that required answers, and this time he would not be so easily manipulated.

Patrick winced when he reached the driveway that led to Shannon House but quickly rode through the dilapidated gates when he heard a carriage approaching. He wasn't ready to speak to anyone who might demand to know his business. He had been warned by his father's lawyer that only a minimal amount of attention had been given to the property over the past ten years and it was immediately apparent that Fenton had not exaggerated. Patrick rode down the rutted, weed-strewn drive, staving off depression. He could see at a glance that the fields were hopelessly overgrown, the dry-stone walls were crumbling, and the gardens his mother had taken so much pride in were overrun by nettles and brambles.

He halted Gladiator and took a closer look. The grand old house once reverberated with laughter and a constant sea of changing faces. It now wore its neglect like a shroud, reinforcing Patrick's determination to re-establish his family's good name. His trusting nature had been eroded by the reality of an empty belly and equally empty pockets. Opportunists would be wasting good shoe leather if they called at Shannon House expecting to find a man as easy to dupe as his father had been.

'Well,' he said to his gelding, feeling overwhelmed by the enormity of the struggle he faced. 'Where to start?'

Patrick guided his horse around the side of the house. The stable block was built of solid Derbyshire stone, and at least the severe winter weather hadn't seemed to have made a significant impression upon it. He smelt fresh hay and noticed bales of straw neatly piled in an open-fronted barn.

'What the devil...'

Patrick scratched his head, wondering if someone was using the stables without his permission. He dismounted and noticed that the largest box had been prepared for equine occupation, presumably Gladiator. But by whom?

'Master Patrick. Is that you?'

Patrick turned at the sound of a familiar voice. The years fell away when he was confronted by the weathered face of an old man who still walked with an erect carriage and looked as strong and muscular as the horses he used to care for.

'Mason?' Patrick let go of Gladiator's reins and strode across the yard to meet the man he'd known since birth. 'Good God, Mason, I had no idea you were still here!'

'Where else would I be?' He took Patrick's outstretched hand in a firm grasp. 'Someone had to take care of the place.'

'Fenton told me everyone had been found alternative positions. I assumed that included you and Mrs Mason, otherwise I would have seen to the matter myself.'

'Mrs Mason and I refused to quit Shannon House.' He chuckled. 'Caused a bit of an upset, that did, but I wasn't being driven off by some fancy lawyer still wet behind the ears.' Mason removed his cap and scratched his head. 'Knew you'd come back sooner or later.'

'You cannot know how glad I am to see you. If I'd known…'

'Aye, I dare say,' Mason replied gruffly. 'I had a feeling, begging your pardon, that someone was trying to pull a fast one. Figured it was best to keep an eye on things.'

'We need to have a good talk about what's been going on in my absence,' Patrick replied. 'But let's give this fella his supper first.'

'Nice looking gelding,' Mason said, casing an expert eye over Gladiator as he led him into the stable.

'Fenton told you I was on my way?' Patrick asked, watching the old man as he efficiently removed Gladiator's saddle and bridle and rubbed him down.

'Aye, the man sent word.'

'But he never told me you were here,' Patrick muttered. 'What's more, I never asked him what had become of you both. It's inexcusable of me not to have made sure that at least you and Mrs Mason were taken care of.'

'You had more than enough to worry about, lad,' Mason said gruffly. 'There now, he'll do fine.' They stood back and watched Gladiator attack a fresh manger of hay. 'Come along into the house now. Mrs Mason will be anxious to see you. She's been fretting for days.'

Patrick slapped Mason's shoulder as they walked together. 'Seeing the two of you is the best welcome home a man could have.'

Mrs Mason shrieked with delight when Patrick entered her kitchen.

'Master Patrick, you're home at last!' She wiped a tear from her eye. 'You look the image of your father.'

'I am very glad to see you again, Mrs Mason,' Patrick said. 'How have you been?'

'Oh, the same as always.' Her smile emphasised the deep wrinkles etched in her face. 'But a sight better now you're home, safe and well and all grown up. Now sit yourself down while I make some tea. You'll take a slice of my cake? I made it special, knowing you were coming.'

'Absolutely. No one makes a better cake than you, Mrs M.'

'Go on with you now.' Mrs Mason's round face flushed with pleasure. 'You're as bad as your father used to be with your flattery.'

I hope not.

Patrick drank his tea and consumed two slices of Mrs Mason's cake, after which he could no longer avoid asking about the state of the house.

'It's in urgent need of restoration,' Mason replied, stating the obvious.

'We've done what we could,' his wife added anxiously.

'I'm perfectly sure you've done more than your duty, both of you.'

A quick tour of the ground floor was depressing and at the same time encouraging. The rooms held the musty air of disuse but flooded his mind with myriad happy memories. His father's good humour had been infectious, even if people had exploited his hospitality. It was a mistake Patrick had no intention of emulating. He lifted the corner of a sheet covering a much-loved sideboard and discovered that it was waxed to a high sheen.

'We had to do what we could,' Mason explained, echoing his wife's earlier words. 'Priorities, like.'

'This furniture will last centuries,' Mrs Mason added. 'Just so long as it's kept polished.'

Patrick shared a smile between them. 'Thank you so very much for your dedication.'

'Your father gave us both a home when we were destitute,' Mason reminded Patrick. 'We ain't never properly repaid him for that, until now.'

'What do you think?' Patrick asked, suddenly full of energy and enthusiasm. 'Shall we bring the house back to life?'

'Is there... well, begging your pardon, but is there any money?' Mason asked.

Patrick laughed. 'Money is the least of our concerns. Tomorrow, Mrs Mason, I want you to bring in as many girls from the village as you need to get the house opened up again. The same goes for you, Mason. The first priority is the gardens. My mother would not like to see them as they are now.'

The Masons flashed identical toothless grins.

'You just leave it to us, sir,' Mason said.

'Good man,' Patrick said, nodding his approval.

'Your old room's ready for you and the bed has been aired,' Mrs Mason said. 'Although you might prefer to move into the master bedchamber now.'

'All in good time. I have a valise that's being sent on from Derby and a trunk on its way from London. In the meantime, I shall have to make do.' Patrick rubbed his hands together. 'Now then, Mrs Mason, some hot water, if you please. I must make myself presentable. I have an appointment with Mr Darcy this afternoon.'

* * *

'Drive slowly along this lane,' Caroline Bingley told her brother's coachman.

The carriage slowed and Caroline peered intently at the passing scenery.

'What is your interest in this particular road?' Louisa asked.

'Nothing special. Are you anxious to be somewhere? If so, I shall have John drive on.'

Louisa wagged a finger at her sister. 'I know that look, Caroline.

You're up to something. Won't you tell me what it is? I could do with a diversion.'

Caroline shaded her eyes with her hand, certain the place she sought was close by, but she was unable to see it yet. 'You're bored because you have been deprived of Mr Henley's society for too long,' Caroline replied, referring to her sister's lover.

Louisa chuckled. 'I'm more concerned about you. I thought you had recovered your spirit but you fell into a depression again during our latest visit to Pemberley.'

'If you think I still yearn for Mr Darcy then you quite mistake the matter.' Caroline tossed her head, striving to appear disinterested in the mention of Darcy's name. Since that humiliating business two years ago when she had been drawn into Wickham's schemes and overplayed her hand, she had learned to keep her emotions under much closer guard. 'He seems perfectly content with his fine-eyed wife. His taste disappoints me, I will admit that much, but I seldom think about him now.'

'I'm glad you feel that way, Caro. It does no good to interfere between husband and wife.'

Caroline barked on a laugh. 'Even if you don't practise what you preach.'

Louisa arched a brow. 'Because I spend as much time with Mr Henley as I do with my own husband?'

'That thought did cross my mind.'

'Mr Henley isn't married and Mr Hurst doesn't mind what I do to entertain myself, provided I'm discreet. It leaves him free to spend all his time at his clubs with a clear conscience.'

'Doesn't Mr Hurst worry that you might present him with another man's child?'

Louisa appeared remarkably untroubled by the possibility. 'We have never discussed the subject but I imagine I must be barren. I have been married for a long time, and involved with Mr Henley for several years, without breeding.'

Caroline forgot the scenery and gaped at her sister, astonished by her candour.

'Barren women are pitied,' Caroline said, a spiteful edge to her voice. 'Don't you mind?'

'Not in the least. Babies are such a nuisance and ruin a woman's figure.'

Caroline nodded. 'I have had more than enough of them recently. I thought Jane, Georgiana and Mrs Darcy would never stop discussing the wretched subject.'

The sisters fell silent again and Caroline mused upon Louisa's situation. It had taught her a valuable lesson about the enduring nature of even the most passionate of marriages. Not that Louisa's marriage, to Caroline's precise knowledge, had ever been blessed with passion... but there were many others she had observed which had been and no longer were. Mr Darcy's, for instance. She had been out of her wits for a while when her part in Wickham's deception was revealed and she had been banished from Pemberley. Charles and Jane subsequently learned of what she'd done and her humiliation was complete. She thought she had burned her bridges with Mr Darcy but was delighted to be invited back to Pemberley for Georgiana's betrothal ball. Mr Darcy had been remote with her, but she didn't mind that. If he hadn't wanted her there, didn't feel something for her, the invitation would not have been issued.

Caroline was content to bide her time now that she had been readmitted to his circle, forgiven. On this latest visit, Mr Darcy had treated her with great civility, instigating conversations with her and seeking her opinion on a number of topics. Caroline was careful to keep her reactions neutral. Mr Darcy was singling her out for a reason, she sensed it, and she would encourage his interest by not appearing too eager for his society. Caroline accepted that Darcy wouldn't throw Eliza aside, especially not now that she had given him three children, but the gloss would wear off the union – was already doing so – because Eliza would put her children's interests first and neglect her husband.

Darcy was in need of a circumspect mistress and that was why he was making himself so agreeable to her. Caroline had no pride left upon which to stand and would happily fill that position. But in order to do so she would first need to find a husband with an estate close enough to Pemberley to make such an arrangement workable. And by the greatest of good fortune, she had literally bumped into the ideal candidate during a recent visit to London.

The alternative to marrying a man she didn't love was to become an object of pity, past marriageable age – an ape leader. Such ignominy was unthinkable. Besides, she was tired of being passed between Louisa and Charles like the inconvenient responsibility she knew herself to be.

'Whose house is that?' Louisa asked as Caroline peered through the carriage window a little too intently at Shannon House. 'It looks rather neglected. I haven't noticed it before.'

'It belongs to the gentleman we encountered in Bond Street just before we returned to Derbyshire,' Caroline replied casually. 'It does look rather abandoned but Mr Shannon mentioned he had been overseas these past ten years, so I expect the house has been closed up.'

'Ah, now I understand.' Louisa flashed a complicit smile. 'Mr Shannon has engaged your interest. Well, that's hardly to be wondered at. He's a charming and personable young man. You could do a lot worse.'

'I know you're anxious to marry me off, Louisa, but I think you're being a little precipitate. I will admit I was curious to see where Mr Shannon lived, but nothing more.'

'I hope he managed to make a fortune while he was in America,' Louisa remarked. 'He will need one to put that estate back into good order.'

Then it was a very good thing that Caroline had a fortune of her own, and she would ensure Mr Shannon was made aware of it when they next met. She didn't doubt her ability to engage Mr Shannon's affections, but the added incentive of a substantial dowry ought to make that task a little easier.

'Drive on,' she told the coachman, watching as a man on a grey horse turned into the driveway of Shannon House.

'Isn't that your Mr Shannon?' Louisa asked.

Yes, Caroline thought, it was. It was also a sign that her luck had finally taken a turn for the better. What were the chances of their passing Mr Shannon's property at the precise time he returned if it was not fate interceding?

4

'Lydia and I had a very frank talk this morning,' Lizzy told Will when they found themselves alone in the middle of the afternoon. 'She feels guilty because she can't mourn Wickham in the way she thinks she ought to.'

'Then I am very glad she can look back and see him for what he was.'

'As am I, but still, I'm worried about her.' Lizzy sighed. 'She is not herself.'

'She needs time to adjust. I doubt whether she got much privacy with your mother dramatising her circumstances.'

'Yes, that's true. She has had to mature remarkably quickly.'

'Your youngest sister was a silly goose when I first knew her, but then how else could she get the attention she craved?'

'Will!'

He gently caressed Lizzy's face as one side of his mouth hitched into a smile. 'She had to compete with your intelligence and Jane's goodness and sense. Mary set herself apart and only Kitty was compliant to Lydia's wild ideas. Your mother indulged Lydia's every whim and your father didn't trouble himself to chastise her.' Will shrugged. 'And so she became what we shall charitably describe as boisterous.'

'A charitable description indeed.' Lizzy rolled her eyes. 'Be that as it may, she's now consumed with guilt for almost ruining us all.'

'Whereas I have a very soft spot for her. Had I not forced Wickham to marry her, you might never have had a change of heart about me.'

'Oh, Will!' Lizzy leaned into him and pressed her lips to his. 'The moment I received your letter explaining all the things I had got wrong about you, I regretted refusing your proposal. Well,' she added with a playful smile, 'perhaps I regretted it a little more when I came to Pemberley with my aunt and uncle and actually saw what I had turned down.'

Will chortled. 'You are many things, Mrs Darcy, most of them admirable.'

Lizzy hoisted a brow. 'Only most?'

'Definitely most,' he replied with a teasing smile. 'But one thing that does not influence a person with your principled nature is monetary gain.'

'And yet it ought to have done, if only for the sake of the rest of my family. I can be quite as selfish as Lydia, you see.'

'I had become so accustomed, I suppose, to expecting my position to impress everyone and didn't stop to consider those truly worthy of my regard would discount it.'

'Let that be a lesson in humility to you, Mr Darcy,' Lizzy chided.

'As to Lydia,' Will said after a short, reflective pause. 'If it will ease your concern for her, think of your sister as being in a temporary state of seclusion.'

'Lydia, in a convent?' Lizzy shook her head and bit back a laugh. 'She is much altered but not *that* much. But still, I do see what you mean, I suppose. She does need time to reflect but has few options available to her. She can either marry again or spend her life living between her sisters.'

'She can rattle around Pemberley, be as unsocial as she likes and never see us at all if she would prefer not to.' Will shrugged. 'I don't see the difficulty.'

'The difficulty is that Lydia feels undervalued and wants to make amends for the mistakes she has already made. A life of idleness no longer appeals to her, but she doesn't think she has any talents. I even suggested we went shopping for gowns and she wasn't interested.'

Will raised a brow. 'That bad, huh?'

'She's lost her vitality and doesn't believe she deserves to be loved for herself because she has nothing to offer.'

Will smiled. 'Your sister still clings to her sense of the dramatic.'

'She actually believes what she says. I have always been able to see through her efforts to draw attention to herself. Anyway, I've suggested she starts a journal—'

'That's an excellent idea. It will help her to see things more clearly.' Will cupped Lizzy's chin between his thumb and forefinger and sent her a sensual smile. 'You are a wise woman, Mrs Darcy.'

'I suppose I must be. After all, I married you.'

'Eventually,' Will replied with a wry smile.

Lizzy rested her head against her husband's shoulder. 'What did you make of Caroline Bingley's behaviour on this visit?'

'She seemed more like her old self again. I certainly didn't sense any animosity towards you or suppressed longing for my society. In fact, I tested that theory by engaging her in conversation. I expected her to hang on my every word, but she actually excused herself and walked away.'

Lizzy nodded but did not share her husband's optimistic view. She was convinced that Miss Bingley still bore her ill-will but had become more skilled at disguising it. Walking away from Will was a perfect way to deflect suspicion. But she had caught her nemesis at unguarded moments, staring at her with unmitigated dislike.

'Jane tells me Mr Bingley despairs of her ever marrying.'

'It's not too late.'

'And I would be the last person to suggest marriage as an alternative to remaining single. However, Caroline is at an age and has the means to respectably establish a home of her own rather than inflicting herself upon Jane the entire time.'

'Has Jane complained?'

Lizzy laughed. 'When does Jane ever complain about anything?' Will conceded the point with a smile. 'But I know my sister feels uncomfortable about the trouble Caroline tried to create for us and will never feel entirely comfortable with her again.'

Simpson appeared in the open doorway and cleared his throat. 'Mr Shannon is here, sir.'

'Ah, good, show him in.'

Lizzy removed her head from Will's shoulder and straightened herself up. 'I shall leave you to it then.'

'No, stay and meet Shannon. I shall be interested to see what you make of him.'

'If you like.'

'Mr Shannon, sir,' Simpson said, standing back to allow their visitor access to the room.

Lizzy studied him as he strode into it. He was a tall gentleman, broad shouldered and impeccably attired, with a shock of light brown hair and equally brown eyes. He wore an aura of authority and looked to have prospered during his absence from Derbyshire.

'Darcy,' Mr Shannon said, hand outstretched. 'It's good of you to see me.'

'Shannon,' Will replied, shaking his hand. 'Welcome home.'

'Thank you. It's good to be back.'

'May I introduce my wife?'

Lizzy stood and shook their visitor's hand also.

'I am very glad to make your acquaintance, Mrs Darcy.'

'And I yours, Mr Shannon. I dare say Derbyshire has changed since you were last here.'

'I have not been back for long enough to notice many changes, other than the deterioration to my own property. However, that will soon be rectified.'

'Some refreshments, if you please, Simpson,' Lizzy said as they seated themselves.

'And you, Mrs Darcy,' Mr Shannon said with a charming smile that illuminated his handsome features. 'Are you pleased with Derbyshire?'

'Very much so. It is very different to my native Hertfordshire, but I have two of my sisters settled close by and a third is actually living here at Pemberley for the time being, so I cannot claim to miss my family.'

'I believe I was introduced to a relation of one of your sisters while in London.'

'Oh?' Lizzy arched a brow. 'Which sister? None of them has mentioned it.'

'I happened to bump into a Mrs Hurst and Miss Bingley.' That charming smile again. 'Quite literally as it happens, in Bond Street.'

Mr Shannon paused while refreshments were delivered and Lizzy poured for them all.

'Thank you.' Mr Shannon accepted a cup from Lizzy. 'It was my fault. I wasn't looking where I was going and managed to knock a parcel from Mrs Hurst's hands. Happily no harm was done. I apologised and fell into conversation with the ladies. When I happened to remark that I was returning to Derbyshire, the connection was made.'

Lizzy's sense of foreboding intensified, which was not at all rational. Caroline's meeting Mr Shannon could not have been deliberately contrived. Even if she had realised quite what a close neighbour he was to Pemberley, there was no occasion for her to mention having met the gentleman to Lizzy or Will. That she had not spoken to Jane about it did seem odd. And she could not have done so or Jane would have told Lizzy. Lizzy tried to convince herself that Caroline couldn't possibly use her slight acquaintance with Mr Shannon to cause trouble at Pemberley, but the possibility refused to disengage from her brain.

'My sister Jane is married to Charles Bingley,' Lizzy explained. 'Jane and Mr Bingley have recently purchased Campton Park in Denton.'

'Ah, I have vague recollections of the estate,' Mr Shannon replied, sipping at his tea. 'It must be comforting to have your sister so close by.'

'Quite so.' Lizzy placed her empty cup aside. 'But now you must excuse me. You gentlemen have matters to discuss.'

'Please don't leave on my account, Mrs Darcy. There is nothing I have to say that you cannot hear. In fact, if you can spare the time, I should appreciate a lady's opinion.'

Lizzy resumed her seat, her curiosity piqued. 'Then I shall be happy to listen.'

'You look as though you have done well for yourself, Shannon,' Will said. 'We were concerned when you disappeared so soon after your father's death. We were expecting you up at Cambridge.'

'And I was looking forward to seeing you there, but alas it was not to be.' Mr Shannon's reflective expression was tinged with anger. 'I went to London as soon as we had buried the pater and visited his lawyer. I was not of age but I thought my father's business was prospering and his managers would continue to run it until I completed my education and was in a position to assume full responsibility.'

'Your father's water-driven mill was the talk of the district,' Will said. 'A brave and forward-thinking move that provided a comfortable living.'

'That's what I believed, so imagine my shock when Fenton informed me that the enterprise was on the brink of collapse.'

'What!' Will looked astounded. 'How could that possibly be?'

Mr Shannon shrugged. 'After ten years, I still don't have an answer, which is one of the reasons why I have returned. I was a raw youth at the time, grieving for the loss of a most excellent father and struggling to come to terms with what Fenton told me about my inheritance. I had neither the wit nor inclination to question him too deeply about the downturn in my fortunes. My father had trusted the man. Admittedly, that's not saying much. The pater trusted everyone and that trust almost certainly contributed to his downfall.'

'He never turned a man away with an empty belly,' Will said thoughtfully. 'Your mother likewise. That is my abiding memory of them. Two kinder people never graced this earth.'

'It's good of you to say so.' Mr Shannon inclined his head. 'My suspicions about their philanthropic natures being responsible for their ensuing problems is a subject we shall return to. Suffice it to say, I will not be so easily gulled. But first I need to explain where I went and why since you have not yet heard the extent of the devastating news I received from Fenton.' Mr Shannon paused and Lizzy could see that he was also struggling to compose himself. 'I inherited Shannon House and a very modest sum of money.' Again, he paused and fixed Will with a probing gaze. 'But the silk business had been left in its entirety to a man I had never heard of in my life before.'

'Good God!' Will said, surprise taking precedence over good manners.

'Precisely my reaction.' Mr Shannon ground his jaw. 'This man was my father's equal partner in the business, although I'd absolutely no idea he had taken a partner. Fenton either didn't know or was unwilling to reveal why the pater had acted as he did. He was able to tell me that the fortune set aside for me had originally been much greater, easily enough for a man to run an estate the size of Shannon House and live comfortably on if wisely invested. However, in his desperation to save his business, the pater had dipped into that fund, thinking to replace the sums borrowed from it when silk became profitable again.'

'Then the timing of his death could not have been worse,' Lizzy said.

'Is there ever a good time? And to complicate matters, my father's mysterious partner, a man by the name of Makepeace, was resident in the newly formed United States of America.'

'Ah, so that's where you have been,' Will said, nodding. 'Your curiosity got the better of you and you needed to meet this stranger face to face in order to extract an explanation.'

'Precisely. The pater left no clues as to his extraordinary behaviour.' Mr Shannon stood up and strode towards the window in a state of considerable agitation. 'He probably thought he had years left ahead of him but died from gastric problems that came on too quickly for him to foresee his own demise. I dare say he planned to tell me everything once I attained my majority.' He sighed as he resumed his seat. 'But that is pure speculation and I shall never know if I have got it right.' He scrubbed a hand down his face. 'In fact, the more I subsequently learned, the less I thought I knew my father at all.'

'It must have come as a terrible shock,' Lizzy said softly.

'I was shocked on two fronts. Having absorbed the discouraging news about the state of the business, I was absolutely sure I could do something to put it back on track.' A ghost of a smile flirted with his lips. 'Ah, the arrogance of youth! However, I digress. I assumed that the blame for the downturn in our fortunes could be attributed to one of my father's charity cases, or perhaps several of them working in tandem to siphon off the profits.'

'I would have thought that too in your situation,' Will said, nodding.

'The immediate question I asked my seventeen-year-old self was what was to be done? The moment I learned of the mysterious American gentleman, I felt the answer had to lie on the other side of the Atlantic.'

Will nodded thoughtfully. 'It would be impossible not to want to know and it's very hard to gauge from a letter whether or not one is being told the complete truth.'

'It's also easy to ignore a letter if one would prefer not to answer it,' Lizzy pointed out. 'Besides, it must take months for letters to cross the Atlantic.'

'How much control did Makepeace wield over the financial side of the business and how accountable was he for those finances, being situated so far away? Naturally, I asked Fenton but he could cast little light on the matter. So, with nothing left to keep me in England and with no means of support if I took up my place at Cambridge, I used half the money I had been left to purchase a passage to America. The rest of it I left with Fenton. He told me the business was beyond saving; and anyway, I had no say in trying to save it since it had not been left to me. Fenton assured me that excellent characters would be given to the servants who had provided us with loyal service, and positions found for them all. In my naiveté, I believed Fenton could give such assurances. I don't know to this day how successful he was, but now that I'm back I hope to find out.' He sighed. 'Ten years too late.'

'You cannot castigate yourself,' Lizzy said. 'As you rightly pointed out, you were still a boy at the time.'

'The rest of the cash was to be used for the basic maintenance of my property and I could leave all the arrangements to Fenton.' He made a wry face. 'In retrospect I can see that I was too trusting.'

'It was very brave of you to venture off to America,' Lizzy said. 'Presumably you did not forewarn Mr Makepeace to expect you, could not know how he would react and had little money to support yourself in the event that he turned you away. But it's also obvious that you prospered. I confess to being curious about what you found when you arrived.'

'Going off was not perhaps the most sensible thing to do, I'll grant you, but I was angry and resentful that my father should take on a partner I knew nothing about.' He spread his hands. 'Anyway, I was burning to know the truth and had not thought beyond confronting the man. How I would have supported myself if Edward Makepeace chose not to receive me I have no way of knowing. All I can say is that it was an exciting time in America with great opportunities available for those with the wit and determination to take chances.' Mr Shannon smiled. 'It was exhilarating.'

'So I have heard said,' Will replied. 'I take it Makepeace did not turn you away.'

'Certainly he did not. The moment I gave my name at the door to his rather imposing mansion I was welcomed with open arms.'

'In what part of the United States did he reside?' Will asked.

'In New York.'

Will nodded. 'I hear it is an area of rapid expansion.'

'Quite so. The end of the American Revolution unleashed a westward migration. New York was the new frontier and Americans looked to acquire land there to exercise their liberty and the pursuit of happiness they had just fought a revolution to protect.' Mr Shannon gazed at a picture on the opposite wall, a faraway look in his eye. 'The land was an untamed wilderness, fraught with dangers and yet full of opportunity for those prepared to take risks. There were no roads, no pastures, no fields and no homes. Everything the settlers needed to survive had to be carved out of the backwoods through back-breaking effort. But the settlers were undeterred and bought up homestead plots from land speculators at an astonishing rate.'

'And Makepeace was a land speculator, I imagine,' Will suggested.

'He was indeed. He recognised what he described to me as a once in a lifetime opportunity and purchased forty thousand acres of land in New York state. He then resold it all in small plots within a month.'

'How very enterprising of him,' Lizzy remarked, impressed.

'It didn't stop there,' Mr Shannon said. 'Not all of the settlers possessed the ability to build their own homes and were prepared to pay someone else to do it for them.'

'I recall you designing a new barn for your father's land when you were still thirteen or fourteen,' Will said. 'I'll wager Makepeace recognised that talent in you and set you to work designing housing for his settlers.'

Mr Shannon smiled. 'That's precisely what he did.'

'But why?' Lizzy asked, shaking her head. 'You have yet to explain what connection he had to your father and what possessed him to become your mentor.'

'Oh, I beg your pardon, Mrs Darcy. I ought to have made myself clearer. The moment I was introduced to Makepeace, no explanation was necessary. Looking upon his face ten years ago was little different to looking upon my own reflection today.' He smiled. 'You see, Edward Makepeace is the half-brother I had no idea I possessed.'

5

'Good heavens!'

Darcy's reaction perfectly mirrored Patrick's own at the time he made the discovery.

'Quite so,' he said. 'I was bursting with curiosity, but before Edward answered any of my questions he politely invited me to make the acquaintance of his family. His mother was still alive and, not unnaturally, she was the person I most particularly wished to meet.'

'Did she also look upon you favourably?' Mrs Darcy asked.

'She was delighted to make my acquaintance and very anxious to hear news of her native Derbyshire, asking all manner of questions about people she had once known.' Patrick paused. 'Upon meeting Mrs Makepeace I better understood my father's determination to be fair minded with all classes of society. She explained to me with refreshing candour what had occurred ten years before my birth; a point in time when my father had only been seventeen himself.'

'I think we can imagine well enough,' Darcy said hastily.

'Quite. It was not my intention to go into detail.'

'Well, I want to hear it all, Will,' Mrs Darcy said firmly.

Patrick smiled at Darcy's wife, to whom he had taken an instant

liking. 'It was obvious that Mrs Makepeace must have been a very handsome woman in her youth. She still bore traces of that beauty as she
aged and had a gentle manner that could not fail to appeal. She was the
daughter of my grandfather's butler.' He waved a hand. 'I know it's
unusual to employ married butlers but my family has never been
conventional. Besides, Jenson was a widower when my grandfather took
him on. Suffice it to say that my father and Mrs Makepeace were
attracted to one another, and Edward is the result of their passion.'

'Upon discovering her condition, your grandfather packed the girl
and the child off to America to avoid a scandal,' Darcy surmised. 'Isn't
that a little extreme? Excuse me, Lizzy, but gentlemen of consequence do
have by-blows and keep them on their estates, or provide for them in
other ways without feeling the need to banish them from the country.'

'That was my first question. Mrs Makepeace had no particular wish
to leave England. She was desperately in love with my father even
though she knew they would never be permitted to marry. It was her
father who insisted upon leaving England. He was beside himself with
anger and disappointment. He had ambitious plans for his daughter that
did not allow for an illegitimate baby. Grandfather asked his butler how
he could make matters right, and it was he, the butler, who insisted upon
a new start in America.'

Darcy flexed a brow. 'Extraordinary.'

'As it transpires, the butler was in the right of it. Once they arrived,
suitably recompensed monetarily by my grandfather, they discovered
that well-trained English butlers were in great demand, and Mrs Makepeace's father found employment with a society family.'

'If she was as attractive as you imply, I would imagine Mrs Makepeace soon had her share of admirers and could put her disappointment
in being parted from your father behind her,' Mrs Darcy said.

'She was passed off as a widow, and Makepeace, a wealthy banker,
was an especially ardent suitor. He was even prepared to adopt Edward
and afford him the protection of his name. They married and Mrs Makepeace didn't have any more children, and so Edward became the centre
of their lives. Makepeace is dead these several years and Edward inherited his wealth.'

'Your father kept in touch with his first son?' Darcy asked.

'Yes. Mrs Makepeace didn't actually say so, but she left me with the impression that my father was the love of her life. She and Makepeace told Edward the truth about his birth when he was old enough to understand. He wrote to my father, apparently, and since my mother, who knew nothing of Edward's birth, was by then dead, my father eagerly entered into correspondence with his first born. The rest I dare say you can piece together for yourselves.'

'Your father's silk business hit difficulties and Edward offered to help?' Darcy suggested.

'Yes, and in return my father insisted upon making him a full partner and leaving the business to him. Edward assured me he didn't want it and, had it been profitable, he would have turned it straight back over to me.'

'What a very understanding family,' Mrs Darcy said with a nod of approval.

'My half-brother is like my father in so many ways, except he is not so easily duped. He is happily married with two sons and two young daughters and their house is full of laughter, just as ours always was. Edward wanted to know what my plans were.' Patrick spread his hands. 'Of course, I had none. Upon learning of my interest in architecture, he insisted that I reside with them and that I was just the person he needed to help with his building programme. I couldn't believe my good fortune, had no pressing desire to return to the mess my father had left behind in England, and so I readily agreed. I made many mistakes but was willing to work hard and learn as I went along. Eventually the financial rewards came and Edward was generous in sharing his profits with me, even though all the risks sat upon his shoulders.'

'What finally persuaded you to return to these shores?' Mrs Darcy asked.

'Ah, the timing seemed right. I was being... er, how shall we put it—'

'Pursued by ladies with their eye upon matrimony?' Mrs Darcy suggested with a smile.

Patrick looked at her askance. 'You are very perceptive.'

Her eyes twinkled. 'My mother would tell you that a young man in possession of a fortune must be in want of a wife, Mr Shannon.'

'A lot of American ladies would agree with her.'

'So too will their English counterparts, Shannon,' Darcy warned him. 'Be on your guard.'

'I have no immediate plans to become leg-shackled.'

'Find the right lady and you will have a change of heart,' Darcy replied, sending his wife a look of such total adoration that Patrick felt as though he was intruding.

'Edward knew nothing about the losses that scuppered the pater's business. He had certainly not taken advantage of him. All he did was supply funds from afar. He had nothing to do with the running of the enterprise.'

'And so your original supposition endures,' Darcy said. 'You think workers colluded to defraud your father and you wish to uncover their identities.'

'Quite so.' Patrick shrugged. 'I realise it won't be easy to prove anything after all this time, but I still intend to try. I shall settle at Shannon House and restore the estate to its former glory. But I also intend to track down some of the people who worked for the pater and see what they know.' He fixed Darcy with a steady gaze. 'That is my reason for calling upon you. As the principal landowner in the area, I thought you might know where some of them finished up. Fenton wasn't much help, which leads me to suppose that he didn't take nearly so much care of them as he promised me he would. If nothing else, I need to satisfy myself that they didn't fall upon hard times as a consequence of Fenton's neglect.'

'There is a great deal of your father's philanthropy in you, Mr Shannon,' Mrs Darcy remarked.

Patrick inclined his head in acknowledgement of the compliment and then turned towards Darcy. 'I believe you took one or two of the pater's servants on here at Pemberley.'

'Quite likely,' Darcy replied. 'But I would need to ask my steward about that.'

'Naturally, and I... Good heavens, is that the time?' Patrick glanced at the long clock in the corner of the room as it chimed the hour. 'I have overstayed my welcome.'

'Not in the least,' Mrs Darcy replied with great civility. 'This has been most interesting. Do remain and dine with us, Mr Shannon, if you are not otherwise engaged. Then we will be at leisure to discuss your problems at greater length and see if we can find ways to help you.'

'If you're sure I won't be intruding,' Patrick replied.

'It will be just the three of us and Lizzy's sister,' Darcy told him. 'If you don't mind talking in front of her.'

'I don't mind in the least, provided the lady has no objections.'

'It might be just the thing to bring Lydia out of herself,' Mrs Darcy said, almost to herself.

Patrick wanted to ask why she needed to be 'brought out', but good manners prevented him from voicing such an intrusive question.

* * *

Lydia blinked when she heard the clock chime, and she realised it was time to dress for dinner. Where had the afternoon gone to? Since becoming a widow, the hours had hung heavily on her hands because finding ways to fill them had seemed like too much of an effort.

Not so today.

She had known Lizzy would try to talk her out of her enduring depression once the rest of the family left Pemberley following the twins' christening, and Lydia had not been looking forward to the lecture she probably deserved. But instead of scolding, Lizzy offered sympathy and practical suggestions. Her sister's appreciation of Lydia's dilemma had been as welcome as it had been unexpected. But even so, writing a journal? What good could that possibly do?

Lydia wanted an occupation, something that would make her feel useful. How could writing down recollections from her childhood possibly make any difference? Even so, just to show Lizzy she was no longer flighty, she decided to give it a try. That had been two hours ago and Lydia couldn't believe how many pages she had covered with her rather untidy writing; how many early memories she had relived. She had been forced to examine the undisciplined, attention-seeking behaviour of her younger years and was thoroughly ashamed of herself. In other words, for the first time, she was thinking deeply about her own actions and how they affected others, which Lizzy had most likely anticipated would be the case when she made her suggestion.

Nibbling at the end of her quill, she sat back and read over what she had written.

> *My earliest memories are of the nursery at Longbourn and the rather austere nurse who had charge of all five of us. I couldn't have been more than three years old at the time but I distinctly recall flying into a violent rage because I wanted something of Kitty's and she refused to give it to me. That seemed most unjust of her.*
>
> *I was the youngest and probably thought my sisters were being unkind because I had been a cause of such grave disappointment to Papa. I'm sure I knew that much; had heard it whispered about, seen heads shaken, even if I didn't yet understand what I had done wrong.*

Lydia studied her words for a considerable amount of time, deep in thought. Had she, on the very first page of her journal, hit upon an explanation for her subsequent disruptive behaviour? No one likes to be a disappointment, especially a child who fails to comprehend what she could possibly have done to cause such disappointment. It wasn't until Lydia was much older that she learned of the Longbourn entail and understood that the pompous Mr Collins would take possession of the property upon Papa's death if no son was born to cut off the entail.

Mama had been confident that Lydia would be a boy. Of course, she was not. Mama failed to have more children and Lydia grew up subconsciously believing that she was the cause of all her family's problems.

Shaking her head, Lydia continued to read.

> *Nurse took absolutely no notice of my outburst, which infuriated me, and continued reading aloud to Mary and Kitty. I screamed even*

louder, which brought Mama running to see what all the fuss was about. She looked severely upon our nurse and scolded Kitty for not handing over her toy. Kitty reluctantly did so upon Mama's command but, of course, by then I no longer wanted it. Instead I continued to be inconsolable because, at last, I had everyone's attention, and I do recall enjoying my misery. Can one enjoy misery? Does that make sense? Mama scooped me into her arms and carried me downstairs, sat me on her lap and petted me, feeding me sweetmeats and telling me constantly how pretty I was. Our Aunt Phillips was there and she agreed with Mama that Nurse had been quite wrong to ignore me.

Thus vindicated, I behaved like an angel, enjoying every moment of being the centre of attention. Then Jane and Lizzy came into the room, having been on a walk with one of the servants to supervise them. Mama launched into a long explanation about how badly Nurse had treated me, but my sisters didn't seem remotely interested. I think I knew, as early as three years old, that Jane, and especially Lizzy, would not fall for my antics. Did I know those antics were wrong? I'm sure that I must have. Every child wants his or her own way and I had already discovered that Mama, in an effort not to reveal how disappointed she was that I had been born a girl, was ready to indulge my every whim.

Lydia was still mulling over what she'd written as she tidied away her writing equipment. A light tap on the door preceded its opening and Lizzy poking her head around it.

'We haven't seen you since luncheon and I was worried I might have overset you with my forthright views. I'm well aware that I express them far too readily. It's one of my greatest faults.' Lizzy flashed a rueful smile. 'Ask Lady Catherine if you doubt it.'

'I'm not in the least upset. In fact, I decided to try what you suggested and start a journal,' Lydia replied. 'I haven't got far past my third birthday but already I know I was the worst behaved child in the whole of Hertfordshire.'

Lizzy's smile widened. 'I hope you don't expect me to deny it.'

Lydia scrunched up her features. 'Hardly.'

'It's not entirely your fault that you ran wild. I don't recall ever hearing Mama chastise you. Or Papa either, for that matter. He simply escaped to his library and ignored us all whenever there was a situation he would prefer not to deal with. Much as I love and respect him, I can't absolve him from his share of the blame.'

'Or me?'

Lizzy tugged at one of Lydia's escaped curls. 'Especially not you. Children need boundaries and you were never prevented from exceeding yours. Anyway, I hope you find the journal exercise beneficial.'

'It's early days but it is already providing me with food for thought.'

'Then I'm glad.' Lizzy and Lydia embraced. 'I came to warn you that we have a guest staying for dinner. If you're not in a sociable mood you don't need to come down. I'll have something sent up for you.'

'Who is dining with us?'

'Mr Shannon. He's very interesting.'

Lizzy sat on the edge of Lydia's bed and told her all about their newly returned neighbour.

'Disrupted silk production. Hmm.' Lydia's features settled into a determined expression. 'That is definitely too serious a crime to go unpunished.'

'I'm glad you haven't completely lost interest in fashion.'

'Hopefully Mr Darcy can help track down the people responsible.'

'So you'll come down?'

'Oh, yes. I'm intrigued.'

'Good.' Lizzy stood. 'I shall pop up to the nursery and then get changed. I'll see you in the drawing room directly.'

When Lydia went down, Mr Darcy and his visitor were standing in front of the fireplace drinking whisky. Lydia's first impression of Mr Shannon was that he cut a striking figure. He was as tall as Lizzy's husband, with a shock of thick brown hair that touched the collar of his superbly tailored coat. A broad forehead, gleaming brown eyes, a chiselled jaw, straight nose and wide mouth ought not to have sat well together but somehow combined to produce a ruggedly handsome face. He wore an air of tough resourcefulness brought about, Lydia supposed, by the travails he'd had to endure after his father's death. His attitude was guarded and she would have found it difficult to interpret his thoughts, even if she could summon sufficient interest to make the attempt. He was the sort of man she would once have gone out of her way to impress. And yet upon being introduced to him, she felt nothing more than a mild interest in his problems.

'It's a pleasure to make your acquaintance, Mrs Wickham.' Mr Shannon took her hand and shook it firmly. Lydia felt a brief frisson of awareness streak through her. She quickly reclaimed her hand, unwilling to admit to any form of attraction since none existed.

'Wickham? Not George Wickham?' he asked, looking perplexed. Obviously, he had not been warned.

'My sister's husband died a little over a year ago,' Lizzy said, entering the room in time to hear Mr Shannon's question and saving Lydia from the trouble of explaining.

'I am very sorry for your loss,' Mr Shannon said politely, looking as though he wanted to ask a great deal more about Wickham.

'Thank you,' Lydia replied, because she had to say something.

'Shall we go straight in?' Lizzy suggested.

Over dinner, Lydia found herself caught up in Mr Shannon's tales of his time in America. He answered the questions put to him with great civility and made Lydia curious about a subject that had never before troubled her mind. America was simply too far away to be of any interest to her, but Mr Shannon brought it alive and made it sound incredibly exciting.

'Did you feel uncomfortable as an Englishman in the newly formed United States?' Lydia asked. She sensed Lizzy's surprise and was pleased to have impressed her by asking a pertinent question. 'After all, they had just fought a war to free themselves from our control so one would have no reason to expect a warm welcome.'

'On the whole I was treated with great courtesy. Americans are very easy going, generally speaking. One or two took issue with my presence there but were easily avoided.'

'Perhaps you will go there one day, Lydia, if the country so interests you,' Lizzy said.

Lydia smiled. 'That's hardly likely.'

With the meal out of the way, the gentlemen didn't linger over their port and when they re-joined Lizzy and Lydia, Mr Shannon's problems were finally raised.

'I have reiterated to my sister what you told us earlier, Mr Shannon,' Lizzy explained. 'And so you can speak freely in front of her.'

* * *

Patrick was unsure what to make of Mrs Darcy's tall sister, dressed in a modest dove-grey evening gown that clung to a svelte figure. She was out of mourning but presumably still distraught at her untimely loss. She had arresting grey eyes that dominated a tolerably attractive face, a waterfall of dark hair and an air of distraction that lent her a degree of fragility. Even so, Patrick was on his guard. In spite of appearances to the contrary, she might already be on the prowl for husband number two.

'I've been thinking, Shannon,' Darcy said. 'Whoever ruined your father's business had to be in a position of authority. Are you absolutely sure your lawyer Fenton knows nothing about it? Your father must have spoken with him when things started to go wrong.'

'He isn't my lawyer.' Patrick jutted his chin, anger at that man's inefficiency briefly reignited by the mention of his name. 'I have engaged another man to look after my affairs. But I did call to see Fenton while I was in London. We spoke on several occasions and at my insistence he gave me a list of all the men in positions of authority in my father's business. I have it with me.' He reached inside his coat and produced a piece of paper. 'Do any of these names mean anything to you?'

The Darcys poured over the parchment and both shook their heads.

'I'll show it to my butler and steward, with your permission,' Darcy said.

'Please keep it. I have another copy.'

'It occurs to me, Mr Shannon,' Mrs Darcy said, 'that the majority of your father's employees would have been women. I don't suppose they would have had anything to do with the finances, but they probably saw a lot of what went on.' She smiled. 'Our sex is blessed with a natural curiosity.'

'Is that a polite way of saying we snoop, Lizzy?' Mrs Wickham asked, biting her lower lip in a rather attractive manner, presumably to curb a smile. Did she think it inappropriate to smile simply because she'd been widowed? How foolish. Patrick was filled with a reckless desire to make her smile, even if she would prefer not to. He quickly smothered the urge. Better not to encourage her.

'We have a reputation for spreading gossip and starting rumours, Lydia, so we might as well live up to it.'

'It is possible that those employed in the mill would have noticed the comings and goings in the offices,' Patrick conceded. 'Thank you, Mrs Darcy. I had not stopped to consider that possibility. And, for what it's worth, my experience of ladies... er, rumour mongering, is that the information spread usually has a basis in fact, however obscure.'

'There you are, Lydia,' Mrs Darcy said, feeling no necessity to curb her own smile. 'We *can* make ourselves useful sometimes.'

'The women working from their homes wouldn't have much exposure to my father's overseers,' Patrick added thoughtfully.

'My point in raising the possibility is that the ladies might be more inclined to speak to my sister and me than they would be to you gentlemen.'

Patrick was taken aback by the suggestion. 'I could not put you to the trouble, ma'am.'

'It's no trouble, is it, Lydia?'

'Not in the least, if you think we can help,' Mrs Wickham replied with lukewarm enthusiasm. 'I shall be glad of the occupation.'

'I was pleased to discover that my father's old head groom and his wife have stayed at the house all this time, keeping it in as good an order as their limited resources permitted. I shall certainly ask them if they know what became of my father's old retainers.'

'And we shall make enquiries of our senior servants,' Mrs Darcy assured him as he stood to take his leave. 'But we will not speak to anyone without consulting you first.'

'I am much obliged to you.' Patrick turned towards Mrs Wickham and took her hand. 'And you also, ma'am.'

He was surprised when Mrs Wickham reclaimed her hand sooner than he had planned to release it and turned her attention to a large marmalade cat that had just stalked into the room.

Far from feeling reassured, the lady's disinterest felt more like a challenge.

How very peculiar, Patrick thought as he rode home.

6

'Oh, how interesting.'

Jane looked up from the letter she was reading. A letter from Pemberley. Jane had only parted from her sister a few days previously. What could Mrs Darcy possibly have to write about that Jane found so interesting, Caroline wondered irritably. Something to do with babies, no doubt. She hid a yawn behind her hand and shared a long-suffering look with Louisa.

'What does Lizzy have to say for herself, my dear?' Charles asked.

'Do you remember that house on the road between Lambton and Kympton? The old manor house that looks so neglected?'

Caroline moved to the edge of her seat, her boredom replaced by keen interest.

'Yes, what of it?'

'Lizzy writes that its owner has returned after a long absence. Mr Darcy knows him and they entertained him to dinner the other night. He is a Mr Shannon and has been in America these past ten years. That would account for the neglect to his property, I suppose.'

'Shannon?' Caroline asked, ignoring Louisa's look of amusement. 'What a coincidence. I believe we encountered a gentleman of that name while we were in London, did we not, Louisa? I had quite forgotten about that.' Louisa cleared her throat but managed to keep her countenance. 'Now that I think about it, he did happen to say he hailed from these parts. You really must call upon him, Charles.'

Caroline was mortified when she observed a speculative look pass between Charles and Jane.

'Lizzy says he is extremely amiable, too. He plans to make Shannon House his permanent home,' Jane said, continuing it read. 'She and Lydia thought him charming.'

Lydia Wickham. Blazes, Caroline had forgotten about that scheming little minx. She would take one look at Shannon and throw her cap at him, widow's weeds notwithstanding. She possessed a rather vulgar charm that appealed to men's protective instincts, a fragility and, Caroline hated to admit, a degree of decorum she never would have thought the chit capable of maintaining. And facts had to be faced – she was also considerably younger than Caroline.

Caroline couldn't allow Lydia to spend too much time ingratiating herself with Mr Shannon before he and Caroline had become reacquainted. She felt slightly less anxious when it occurred to her that even if Mr Shannon enjoyed Lydia's society, nothing could come of it. Judging from the state of his property, he was not well situated and would require a wife with a substantial dowry. Although there again, Mr Darcy would probably offer Lydia a generous settlement just to be rid of her.

Caroline inverted her chin, determined that such largesse would do the troublesome child no good. Mr Shannon was destined to become *her* husband although, of course, he didn't know it yet. She was heartily sick of the wretched Bennet clan, and none of them would get the better of her this time.

'Mr Shannon made his fortune in America and is in a position to restore his property,' Jane said, beaming.

Damnation!

'Caroline's right, my dear. We ought to recognise him.'

'I shall call tomorrow,' Charles said good-naturedly. 'I could drop you at Pemberley first, Jane, if you like and you could visit with your sisters.'

Jane's face came alight with pleasure. 'Oh, yes please.' She glanced at Caroline. 'Shall you come too, Caroline?'

It was obvious that the offer had been made out of a sense of duty and that Jane didn't really desire her company. In fact, Jane had not been the same sweet obliging girl since Charles purchased Campton Park and Jane became mistress of it. She seemed to tolerate Caroline nowadays; nothing more. It was extraordinary. Jane was the last person Caroline would have expected to put on airs, which just went to show how an advantageous marriage could change a person's character.

Jane and Charles now knew of the part Caroline had played in Wickham's scheme to compromise Lizzy. That was mortifying for Caroline, and even she could see how difficult that must have made things for Jane. All the doctors Caroline had been forced to consult agreed she had temporarily lost her senses. She had willingly perpetuated that myth even though it wasn't true since it meant she wasn't deemed culpable for colluding with Wickham.

She was now fully recovered but had overheard one of the physicians warning Charles that she was still very fragile. That was convenient since it meant no one asked her awkward questions and treated her with consideration. Her only regret was that Lizzy had consolidated her position by giving Darcy three children. Even so, no one would ever convince Caroline – who was and always had been of sound mind – that she and Fitzwilliam Darcy were not destined to be together. Caroline would not be satisfied until she had brought that situation about and Patrick Shannon was just the person to help her arrange it.

'No, I shall just be in the way,' Caroline said in response to Jane's invitation. She stood up. 'Excuse me. I feel the need for fresh air.'

Caroline paced out her agitation on the terrace. It was vexatious that Mr Shannon didn't require Caroline's fortune, but he did require a wife. Caroline was ten times better educated than Lydia and could speak intelligently without giggling. She could also sing and play, was well read, spoke fluent French and possessed manners and dignity.

No, she had nothing to fear from Lydia Wickham, but she *did* need to remind Mr Shannon that she was alive. It wasn't as though she was unattractive. She had received a good offer of marriage from one of Mr Hurst's acquaintances when last in London. That gentleman didn't need her fortune either but was taken, as he put it, by her grace and ladylike qualities. If she could attract a man of fortune without even trying, then Mr Shannon was as good as hers.

Thus reassured, Caroline was able to dredge up a smile for Louisa when she joined her on the terrace.

'By mixing with Mr Shannon you will be thrown into more constant company with the Darcys,' Louisa warned. 'Are you prepared for that?'

Caroline shrugged. 'Why would I not be?'

Louisa linked her arm through Caroline's. 'Have a care, my dear. Don't do anything rash simply to make a point to Mr Darcy.'

'If you won't take my word for it, I don't know what I can say to convince you that I no longer have any interest in Mr Darcy.'

Caroline was surprised how easily lies tripped from her tongue nowadays. An unfortunate necessity since Louisa, despite her lover and enlightened ways, would never understand that Mr Darcy needed her.

'I shall be happy to help you attract Mr Shannon, if that's what you have in mind.'

Caroline quirked a brow. 'You think me incapable of engaging a gentleman's interest without your help?'

Louisa sighed. 'You seem determined to pick a fight with me today when I only have your best interests at heart.'

'If I am out of sorts it is because I saw the way Charles and Jane looked at one another when I mentioned Mr Shannon. It's as though they can't wait to be rid of me.'

'I'm sure that is not the case.'

Caroline was equally sure that it was.

* * *

'I've had a think about your father's workers,' Mason told Patrick a couple of days after Patrick had dined at Pemberley. 'The manager of the watermill was a man called Jessup. I've only just remembered that. You could do worse than track him down.'

The name had come up before. Fenton had mentioned him.

'I would if I knew where to find him. The moment my father died, he disappeared, which is damned suspicious. If I knew where he was I would be interested to have a conversation with him.'

'Aye, that's what I thought.' Mason forked clean straw into Gladiator's stable as he spoke. 'I asked a few questions about him and word is he's taken an overseer's position at a new mill in Matlock. Only recently opened up, so it has.'

'Then I shall ride over there tomorrow and see what he has to say for himself.'

Patrick walked back to the house, thinking about Jessup. He had vague recollections of a brutish man with a squint and recalled not taking to him. It would have been a waste of breath to have voiced unfounded suspicions to a father who saw only good in everyone, especially since Jessup was so well-qualified for the position he held.

With all the activity around the house and grounds since his return, Patrick had had little opportunity to delve further into the whereabouts of his father's workforce. There was no immediate hurry, although the matter would continue to play on his mind until he found some answers. He hoped Darcy had met with success. Patrick would ride over to ask him when he had a moment to himself.

'You've got company,' Mason said, pointing to a curricle making its way slowly up the unkempt drive.

Patrick assumed it must be Darcy. No one else knew he was here. But when he rounded the house and stood on the crumbling steps to await the curricle's arrival, he could see it was being driven by a stranger. The man secured his reins and stepped down from the conveyance, hand outstretched and a friendly, open smile gracing his features.

'Mr Shannon? The name's Bingley. Do hope I'm not inconveniencing you. I believe you are acquainted with my sisters.'

'Of course.' Patrick shook Bingley's hand. 'How very good of you to call.'

'Mrs Darcy mentioned to my wife that you were in residence so I came at once to bid you welcome home.'

'I'm very glad that you did. Please come inside, if you can ignore the chaos. The drawing room at least is reasonably presentable.'

It was about the only downstairs room that was. The furniture had been uncovered and put into its proper places, rugs and drapes had been removed, beaten and replaced and a fire blazed permanently, removing the musty air of disuse. It was also relatively tranquil, whereas every-where else, maids purposely scurried about. Outside, repairs to the crumbling stonewalls were already underway and restoration of the gardens would soon commence.

'Some refreshments?'

'Please don't go to the trouble. I can see that you're still getting settled. I simply wanted to introduce myself. We are at Campton Park, you know.'

'I recall the estate. A school friend of mine lived there when I was a boy. Are you pleased with it?'

'Very much so. Mrs Darcy is my wife's sister and now that we have removed to the north, they are only ten miles apart. I left Jane at Pemberley a moment ago. When she knew I was coming to call upon you she couldn't resist a visit to her sister.'

'What ladies find to talk about is a mystery to me,' Patrick said, smiling.

'Me also.'

They chatted for a while about Patrick's plans for his estate and Bing-ley's own for his. They both intended to run sheep.

'I'm thinking of Gritstones,' Patrick said. 'They are hardy devils, well able to withstand our harsh winters.'

'How extraordinary. I was thinking along the same lines. Perhaps we could share the services of Gritstone rams.'

'It's certainly a possibility,' Patrick replied, unprepared to enter into a binding commitment until he was absolutely sure it was the best thing to do.

'Let me know what you decide.'

'I trust your sisters are well,' Patrick said politely when he and Bingley had exhausted the subject of Derbyshire sheep.

'In the best of health, I thank you. They are both in Derbyshire at present. I was never more surprised than when my wife received a letter from her sister mentioning your arrival and Caroline said she had met you. A small world, what?'

'Indeed.'

'Well, I'd best not detain you.'

Bingley stood. Patrick walked to the door with him and shook his hand again. 'Thank you for calling. I do hope on your next visit my home will be fit to be seen.'

'Nonsense. I know how long it takes to get a place in order. Jane is still not completely satisfied with the changes she's made to Campton Park.'

Patrick chuckled. 'Don't expect her to be so any time soon.'

'I would not be so optimistic,' Bingley replied with a broad smile.

Patrick watched Bingley drive away, aware that he would need to return the call and reacquaint himself with Bingley's sisters. He hoped Miss Bingley was not on the lookout for a husband. He had no reason to suppose that she was. There was just something about the nature of their accidental meeting and the questions she had peppered him with when she realised where he lived that had appeared contrived.

He had come north in the expectation of being left in peace by predatory females, so would treat Miss Bingley cautiously.

* * *

'This is a lovely surprise, Jane.' Lizzy hugged her sister and led her into the small sitting room she favoured when they didn't have company.

'The strangest thing happened,' Jane replied, explaining about Caroline Bingley knowing Mr Shannon. 'When your letter arrived telling us of his arrival, Caroline asked Charles to call upon him, which is where he has gone now.' Jane flashed a knowing smile. 'I think Caroline likes Mr Shannon. When his name was mentioned, it was the most animated I have seen her since... well, since you know when.'

'If they met in the street, she can hardly know him.'

'True.' Jane flashed a rueful smile. 'But I still live in hope.'

'Poor Mr Shannon. He mentioned in passing that he left America partly because he was being pursued by ambitious females.'

'Is he an attractive gentleman, Lizzy?'

'Oh yes, and very charming, too. But there is a cynical edge to his personality, I think.' Lizzy told her sister about their new neighbour's problems with his father's estate. 'He believes his father's good nature was taken advantage of and doesn't plan to make the same mistake himself. He looks upon everyone with suspicion, and given his history it's hard to fault him for that.'

'Poor Mr Shannon.' An anxious smile played about Jane's lips. 'And poor Caroline, too. If she does have designs upon him, that is.'

'And you would like rid of her—'

'No!'

'Yes, Jane.' Lizzy patted her sister's hand. 'I know it's difficult for you to admit to such a wicked aspiration, but that doesn't make it any the less true.'

'You're right, as always.' Jane relaxed her rigid shoulders. 'I resent Caroline for what she tried to do to you. How could I not? And yet she's Charles's sister and his responsibility.'

'And you would much prefer her to be someone else's?'

'I would.' Jane smiled. 'There, I've said it!'

'Good girl!'

'Anyway, Caroline seems like her old self again. If she finds a gentleman who engages her affections she will also find the contentment that eludes her and be a nicer person as a consequence.'

'There's hope for you yet, Jane.'

'Possibly, but I wouldn't speak that way in front of anyone else. Not even Charles.' She paused. 'Especially not him.'

'But if Caroline were to find a husband you would be happy to have her out of your lives.' Lizzy grinned. 'There you are, Jane, we have managed to make everyone happy without your being obliged to think too badly of anyone.'

'Stop teasing me, Lizzy.' Jane waved a hand in half-hearted protest.

'In that case, Caroline is welcome to do her worst with Mr Shannon. I dare say he's able to look out for himself.'

When the footman bearing refreshments had withdrawn, Lizzy told her sister about Mr Shannon's determination to discover who had exploited his father's good nature.

'But you must keep everything I have told you about his affairs to yourself, Jane. Mr Shannon didn't give us leave to make it public.'

'Certainly I shall say nothing. It must have been a terrible shock for him. Is Mr Darcy doing anything to help his investigations?'

'He's trying and so are Lydia and I.'

'How is Lydia?'

'Still very downcast. She is writing a journal at my suggestion, starting with her earliest memories. I thought it might help her to see things more clearly, but now I wonder if it is such a good idea.' Lizzy wrinkled her brow. 'It's making her think too deeply about things that can't be changed.'

Jane looked confused. 'What harm can it possibly do?'

'Well, she wasn't aware until she commenced the project that her first memory was of being a "disappointment".'

'A disappointment?' Jane looked bewildered. 'But she was our mother's favourite.'

'She thinks that's because she was expected to be a boy.'

Jane sighed. 'We all were.'

Lizzy sighed. 'Yes, but Papa had had four disappointments before Lydia's arrival and she was supposed to be the baby who finally cut off the entail. She heard it talked about in whispers and hadn't remembered until she started writing things down. She thinks that's why she behaved so badly.'

'Bah, that was because she was allowed to do as she pleased.'

'You and I know that, but Lydia will never be convinced. She also feels guilty because she isn't as sorry as she thinks she ought to be about Wickham's death.'

'And overcompensates by still wearing grey?' Lizzy nodded. 'Well then, perhaps the journal is not such a very bad thing. By the time she gets to her elopement and subsequent marriage, if she can be honest with herself I am sure it will help her to see just how shamefully Wickham used her innocence to his advantage.'

'Very likely.'

'How did she respond to Mr Shannon?'

'With indifference.'

'Good heavens, now you have really worried me.' Jane widened her eyes. 'If what you tell me about him is true, he is pleasing to the eye, comfortably situated and possesses great charm. Since when did Lydia resist such temptation?'

'Since she became a "disappointment", apparently. However, she has agreed to try and help Mr Shannon find some of the people who worked for his family. We have decided that she and I ought to speak to the women rather than Mr Shannon. Anyway, whether or not we succeed, at least it gives Lydia an occupation that keeps her cheerful.'

The appearance of Lydia herself brought the discussion to a close.

'Jane, what are you doing here?'

'It's lovely to see you as well, Lydia,' Jane replied with a wry smile, embracing her youngest sister.

'I just meant Lizzy didn't warn me you were coming.'

'That's because I didn't know,' Lizzy pointed out. 'You look as though you're bursting to tell me something.'

'There's a family here on the estate called Hobson,' Lydia replied. 'Mrs Reynolds tells me that Mrs Hobson, before her marriage, was one of Mr Shannon's spinners at the mill.'

'I think I know the family,' Lizzy said. 'Her husband is one of the keepers and they have a cottage in the spinney. We could go together and speak with Mrs Hobson this afternoon.'

'Yes, all right.' Lydia threw herself into a chair and tapped her slippered foot on the boarded floor, not because she was bored necessarily but because sitting still, especially when something excited her, was beyond Lydia's capabilities. 'It will probably be a waste of time though, so we might as well not mention it to Mr Shannon and raise his hopes unnecessarily.'

'Ah, here's Mr Bingley, Jane. And just in time for luncheon, too.'

7

'You must excuse me from visiting Mrs Hobson with you,' Lizzy said breathlessly, poking her head around the door to Lydia's chamber. 'Spencer is running a slight fever. Will has insisted upon sending for Dominic.'

'I hope Spencer will be all right,' Lydia replied.

'I am sure we are worrying about nothing,' Lizzy said, not sounding sure at all.

'Then shall you mind if I go and see Mrs Hobson alone?'

'Not in the least.' Lizzy flashed a distracted smile. 'I can see you have your heart set on a little sleuthing. The cottage you want is in a cluster of several about a mile beyond the woods, in a pretty clearing.'

'I know the place. You pointed the cottages out to me once and told me about the repairs Mr Darcy had put in hand.'

'Then go, but be cautious in your approach with Mrs Hobson,' Lizzy advised. 'There's no way of knowing whom she still associates with from her time at Shannon's Mill, and your questions might inadvertently alert the culprit of Mr Shannon's interest in him.'

'I wouldn't imagine Mrs Hobson was involved in any wrongdoing.' Lydia frowned. 'Although why I should think that when I haven't even

met her is beyond me. Women are just as capable of resentment, ingrati-
tude and criminal activities as men.'

'Precisely so.'

'Go back to Spencer, Lizzy!' Lydia shooed her away with a flapping
motion of her hands.

Lizzy smiled distractedly and took herself off.

A short time later, Lydia left the house and strolled through
Pemberley Park, a soft summer breeze caressing her upturned face. She
enjoyed the solitude she had once found so disagreeable but now craved.

She had added more recollections to her journal over the past two
days; oddities that had stuck in her mind because they were out of the
ordinary, even by her own disruptive standards. Throwing Mary's collection of ribbons on the fire and pulling Kitty's hair until she cried was *not*
normal behaviour, but Lydia couldn't recall being chastised for any of
her transgressions.

No wonder she was such a 'disappointment'. But she could not
possibly have been aware of the inconvenience being born a female had
caused when still so young and so couldn't use that as an excuse for her
conduct. Indeed, the time for excuses was past and Lydia was obliged to
accept there must be something inherently bad about her character.

Her rambling walk and even more disjointed thoughts brought her
to the clearing, dappled in sunshine, which housed the cottages she
sought. A grubby little boy with a toothy grin pointed out the one inhab-
ited by Mrs Hobson. Smoke billowed from the chimney, the small front
garden was a mass of flowers in bloom, and she could see long, neat rows
of vegetables planted to one side of the building.

Lydia tapped on the door, and it was answered by a barefoot, straggly
haired little girl of no more than about four.

'Is your mama home?' Lydia asked, crouching down to the child's
level.

The girl merely stared at her through vacant eyes and sucked her
thumb. A baby cried in the background, at which point the little girl
looked over her shoulder and trotted off in that direction, leaving the
door open. Unsure what else to do, Lydia followed her into a neat, over-
warm kitchen. A stout woman with a red face, wearing a dirty pinafore,

bent over the crying infant, rocked its cradle and made impatient crooning noises. Lydia stood on the threshold, watching the woman alternately trying to calm the baby and continue with the baking its cries had interrupted.

'Mrs Hobson?' she asked.

The woman whirled around. 'And who might you be?' she asked accusingly.

'I did knock but...' Lydia placed a hand on top of the little girl's head and smiled at her. The child stared emotionlessly back at her.

'Maisie don't talk much.' Mercifully, the baby had stopped crying. 'What do you want?'

'I am Mrs Wickham, Mrs Darcy's sister.'

If Mrs Hobson was impressed to receive a visit from the mistress's relation, she gave no sign. 'Aye, I've seen you about.'

'Would it be all right if I sat down?'

Mrs Hobson shrugged. 'Suit yourself.'

Lydia pulled out a stool and sat at the scrubbed wooden table. 'I believe you once worked for Mr Shannon at his mill,' she said, getting to the point before Mrs Hobson was again distracted by the grizzling baby.

'The mill?' A brief expression of anxiety creased Mrs Hobson's features. 'That were years ago. I was just a gal.'

'You were one of the senior spinners?'

'Why are you dragging all that up?' Mrs Hobson squinted suspiciously at Lydia.

Lydia wondered why she was so reluctant to talk about her former employment and how she had finished up so advantageously married to Hobson. She wasn't an especially handsome woman and Lydia couldn't detect any signs of her having been so before a succession of children had robbed her of her figure. Hobson, as one of Mr Darcy's keepers, would have been considered a good catch. It might have been a love match, Lydia reminded herself. Surely her romantic nature was not so crushed that she could overlook such an obvious possibility?

'Mr Shannon's son has just returned to Derbyshire.' Mrs Hobson would soon learn of it, if she didn't already know, so Lydia saw no harm in mentioning it. 'I understand the mill didn't prosper?'

Mrs Hobson puffed out her considerable chest and took immediate offence. 'Not for lack of hard work on the part of us spinners if that's what you're implying.'

'Not in the least.'

'It don't do no good, raking over the past.' Mrs Hobson's attitude bordered on the uncivil. Lydia suspected that if she had been anyone else, she would have been encouraged to leave before now. 'What can't be cured must be endured.'

'Mr Shannon is curious about the circumstances surrounding the failure of the mill. He told Mr Darcy that he was too young to ask questions at the time. But now that he's back in England he's keen to know what happened. I'm sure I would feel the same way in his situation. When I heard that you were once one of old Mr Shannon's most valued spinners, I thought I would come and chat with you.'

'Well, you've wasted an afternoon,' Mrs Hobson replied belligerently. Was there a hint of anxiety in her eye again, accounting for her bluster? 'Now, you'll have to excuse me.'

But Lydia wasn't ready to be dismissed. 'You must know...' She glanced down when something tugged at the sash dangling beneath her pelisse. To please Lizzy, Lydia had replaced her grey sash with a bright yellow one and Maisie was clearly fascinated by it. With her mouth hanging open, she twisted its ends around her tiny fingers, humming to herself. 'That's yellow,' Lydia said, smiling at the child. 'Do you like it?'

'Sun,' the little girl said. 'Sun. Sun.'

'I'll be blowed!' Mrs Hobson looked astounded. 'That's the first word Maisie's uttered in days.'

Lydia lifted the little mite onto her lap and stroked her hair. 'Do you like the sun, Maisie?'

'It's what her pa calls her. He picks her up, points to the sun and calls her his little ray of sunshine. We have three boys, including this one.' She indicated the grizzling baby with a jerk of her thumb. 'But Maisie is her pa's favourite. He dotes on her, so he does.'

But not to the extent that he encourages her to talk.

'We thought she were right simple.' Mrs Hobson shook her head. 'Perhaps she's just a bit slow.'

'Most likely.' Lydia removed her sash and tied it around the little girl's middle with a flamboyant bow. 'There, that's for you,' she said.

The little girl's eyes widened with wary anticipation.

'That's right nice of you, ma'am.' Mrs Hobson watched Maisie slither from Lydia's lap and dance around the kitchen with the ends of the sash grasped in her hands. 'Now, what did you want to know about Shannon's mill?' she asked in a more civil tone.

'What were they like to work for?'

'Better than most. Mr Shannon was a right gent, firm but fair, although sometimes a bit too trusting.'

'In what respect?'

'Well, he would only need to hear that someone was down on their luck and he was there with an open purse, ready to lend a helping hand. Word got about and people took advantage.'

'How shocking.'

'Not so very shocking. More like human nature, if you ask me.'

'What about the people in positions of authority? Did they take advantage?'

Mrs Hobson settled her bulk more comfortably at the table and gave the question some consideration. 'We had a new manager foisted upon us about a year before Mr Shannon's passing. A right brute, he were, by the name of Jessup. Mr Shannon might have been too trusting but Jessup veered in the opposite direction. He sacked one girl on the spot for not working hard enough. She had a fever and could hardly stand at her loom, but did he care? Did he heck as like. Needless to say, the lass went to Mr Shannon and he found her work at his house. There was a right to-do over that. I heard Jessup shouting at Mr Shannon, saying he couldn't keep proper order if Mr Shannon kept undermining his authority.'

'If this Jessup was manager he wouldn't have supervised the floor, would he?' Lydia's knowledge of the workings of a silk mill were vague. 'Presumably there were overseers for that purpose.'

'Jessup liked to stride around, changing the orders given by his overseers just so everyone knew who was in charge. But he also spent a lot of time locked away in his office, now that I think about it.' Mrs Hobson screwed up her eyes as though it was an effort to recall, although Lydia was left with the impression that she remembered very well. 'Lots of comings and goings, so there were.'

'What do you mean by that?'

'Buyers, we heard they were. Jessup was looking for new markets, but buyers had never come to the mill before Jessup took control. We all thought it was a bit odd, especially since they didn't come and look at the silk being woven, but it wasn't our place to ask questions.'

'Do you remember any of their names?'

Mrs Hobson shook her head vigorously before Lydia finished voicing the question. 'No, but I expect they'll be recorded in the ledgers, if indeed they did make purchases.'

'I'm sure they must be.' It hadn't even occurred to Lydia that books would have been kept. Presumably, Mr Shannon had seen them and they had not been much help. 'However, if you could just cast your mind back—'

'I was always taught to mind my own business and let others mind theirs,' Mrs Hobson said, finality in her tone. 'That's good advice and you could do worse than to remember it. Now, you really will have to excuse me. There's nothing more I can tell you, and I have work to do.'

Lydia thought there was a great deal more Mrs Hobson could tell her, but she seemed afraid to speak out. Aware that she would learn nothing more, Lydia thanked her most civilly and left the cottage. She stepped outside into bright sunshine that hurt her eyes and noticed a young man leaning against the wall of the cottage opposite. He was dressed in scruffy working clothes, and he fixed her with a surly expression as he watched her without blinking. He didn't so much as doff his cap, as he most assuredly ought to have done. She glanced over her shoulder and saw that he was still watching her as she walked away. Then he pushed himself from the wall and sauntered off in the opposite direction. He had made her feel uncomfortable and she hastened to put distance between them even though he wasn't following her.

As she walked back to Pemberley, she mulled over what she had just learned. It wasn't a great deal. Perhaps Mr Shannon would see something useful in her discoveries that escaped Lydia. She felt an overwhelming need to be useful to their neighbour for no reason other than it might atone in some small way for the selfish manner in which she had lived all these years. She couldn't think of a single occasion before today when she had put anyone else's interests ahead of her own.

Sighing, Lydia walked into the house and found Lizzy in the drawing room.

'How is Spencer?' Lydia asked.

'Crisis averted. Just a touch of colic apparently.' Lizzy looked less than her normally composed self. 'Honestly, no one warned me that being a mother would be quite so terrifying. I am sure I must have aged ten years today.'

'I'm glad.' Lydia smiled. 'Not that you feel older, but that Spencer is not seriously ill.'

Lizzy chuckled. 'I knew what you meant.'

Lydia fell into the chair beside Lizzy's and smiled at Mr Darcy as he hovered in front of the fireplace. It was strange how she felt so much more at ease in his company since Wickham's demise. She used to think Mr Darcy cold and aloof and had not envied Lizzy, in spite of all the wealth and consequence that went with her marriage. Now she saw a very different side to the owner of Pemberley, knew that his love for Lizzy was deep and abiding – something she *did* envy – and appreciated all he had done for his nemesis's wife when he could so easily not have troubled himself.

'How was your afternoon, Lydia?' he asked with great civility.

'Very interesting, actually.'

Lydia described Mrs Hobson's circumstances and explained how reluctant she had been to talk about the mill.

'She looked frightened,' Lydia said, frowning. 'I feel persuaded she knows a great deal more about the mismanagement of the business than she actually revealed.'

'It doesn't seem so strange that buyers would be closeted with the manager,' Mr Darcy said musingly. 'I dare say he had samples of the silk in his office to show his customers, saving them from watching the production first hand and not being able to make themselves heard over the noise. Just because things weren't done that way before Jessup took up his position... Well, everyone has a different way of working.'

'Even so, Will,' Lizzy said. 'If Lydia thinks Mrs Hobson knows more than she's saying then Mr Shannon ought to be made aware.'

'Of course. Shall we call on him tomorrow, Lydia, and you can tell him yourself?' Mr Darcy asked.

'Is that really necessary?'

Lydia noticed Lizzy and her husband share a glance.

'If you'd rather not—'

'You can tell him for me, Mr Darcy. There's nothing more I can add, although...' Lydia wrinkled her brow. 'Actually, there is one thing I'm curious about. How did Mrs Hobson come to marry your keeper, Mr Darcy? He is some years older than her, I understand, and holds a senior position at Pemberley. Would he not have considered himself above the likes of Mrs Hobson? She isn't an especially handsome woman and... Well, it just seems odd.'

'Stranger unions have been known to work, Lydia,' Lizzy said with a wry smile, her attention fixed upon her husband.

'I confess to having no idea about Hobson's background,' Mr Darcy added. 'But to satisfy your curiosity, Lydia, I will ask my steward about him.'

'Don't go to any trouble. I dare say there's nothing to it.'

'Probably not,' Mr Darcy said, smiling at her. 'But I like to be thorough.'

8

'How much longer must we wait for Mr Shannon to return Charles's call?' Caroline tapped her fingers restlessly against the arm of her chair. 'It's been three days now which borders upon the uncivil.'

'He's probably occupied with his property.' Louisa's indolent tone irritated Caroline. 'He will come eventually.'

But all the time he delays, Lydia will be ingratiating herself with him; the shameless hussy! The unpalatable truth was that Caroline couldn't have made much of an impression upon Mr Shannon if he was so reluctant to renew their acquaintanceship. That realisation gnawed away at her like a persistent toothache, souring her mood and making her short-tempered with everyone.

'Your patience is about to be rewarded,' Louisa said with a wry little smile as she glanced out of the morning room window.

Caroline followed the direction of her sister's gaze and observed a gentleman riding a grey horse up the drive. Her heart fluttered with nervous determination at the prospect of finally instigating her plan. Her feelings for Mr Shannon were entirely imaginary, but his delay in returning Charles's call also made him a challenge. She would not be passed over for a second time, especially not in favour of another Bennet.

Caroline stood up and straightened her gown. She checked her reflection in a nearby mirror, adjusted a curl that had dared to slip from its appointed place, pinched her cheeks to add a little colour to her wan complexion and was as ready as she would ever be.

Mr Shannon greeted Caroline and Louisa with reserved civility. He was taller than she remembered and a great deal better looking. Nothing compared to Mr Darcy, of course, but he still cut an imposing figure. Caroline was glad about that. She would find it difficult to marry an 'ordinary' man, even for Mr Darcy's sake.

'I hope calling upon us has not taken you too far out of your way,' Jane said.

'We're only ten miles from Pemberley, Jane, as you well know since we are there all the time,' Caroline pointed out before Mr Shannon could respond. 'And less than that from Shannon House. It's no distance at all.' When everyone looked at her with varying degrees of incredulity, Caroline felt her cheeks warm. She had shown too much interest in Mr Shannon's situation and had possibly alerted him to her intentions. Perdition, what was wrong with her? 'A good horse makes such distances inconsequential,' she finished lamely.

'It was a pleasure to reacquaint myself with the district and a fine day for a ride,' Mr Shannon replied with great civility.

Conversation became general while refreshments were served.

'How are you enjoying your return to Derbyshire, Mr Shannon?' Caroline asked a short time later, desperate to show herself in a less... desperate light.

'I am being kept very busy with the restoration of my house, ma'am,' he replied. 'It has been neglected but I am happy to say that situation is changing, thanks to the army of servants my housekeeper has engaged.'

'It must seem rather strange to be back in England after so long,' Jane said.

'I'm very glad to be here.' He sent Jane a warm smile. Caroline was aware such warmth had not been directed her way. She felt justifiable annoyance at the Bennet clan collectively, still unable to understand why every male they encountered appeared to find the whole lot of them irre-

sistible. 'I should not have stayed away for so long. I have responsibilities.'

'I hope they will not deprive us of your society,' Caroline said,
ignoring Louisa's raised eyebrows.

'I will not allow that situation to arise.'

Mr Shannon spoke with absolute politeness, but Caroline was
discouraged when he encompassed the entire company when he made
that remark. She told herself she was expecting too much too soon. After
all, he barely knew her.

'Shall you spend much of your time in London, Mr Shannon?' she
asked. 'There are many gentlemanly distractions to be had in the capital,
and I dare say you are anxious to renew old acquaintanceships.'

'If you refer to the clubs, then you mistake the matter.'

'You don't care for a decent game of cards?' Mr Hurst asked disap-
provingly.

'I enjoy a game of chance as much as the next man, but I certainly
would not go to London simply to gamble away my fortune.'

'Well said,' Charles remarked.

'I shall not be frequenting the clubs, Miss Bingley. I prefer to remain
quietly in the country and if that makes me unfashionable, I cannot
bring myself to apologise for it.'

'You find us in the country for the same reason, sir,' she replied with
a serene smile.

Mr Shannon made no direct response to her, turning instead to
Charles and replying to a remark he had just made. Caroline was
conscious of Louisa struggling to contain a smile. Caroline had talked
Louisa's ears off over the years about her preference for the liveliness of
London society and how bored she became if she remained in the
country for too long. But Louisa knew very well why Caroline was
putting up a pretence, and the least she could have done was to utter a
word or two in support of her.

Caroline was afflicted by the swirling anger that sometimes
gripped her if things didn't go her way, and which was responsible for
her occasional and perhaps very slightly irrational behaviour. Her
'episodes', as one of her expensive London doctors had euphemisti-

cally referred to them. Her temple thudded, black spots danced before her eyes and she was obliged to clasp her hands in her lap to prevent them from trembling, breathing slowly and deeply until the episode passed.

'I do hope you will be able to dine with us on Friday evening, sir.'

Jane's unexpected invitation caused Caroline's heart to lift along with her anger. She had behaved like a simpering idiot this morning, but if she had advance notice of Mr Shannon's next visit, Caroline vowed that he would be confronted by a very different creature. An elegant female, cool and composed and impossible not to admire, would replace the inept Caroline Bingley he had met today.

'My sisters and Mr Darcy will be here, as will Doctor and Mrs Sanford. I don't suppose you remember Georgiana, Mr Darcy's sister. She was still a young girl when you left Derbyshire, but she is now Doctor Sanford's wife.'

Damnation, Caroline thought. She had forgotten the Darcys were engaged to dine, which meant Lydia Wickham would be a member of the party. Still, perhaps that was not such a bad thing. If Mr Shannon saw her and Lydia in the same room, he couldn't possibly admire Lydia's rather common manners over Caroline's breeding and sophistication.

'Thank you, Mrs Bingley, but I am not yet in a position to return invitations.'

'Ours was not issued in anticipation of reciprocation,' Jane replied.

'Then I shall be delighted. I have little recollection of Darcy's sister but I do remember Sanford and shall be glad to renew that acquaintanceship. I have already had the pleasure of meeting Mrs Darcy and your sister, Mrs Wickham. In fact, Mrs Wickham and I are engaged upon some sleuthing.'

Blazes! Louisa gave her a nudge and Caroline, through a supreme effort of will, stopped scowling. That scheming minx Lydia Wickham had taken no time sinking her hooks into Mr Shannon, and he seemed perfectly content with that situation. So content that he had barely spared Caroline a lingering glance. No, he had *not* spared her one. Barely didn't come into it. Well, they would just have to see about that.

'Oh, how intriguing. Lydia didn't mention anything,' Jane said.

'And I should not have done so either,' Mr Shannon replied. 'Not that there's any great mystery about it. Merely a local matter.'

'Oh, do tell us more,' Caroline begged. 'Perhaps we can help, too.'

'I would not trouble you with my problems.'

No, but you've troubled Lydia. 'It would be no trouble.'

'I dare say Shannon will let us know if we can help,' Charles said amiably. 'Don't badger the poor man, Caroline.'

'Badger, Charles?' Caroline adopted a haughty expression. 'What a very charming turn of phrase.'

Charles merely smiled at the snub. 'We must talk some more about sheep when you have time, Shannon,' he said. 'I've had a few more thoughts about that. Not that I mean to rush you, but once I get a passion for a scheme there's no stopping me.'

'By all means, but now you really must excuse me. I have another appointment.' He stood up. 'Until Friday then, ma'am,' he said, bowing over Jane's hand.

* * *

Patrick left Campton Park and cut across country, thereby considerably reducing the distance he would otherwise need to cover to reach Pemberley. Gladiator was keen to stretch his legs and they arrived in less than an hour only to be told that Mr and Mrs Darcy were not at home. It was stupid of him to arrive without an appointment.

He had been tempted to call at Pemberley first thing that morning instead of returning Bingley's call, but good manners prevailed. Even so, he resented the necessity and was glad it hadn't detained him for long. Mrs Bingley was a delight, but Patrick was less enamoured of Bingley's sisters, particularly the unmarried one whose predatory attitude had made him feel distinctly uncomfortable. Caroline Bingley wasn't unattractive but had reached the age of about twenty-three or twenty-four, he estimated, without embracing matrimony. He had heard rumours that she possessed a fortune, but Patrick had no need of her money and certainly wasn't in the market for a woman other men found so easy to overlook.

Patrick was adamantly opposed to the whole idea of matrimony. His decision was coloured largely by his father's trusting nature and the problems that had caused for him. The long and the short of it was that people didn't hesitate to take advantage of a man with good intentions. Therefore, he definitely had no plans to marry in the near future – perhaps not ever – and it would be unfair to encourage the likes of Miss Bingley to think otherwise.

'Perhaps you will tell Mr Darcy that I called,' Patrick said to Simpson.

He was about to leave when he heard someone on the stairs and looked up to see Mrs Wickham descending them. She was dressed in a similar grey gown to the one she had worn when he first met her. He didn't think she had come down because she had heard his voice, and unlike Miss Bingley, she didn't seem particularly pleased to see him.

'Oh, Mr Shannon,' she said as she reached the vestibule. 'I'm afraid my sister and Mr Darcy are out.'

'So I understand.'

'I imagine Mr Darcy already told you what little I managed to learn from Mrs Hobson.'

'No, unfortunately not. He called yesterday when I was not at home. Now I have returned the favour.'

'Then come through and I'll tell you what I found out.'

Patrick passed his hat and gloves to Simpson and followed Mrs Wickham into the drawing room, not feeling wary at the prospect of being alone with her. She seemed incapable of looking him directly in the eye and showed no particular interest in him as a man. An enveloping melancholy clung to her. It must be very hard to be widowed at such a young age, and it was evident that she wasn't coping well with her new status. He had visited the inn at Lambton the previous day. He mentioned Wickham's name in passing and was soon privy to all the details of his death, probably embellished and exaggerated, but the crux of the matter was that he'd fallen from a horse of all things, and on Sanford's land too. Patrick was well aware that such accidents happened, but he seemed to recall that Wickham was an expert horseman. It was deuced odd.

Seated in the drawing room, which seemed very quiet when

Simpson withdrew, Mrs Wickham continued to avoid his gaze but seemed incapable of sitting still. Her posture was rigidly upright but she constantly either tapped her fingers on her knee or her toe on the rug. Nervousness at being alone with him, or anxiety? Patrick was unable to decide. Mrs Wickham's attention was claimed by the same marmalade cat that had engrossed her before, eliciting a sad little smile from her that lit up her features and, annoyingly, brought out Patrick's protective instincts. She had an engaging smile. The cat climbed onto her lap but was so large that it slipped over the sides of it, purring loudly. Mrs Wickham commenced stroking it, which gave her something constructive to do with her hands. Very small, delicate hands for such a tall lady, he noticed.

'You had something to tell me,' he reminded her when the silence was in danger of becoming embarrassing.

'Oh yes, excuse me. Clarence has a way of demanding attention that is difficult to ignore.'

Lucky Clarence.

She then told him all about a visit she had made to Mrs Hobson.

'It is strange that she should have mentioned Jessup,' Patrick said when she ran out of words. 'I was given his name also and was told that he now holds a position in a mill in Matlock. I rode over yesterday to speak with him. Imagine my surprise when I discovered that he is not the manager of that mill, but the owner.'

'Good heavens!' Her head shot up and he finally had her full attention. Clarence objected with an indignant meow when she abruptly stopped stroking him and jumped to the floor, tail swishing. 'I wonder where he found the money to purchase a mill of his own.'

'As do I, but I could hardly ask. The obvious answer is that he stole it from my father over a period of time, but knowing it and proving it are two very different matters.'

'What did he have to say for himself?'

'Not a great deal, unfortunately.' Her eyes weren't grey, Patrick noticed. In this light they appeared more silver. Silver with green flecks. Luminous, too large for the delicate face that housed them. 'He received me with affability but said he knew nothing of the finances of the mill. It was his opinion that my father was too philanthropic in his approach to those with troubles, which did not exactly come as a surprise. Apparently Jessup warned the pater on several occasions about being so generous.'

'Mrs Hobson overheard one such argument between them.'

Patrick noticed that Mrs Wickham's fingers were now playing with her wedding band. She was twisting it round and round her finger without appearing to realise what she was doing. 'Jessup said he had been trying to find more markets for our silk, which ties in with his mysterious buyers Mrs Hobson told you about.'

'She also said that any purchases would be recorded in the company's ledgers,' Mrs Wickham pointed out. 'Did you examine them?'

'If I had,' he said with a rueful smile, 'I would know a great deal more. The problem is that they've disappeared. Fenton insists they were kept at Shannon House and that he hasn't seen them since the mill closed.'

'Really?' Mrs Wickham elevated a brow. 'Surely he would have needed them to... well, to do whatever he needed to do to deal with your father's affairs.'

Patrick shrugged. 'Evidently not. And they are not at Shannon House. I've turned the place upside down and can't find any trace of them. I can only assume that they passed into the hands of the new owners.'

Mrs Wickham wrinkled her brow. 'How could Fenton have dealt with the workforce who were not fortunate enough to retain their positions if he didn't have their names?'

'What a very astute question, Mrs Wickham.'

'Is it?' She appeared surprised by a compliment she hadn't expected.

'I asked Fenton the same thing. He was furnished with a list of names but destroyed it after several years since it was of no further use to him. And his clerk is no longer alive so I couldn't test his memory.'

'That seems rather convenient. About the records being destroyed, not about the clerk's death.'

Patrick sighed. 'Convenient and irrefutable, without proof to the contrary.'

'Ten years is a long time, Mr Shannon. People move away, women marry.' She paused, her disillusioned expression drawing both his gaze and his curiosity. 'People die,' she added, so softly that he barely heard her.

Patrick was conflicted. Part of him wanted to make his excuses and leave her to her grief, upon which he was clearly intruding. Her despondency stirred dangerous feelings in Patrick, and the urge to offer words of comfort was too strong to be ignored. Words, he reminded himself, not deeds. Especially since the lady was still mourning the loss of the husband she had adored. Not that he was in the habit of behaving inappropriately with any lady of quality, regardless of her circumstances. Perhaps her lack of interest in him had dented his manly pride, accounting for his unusual reaction to Mrs Wickham. Patrick suppressed a self-deprecating chuckle at the thought.

'I knew him slightly,' he said softly.

She sent him a distracted sideways look, so absorbed by her own thoughts that it was as though she had forgotten he was there. 'Knew whom?'

'Your husband.'

'Good heavens!' Her head shot up. 'Whatever made you mention him?'

'I have been indelicate, for which I apologise.'

'Not in the least.' And amazingly she did seem more curious than perturbed. 'I simply wondered why you would mention Wickham when we were discussing your problems.'

'You looked so sad when you spoke of people dying. I thought you must have been thinking about him.'

'I avoid thinking about him as much as I possibly can.'

Patrick had absolutely no idea what to make of that cryptic comment but assumed the recollections were simply too painful to be endured. If she didn't want to talk about Wickham, that was all to the good. Having brought up his name, Patrick should in all conscience say something complimentary about the man. Yet short of indulging in an outright untruth, he had no fond memories to share with his widow.

'In that case,' he said, smiling at her, 'you will not hear his name from me again.'

'Thank you.' She plucked at the fabric of her skirts and resumed tapping her toe. 'Returning to the subject of Mrs Hobson, she knows more about the situation at your father's mill than she was prepared to tell me, I'm absolutely sure of that. Mr Darcy promised to find out how she managed to marry so advantageously, but he hasn't said anything more to me on the matter. Perhaps he's waiting to see you.'

'That hardly seems fair. Thus far you are the only one to have uncovered useful information.'

She lifted her shoulders. 'I'm not sure it's useful.'

Once again they fell silent and Patrick started to feel he had outstayed his welcome. He was about to take his leave when she spoke again.

'There was a young man loitering outside Mrs Hobson's cottage when I left it,' she said reflectively. 'I thought at the time that he was watching me, but I can't think why he would. I'm sure there must be a perfectly rational explanation for his presence there, and I was probably seeing shadows where none existed.' The cat reappeared and leapt agilely onto her lap again.

'You mustn't put yourself in danger to help me, Mrs Wickham.' He fixed her with a severe look as he reached forward and scratched the cat's ears. The wretched creature hissed at him. 'I shouldn't be able to live with myself if something happened to you because of it.'

She laughed then, properly. The gesture transformed her entire face, eradicating all signs of melancholy. Patrick was momentarily transfixed by the sight. 'Nothing will happen to me on Mr Darcy's land,' she assured him.

'I should hope not,' he replied, scowling.

'I should not have mentioned the young man. It was a coincidence.' The cat had stopped hissing and was purring again since Mrs Wickham was vigorously stroking his sleek back. 'He couldn't have known I would call upon Mrs Hobson and ask questions. Besides, what was it to him if I did? He looked too young to have worked for your father.'

'Word spreads fast in the country, Mrs Wickham. I have been asking questions at the inn and Mr and Mrs Mason have been talking to everyone they know. I'm convinced there's something sinister about the collapse of my father's business, especially since meeting Jessup, and there's no telling to what lengths people will go in order to protect themselves.'

'I think you exaggerate.'

'But you said yourself Mrs Hobson knows more than she's willing to tell. All I'm saying is that you should take care.'

She looked as though she was about to protest when voices from the hall suggested the return of Mr and Mrs Darcy.

'Here's Lizzy now,' Mrs Wickham said.

The Darcys joined them and Patrick stood to greet them.

'I apologise for arriving unannounced,' he said, shaking Darcy's hand. 'I've just come from visiting Bingley and so detoured here on my way back. I am to dine with them on Friday.'

'Oh, then perhaps you will accept a seat in our carriage,' Mrs Darcy said civilly.

'Only if you're sure I won't crowd you.'

'Not in the least,' Darcy replied. 'It makes no sense for you to ride when we shall be passing your door and can easily collect you. Sanford and Georgiana are going in their own conveyance so there will be plenty of space in ours.'

'Then thank you.'

'Has Lydia told you about her meeting with Mrs Hobson?' Mrs Darcy asked, taking the seat beside her sister.

'Yes, we were just discussing it.'

Patrick told them about Jessup's improved circumstances.

'Strange,' Darcy said thoughtfully. 'I've been meaning to tell you, Lydia, that Hobson was a confirmed bachelor—'

'Is there such a creature?' Mrs Darcy asked with a mischievous smile. 'I have often heard of men who proclaim no interest in matrimony, but that resolve seldom survives the attentions of a worthy woman.'

'Speaking personally, ma'am,' Patrick replied, 'I am living proof that one or two of us still survive.'

'And you have my assurance that I shall respect that confidence, Mr

Shannon. Otherwise half the single female population of Derbyshire would take it upon themselves to try and alter your circumstances.'

Patrick made a wry face. 'I don't doubt it.'

'As I was saying,' Darcy continued, 'Hobson was considered a bachelor and by all accounts was perfectly content with his life as one of my keepers. Then he surprised everyone by announcing that he was to marry Elsie Fletcher, as she then was. According to my steward, no one knew anything about the woman or how they had met, and the marriage took place very quickly. So quickly that gossip abounded, but when she didn't produce their first child until after a year of marriage, tongues ceased to wag and everyone assumed it was a love match.'

'I knew it!' Mrs Wickham said. 'She was frightened and defensive the whole time I was speaking with her.' There was a restless animation about Mrs Wickham that Patrick found enticing. 'She knows something and was offered the opportunity to marry Hobson in exchange for her silence, an offer she would have found difficult to resist because it was a good match for her and because she had reached an age where she was in danger of being left on the shelf.'

'Possibly,' Patrick agreed. 'But how do we prove it?'

'There's an old lady who lives in a cottage in the village,' Mrs Darcy said. 'I sometimes call on her. She has taught me a lot about local life and knows absolutely everything about everyone. She might be old, but her mind is sharp and she forgets nothing.' She turned towards her sister. 'Perhaps we'll call on her together, Lydia, and see what she can remember about Elsie Fletcher.'

9

For the next few days Lydia diligently worked on her journal, wondering what masochistic tendencies compelled her to persevere when the only events she could recall with clarity failed to show her in a good light. A conscience that had not previously troubled her forced her to accept that there must be something intrinsically bad about her character. Tears blurred her vision as she wrote about Jane's first ball gown and how lovely she had looked in it. It had seemed grossly unfair to Lydia that she was not permitted to attend the ball too. Unaccustomed to not having her way, she threw a tantrum, her screams audible in every corner of the house. When even that ploy failed to change Mama's mind, Lydia had tried to damage Jane's gown in retaliation.

She threw her quill aside and shook her head in abject shame. Years of atonement would never make up for the trouble she had caused.

In search of a less mortifying occupation, she turned her mind to Mr Shannon's investigation. She'd been looking forward to visiting the old lady in the village with Lizzy, but Marcus had developed a cold and Lizzy had scarce left his side for two days. It seemed at one point that the dinner at Jane's would have to be cancelled. But this morning, Friday, Marcus seemed much improved and so for Campton Park they were all bound.

Lydia stood as her maid helped her into her dove-grey silk evening gown.

'Oh, ma'am,' Nora said, wistfully eyeing the more colourful gowns inherited from Kitty that now filled Lydia's wardrobe. 'Are you sure you don't fancy a change?'

'Quite sure, Nora.' No one took much interest in her, and that was the way she preferred it nowadays. The gown emphasised her curves, she noticed with an indifferent shrug as she glanced in the glass. The neckline was modest, the grey offset by a trimming of lavender lace. 'Dress my hair and then you may have the evening off.'

Lydia had become accustomed to her greyness and saw no occasion to stop wearing the colour simply because society no longer expected her to mourn. Not that she *had* mourned Wickham's passing. She had lost the capacity to feel anything at all.

Mr Shannon's problems had come as a welcome distraction from her own unsettled state of mind and she was now fully taken up with her quest to find the truth. She grudgingly conceded that a part – a very small part – of her dormant heart had stirred with the arrival of Patrick Shannon in Derbyshire. He was a highly eligible gentleman: handsome, engaging *and* a man of property. She might be a 'disappointment', but she was not blind. All sorts of rumours abounded about how he had amassed a fortune during his absence from England. Lizzy had laughingly repeated exaggerated stories that ranged from smuggling to criminal activities and even white-slaving.

The air of mystery that surrounded him and his disinclination to embrace local society generally added to his mystique. Nora had told her that at least half a dozen local ladies with daughters of marriageable age had found excuses to call at Shannon House. Whether Mr Shannon had received them, Lydia didn't know. Nor did she care. Well, not all that much. She idly wondered if Miss Bingley had fixed her interest upon him. Jane had mentioned her suspicions in that regard in a note to Lizzy. Lydia, well aware what lengths Caroline would be prepared to go to in order to get her way, felt a moment's unease at the prospect of Mr Shannon being united to such a woman. Then she reminded herself that he was a grown man, well able to look out for himself, and that his affairs were no concern of hers.

'Are you ready?' Lizzy asked, poking her head around Lydia's door. 'The carriage will be round in a moment.'

'How is Marcus?' Lydia asked, picking up her reticule and following Lizzy from her chamber.

'Oh, everyone tells me I need not worry, which only makes me worry more. You will discover how that feels when you become a mother yourself.'

Which will never happen.

A short time later, their carriage halted at the steps to Shannon House and Mr Shannon walked through the door looking very distinguished in his evening clothes. He greeted Lizzy and then Lydia with the utmost civility before taking his place beside Mr Darcy, his back to the horses. He was directly across from Lydia, and it was necessary for him to stretch his long legs towards the door in order to avoid clashing knees with her. A spark of inappropriate desire spiralled through Lydia at his close proximity. She turned away, only for her gaze to land upon muscular thighs, encased in tight-fitting buckskin. She stared at the passing scenery, determined not to be impressed by his... well, by the impressive figure that he cut.

'Perhaps we could finally call upon Mrs Bathgate tomorrow, Lydia,' Lizzy suggested after they had travelled for some distance and Lydia had not contributed a word to the conversation. 'We were unable to do so before now, Mr Shannon, since my son has been unwell. But he is quite recovered now.'

'I am entirely at your disposal,' Lydia replied, her wandering attention recalled.

'Fenton managed to find the list of my father's employees,' Mr Shannon told them. 'I received a letter from him enclosing it just this morning. Apparently it had been put in the wrong place and forgotten about. I'd like to show it to you tomorrow, Darcy, if you can spare the time. There might be names on it that you recognise. Jessup's is on there, and Elsie Fletcher's, but none of the others mean anything to me.'

'Call in the afternoon and I will take a look at it,' Mr Darcy replied.

'We shall have seen Mrs Bathgate by then,' Lizzy added.

'I am much obliged to you all,' Mr Shannon said, his gaze lingering speculatively upon Lydia as he spoke.

Idle conversation saw them complete the journey to Campton Manor in good time. All the while, Lydia was conscious of Mr Shannon's dark, intense gaze frequently resting upon her profile. He couldn't really help that since he was sitting directly opposite her. Even so, she found his close proximity and her physical reaction to it disturbing. It would be very difficult to atone for her past behaviour and be anything other than the epitome of widowed respectability all the while this annoyingly attractive man had the temerity to agitate her passions. Worse, there was something about his studied nonchalance that suggested he knew precisely what he was doing to her. Annoying man!

She was relieved when the carriage arrived at its destination. At least now she would be able to avoid him for the rest of the evening without seeming impolite.

* * *

Having given the matter considerable thought, Caroline settled upon wearing a gown of bronze figured silk, elaborately trimmed with seed pearls, for the dinner party at which she planned to impress Mr Shannon with her appearance, wit and gentility. She had her maid thread matching ribbon through her hair and was satisfied to observe that her eyes sparkled, her complexion was clear and her figure was displayed to its very best advantage in a colour that she had often been told became her well.

Now she was in the drawing room and her confidence had been given a timely boost when several compliments were directed her way, helping to quell her nerves. She was annoyed that her efforts to discover what it was that Lydia Wickham was helping Mr Shannon to investigate had met with failure. It gave Lydia an unfair advantage. Jane appeared to be as much in the dark about Mr Shannon's quest as Caroline was. Not that that would prevent Caroline doing everything in her power to interpolate herself into his investigation. If all else failed, she would befriend Lydia and persuade her to tell all. The woman was easily duped.

'If I didn't know better,' Louisa said to her in an amused aside, 'I might think you were trying to impress someone.'

Caroline fixed her sister with a haughty expression. 'Are you suggesting I may not succeed?'

Louisa elevated one shoulder and glided away from her, leaving Caroline in a renewed state of indecision. Perdition, Louisa was supposed to be on her side!

All of Jane's guests had arrived, including Georgiana and her husband. Only the party from Pemberley had yet to appear. And Mr Shannon too, of course. Caroline was not best pleased to learn that he was coming in the same carriage as the Darcys and Lydia Wickham.

'I'm so sorry if we've kept you waiting,' Lizzy said as she walked into the drawing room. 'I wanted to see Marcus settled.'

Jane embraced her sister and hastened to assure her she wasn't late at all. Caroline stood back, doing her utmost not to look at Mr Darcy. Even so, her gaze was frequently drawn to him. She liked him best when he was in evening clothes, and to her he had never looked better than he did on this particular night: dark, distinguished and oh so inaccessible. Caroline died a little inside as she watched him at his wife's side, smiling at her, kissing Jane's cheek, shaking Charles's hand. Then he glanced in her direction, sent a smile over the guests' heads for her exclusive enjoyment and her doubts fell away. It no longer mattered what obstacles she had to overcome to win his regard. They would simply make the ultimate reward that much more worthwhile.

Mr Darcy looked away and Caroline's attention was claimed by Lydia Wickham. She still wore a dreary grey gown and had taken little trouble to make the best of herself, which momentarily confused Caroline. She was now officially out of mourning and she had supposed that this occasion would see her back in one of her gaudy creations. Instead she obviously planned to play the part of the wilting widow to the hilt in the hope of evoking sympathy.

Satisfied that Lydia's competition would be easily overcome, Caroline turned her attention to Mr Shannon. He had just approached her and

Louisa, and both ladies bobbed a curtsey. He was ruggedly handsome in his evening clothes, and her heart managed a slight flutter at the sight of him. Were it not for Mr Darcy... But Caroline was not *that* inconstant. Fitzwilliam was the man she had lost her heart to the first time Charles had introduced them five years ago and had made her impervious to the charms of all the other men she had subsequently met.

'How is the restoration of your property coming on?' Louisa asked when pleasantries had been exchanged.

'Chaotically,' Mr Shannon replied, glancing around the room and acknowledging Dr Sanford. 'Is that Darcy's sister at Sanford's side?'

'Yes,' Caroline replied. 'Georgiana *is* a great credit to her brother and very accomplished. Louisa and I have a hard time of it keeping pace with her. She plays and sings like an angel.'

'*All* young ladies sing and play.'

'Not all and not necessarily well,' Caroline replied with a darkling glance in Lizzy's direction. 'I pride myself on having had some small influence over Georgiana's musical progress prior to her marriage.'

Mr Shannon looked surprised at Caroline's assertion. 'I dare say,' he replied. 'Will you excuse me, ladies? I'm anxious to reacquaint myself with Sanford and his accomplished wife.'

'And I with Mr Glossop.'

Caroline watched Mr Shannon walk away, furious with the way she had sounded so desperate to impress. She had promised herself that she would appear aloof and unattainable, but anxiety had made her behave like a braggart. She had no interest in Mr Glossop, one of their neighbours in attendance, but that gentleman had made his pleasure in her society plainly apparent on several previous occasions. Caroline would play upon his partiality to show Mr Shannon that he had competition.

Caroline had swallowed her pride and asked Jane to arrange for Mr Shannon to take her into dinner. She would repair the damage she had caused during the course of the meal when there was no possibility of his escaping her.

* * *

Given a choice, Patrick would have escorted Mrs Wickham into dinner. It was probably just as well that the choice wasn't his to make and that he found himself partnered with Miss Bingley. He was in no danger in her company. As they walked through to the dining room, Patrick tried to decide what it was about Darcy's widowed sister-in-law that he found so arresting. It occurred to him as he held Miss Bingley's chair and waited for her to arrange her skirts to her satisfaction that it was Lydia Wickham's lack of interest in *him* that he found hard to... well, to ignore. A wry smile played about his lips. He had not previously been aware that he placed so much stock by his ability to attract the opposite sex.

'How long do you intend to remain in Derbyshire, Miss Bingley?' Patrick asked.

'Indefinitely, sir. I infinitely prefer the country to the hustle and bustle of town. Although putting in an appearance during the season is unavoidable. People of our standing cannot altogether ignore the demands of society, much as we might wish it to be otherwise.'

'Oh dear.'

Miss Bingley shot him a surprised look. 'Is something wrong?'

'*I* intend to ignore society all together.'

'It's different for single gentlemen. I envy you the freedom to do more or less as you please.' She sighed. 'Mr Hurst enjoys his London clubs and my sister usually persuades me to accompany her whenever he returns to town. Charles makes me very welcome but I don't like to impose upon his family.'

'But you are his family.'

'True, but no longer his first priority.' She flashed a brittle smile. 'I kept house for him before his marriage and was happy to make myself useful in that regard.'

And resent being usurped. 'Not to the neglect of your own pleasures, I hope.'

'We must all do our duty, sir, and I have no complaints to make. However, Charles doesn't need me now that he has a wife.'

Patrick wanted to ask her why she didn't establish a home of her own if she felt she was a burden to her brother. But that would imply she was beyond marriageable age and would be unpardonably rude.

'Is American society very different to English?' she asked, helping herself to a slice of duck breast from a platter offered to her by a footman.

'I can only speak of New York society, which has many similarities to the English system. It's dominated by several influential families.' Patrick moved to one side, allowing a footman to refill his wine glass. 'All those aspiring to be accepted pay court to those families, regardless of whether they actually enjoy their society.' He flashed a sardonic smile. 'Rather as they do in England.'

'I think it important that standards are maintained, Mr Shannon, otherwise there would be anarchy.' She canted her head in a considering fashion. 'Besides, I imagine the New York socialites can trace their roots back to England and have adopted their habits from our tried and tested methods. They could do a lot worse. Everyone needs to know their place in the structure of things.'

'I suppose they do,' Patrick replied, somehow refraining from rolling his eyes as he recalled some of the pretentiousness he had witnessed during his time overseas. He hadn't enjoyed society's strictures then and fully intended to avoid becoming embroiled with them now that he was home; another good reason not to look for a wife. Ladies enjoyed balls and parties and theatres and all the other frivolities that Patrick was at pains to avoid.

'Tell me about the investigation that you have enlisted Mrs Wickham's help with,' Miss Bingley said after a short pause. 'Perhaps I can help too.'

The mention of that lady's name caused Patrick to instinctively glance at her, still trying to establish the precise colour of her remarkable eyes. Every time he thought he had decided the matter, they disobligingly changed hue. But one thing that never changed was the melancholy reflected in them, even when she was smiling. They definitely looked silver in the reflection of candlelight, but the irises were darker, flecked with golden brown... and a hint of russet-green.

She was seated on the other side of the table, several places up from him, between two gentlemen whose names he had already forgotten. One of them was engaging her in conversation and she was responding to him without animation. She *had* been animated, Patrick realised, when they had been alone together in Darcy's drawing room and a little, a very little, passion had briefly broken through her reserves. Animated but not flirtatious. Miss Bingley, on the other hand, was batting her lashes at him and constantly found reasons to lay a hand on his arm. Patrick wanted to tell her that she was wasting her time.

Conscious that he was staring at Mrs Wickham – a fact brought home to him when she looked in his direction and opened the eyes that so fascinated him wide in enquiry – he forced his attention back to Miss Bingley.

'Thank you, but there is nothing you can do. I am trying to locate a few of the people who worked for my late father. Mrs Darcy suggested that she and her sister help me with that search. One or two of them are now employed at Pemberley, you see.'

Miss Bingley's face fell and she looked rather discouraged. 'I see.'

'I'm sorry if you thought there was some great mystery.'

'I expect Mrs Wickham is anxious to make amends.' Miss Bingley lowered her voice to a conspiratorial whisper. 'You must have heard that her marriage to Wickham was a rather rushed affair.'

Patrick flexed a brow in arrogant disdain. 'No, I had not heard that. I have no time for idle speculation on subjects that are none of my business.'

Miss Bingley seemed rather startled by Patrick's putdown. He expected her to drop the subject but she did not.

'Wickham and Mr Darcy were sworn enemies, you know. You are probably aware that Wickham was the son of old Mr Darcy's steward; hardly his social equal.'

'There you go again,' Patrick said, tempering his words with a smile. 'Trading upon social positions.'

'His assumption that he *was* Mr Darcy's equal rather proves my point. It was Wickham's presumption that caused the rift; whereas if he had remembered his place, it need never have happened.' She sighed. 'It must have caused Mr Darcy great anguish to become related to his nemesis, albeit by marriage.'

'Then he must love his wife very much indeed,' Patrick said with minimum civility. 'It is my understanding that the Darcys' union took place after that of the Wickhams.'

Miss Bingley gasped.

'Are you feeling well, Miss Bingley?' Patrick couldn't think what he had said to make her so obviously angry.

'Perfectly so, I thank you.' She appeared composed again. 'A slight headache. It will soon pass.'

'Then I'm relieved.' He paused while a footman removed the empty plate from in front of him, searching his mind for a safer topic of conversation. 'You mentioned earlier that you enjoy music.'

'Very much so. Are you a music lover, Mr Shannon?'

'If it's played with passion then certainly I am.'

'Then I hope that after dinner I shall be able to exceed your expectations.'

'I look forward to it.'

Patrick had neglected the lady seated on his opposite side, mainly because Miss Bingley seemed determined to engage his complete attention. He turned to her now and asked her a question about her family.

10

'You must tell us more about your travels, Shannon,' Mr Bingley said as he took his seat at the head of the table. 'Perhaps after dinner. I'm sure we would all be interested to hear what you have to tell us about America.'

Several voices murmured their approbation.

'If you won't find it a dreadful bore, it would be my pleasure,' Mr Shannon replied.

'Did you meet with savages?' one young lady asked him, eyes wide with alarm.

'What of silk?' Doctor Sanford asked. 'Your family produced some of the finest in Derbyshire. How does that compare to the merchandise you came across in New York?'

'I didn't involve myself with silk. My time was fully occupied with designing houses.'

'You would be able to compare, Lydia,' Lizzy said. 'You dealt with a lot of imported silk at our uncle's warehouse.'

'True,' Lydia conceded. 'I did learn to detect quality without even touching the fabric. The sheen tells one a great deal.'

Lydia was conscious of Mr Shannon's attention focused upon her. He looked surprised. Surprised at her knowledge or because a relation of Mr Darcy's would be required to work for a living? She was unsure which and didn't have the energy to care. Miss Bingley fixed Lydia with a rather superior half-smile. Lydia was filled with a capricious desire to remind Caroline Bingley that her own fortune originated from trade and she had nothing to feel superior about. She took it as a sign of her newfound maturity when she managed to resist a temptation she would previously have succumbed to without thought for the consequences.

The conversation moved on to other subjects. Lydia, who would once have tried to dominate it and enjoy being the centre of attention, had little to contribute. Ever conscious of the fact that she was a 'disappointment', she yearned now for an elusive something; a purpose that would atone in some small way for her behaviour in her earlier years and make her family proud of her.

She sat a little straighter as she enjoyed a rare moment of clarity. Writing her journal had forced her to face up to her inadequacies; but that discomfort had been overridden by the pleasure she took from actually writing the words. Lydia's handwriting was near-illegible, her spelling atrocious, but since no one else would read her journal, that hardly signified. What mattered was that she'd discovered she really enjoyed juggling with words, trying to express her feelings without glossing over her shortcomings.

It occurred to her now that she had recorded her recollections not just to understand her failings but to entertain an imaginary reader. Instead of hanging heavily on her hands, the hours had flown by since she'd embarked upon the project. For the first time in months she had taken satisfaction from an activity that consumed her. A glimmer of optimism broke through the fog inside her head and she knew suddenly what she would do with herself.

Lydia would write a novel!

During the meal she was conscious of Miss Bingley constantly glancing in her direction as though to find fault. She studied Caroline with her burgeoning writer's eye, committing her features and mannerisms to memory so they could feature in her first tome. Lydia disliked and mistrusted Miss Bingley. She suppressed a smile as she decided that the lady upon whom she bestowed Miss Bingley's characteristics would not be an agreeable person.

Lydia became aware of Mr Shannon's attention focused upon her from across the table. The smile he directed towards her had a very disconcerting effect upon Lydia. A surge of acute longing, as unexpected as it was inappropriate, gripped her as their gazes collided. The old Lydia briefly came alive. The widowed Mrs Wickham pushed her irritably aside, watching as Miss Bingley addressed a comment to Mr Shannon twice before he slowly dropped his gaze and returned his attention to her.

When the ladies withdrew, Georgie came to sit with Lydia.

'How are you feeling?' Lydia asked her.

'Fat,' Georgie replied with a sigh. 'But I don't suppose you want to talk about babies.'

'I like babies,' Lydia protested. 'And I enjoy being an aunt. One has all the pleasure and none of the responsibility. Lizzy and your brother have been beside themselves this week with the minor ailments endured by their infant sons.'

'I expect I shall be just as bad.' Georgie smiled. 'Anyway, what is your opinion of Mr Shannon?'

'He seems popular with the ladies.'

Georgie elevated a brow. 'But not you?'

Lydia wrinkled her nose but was saved from the trouble of formulating a response when the gentlemen rejoined the ladies and Jane suggested some music. Lydia wasn't surprised when Miss Bingley took little persuading to perform first. Restless, Lydia wandered out onto the terrace. There were twenty people in the drawing room to listen to Miss Bingley play. No one would miss her. She strolled the length of the wide stone path that cut between the flower beds below the terrace, breathing in the scent of jasmine and other plants she couldn't put names to. If she was to be a proficient novelist then she would need to learn what they were. She practised describing them as she walked along.

'A delicate blue bloom with a heady perfume and pale leaves... A small yet robust pink flower that appears to spread without encouragement... A rambling torrent of wild, untamed beauty...'

Hmm, there was room for improvement but all writers had to start somewhere. Rhododendrons she did recognise. They were in full, magnificent bloom and she paused to admire heavy heads that looked too weighty for the stems that supported them.

'Quite beautiful, are they not?'

She turned at the sound of Mr Shannon's voice and her heart did an annoying little flip as she watched him amble towards her, elegant and self-assured. Had he deliberately followed her or was this meeting a coincidence?

'What are you doing out here?' she asked.

He flashed a wicked smile. 'The same thing as you, I would imagine. Escaping.'

Lydia laughed in spite of herself. 'Shame on you, Mr Shannon. The very least you could do is have the courtesy to listen to Miss Bingley's performance.'

He executed a negligent shrug. 'She won't even notice I am not there.'

'I doubt that very much.'

Lydia strolled on and he fell into step beside her.

'You should laugh more often, Mrs Wickham. Some people are born to smile. You are most definitely one of them.'

'What a very strange observation to make,' Lydia replied, stopping at another rhododendron and burying her face in its bloom.

'A beautiful perfume, no?' he asked indolently. 'They rely on insects to pollinate them, you know. After a pollinator leaves, carrying off his cargo of pollen, the plant wants the next flower visited to be the same species, leading to the most fascinating and intoxicating combination of scents.'

'Are plants really that clever?'

'Apparently so.'

'You are remarkably well informed on the subject,' Lydia said, releasing the bloom and moving on.

'My mother adored her garden and I recall her telling me something of that nature when I was still in short coats. I have a mind that tends to retain trivia.'

'Whereas mine is completely empty.'

'And yet you seemed to be deep in thought throughout dinner.'

Lydia glanced at his profile, surprised that he had noticed her preoccupation, given the amount of interest his presence at dinner had engendered, especially amongst the ladies.

'My private thoughts would not inspire philosophers.'

His smile was warm and engaging and the cynical light she often detected in his eye was nowhere in evidence. 'If that's a polite way of telling me to mind my own business, feel free to tell me to go to the devil.'

'It is to your credit that you're endeavouring to make me seem interesting, Mr Shannon,' she said, sighing, 'but there is absolutely nothing remarkable about me.'

'I beg to differ.'

'Only because you didn't know me when—'

'When you were married?' She nodded. 'You have suffered a devastating loss at a young age,' he said softly. 'It is little wonder that you feel unsettled.'

Lydia widened her eyes. 'No one ever speaks to me about Wickham. In fact, they avoid the subject as much as they possibly can.'

'For fear of oversetting you?'

'Perhaps.'

'Your sister mentioned something over dinner.'

'Yes. That surprised me, too.'

'I had no idea you had practical experience with silk.'

'After Wickham left the army, my uncle offered him a position as manager of one of his warehouses into which all manner of products were imported.'

'And you became involved?'

'It made me feel useful.' Lydia wasn't about to admit she didn't trust Wickham to execute his duties efficiently unless she kept a close watch on him.

'You enjoyed the experience?'

'Very much indeed.' She sighed. 'I sometimes wish I were a man. I should enjoy taking up a career in my uncle's employ.'

Even though they had strolled some way from the house and she couldn't see him clearly in the gathering gloom, she sensed the heat from his gaze focused on her face. 'I am so very glad you are not a man.'

* * *

Patrick had felt stifled by the company and came outside for a respite. No, that wasn't precisely true. He had seen Mrs Wickham wander onto the terrace a little earlier. The drawing room felt like a dreary place without her in occupation of it, and something stronger than his own will caused him to follow her. Quite why he was also set upon flirting with her was a mystery. Unlike Miss Bingley, she had done absolutely nothing to encourage his attentions and seemed embarrassed by them. Perdition, what had got into him?

'There's no need to be gallant,' she said, taking another path. He followed her. 'I did not speak my mind in expectation of being complimented.'

'And I don't offer false flattery. Not to you.'

Her eyes were alight with confusion. 'Shall we speak of something else?'

'By all means.' He treated her to his most charming smile. 'How do you occupy your time now that you are no longer being of service to your uncle?' he asked.

'Actually, I'm writing a journal. It was Lizzy's suggestion and I wasn't very keen to start with. Now I am rapidly becoming obsessed with it. It is forcing me to face up to the fact that I wasn't always very nice to my sisters.'

'I don't have any siblings but it is my understanding that they seldom get along well, especially if they are of the same sex. Boys go off to school and when they are at home they either ignore their sisters or feel protective towards them. Girls on the other hand are stuck at home and amuse themselves by annoying one another, I would imagine. It seems perfectly normal and you ought not to chastise yourself.'

'I wish that were true.' She sighed. 'I am the youngest of five you see and—'

'Ah, well, there you have it. The youngest is always indulged and so your conduct can be excused.'

'Even though I am a "disappointment"?'

'A disappointment?' He stopped walking and stared down at her. 'I don't have the pleasure of understanding you. Why would anyone look upon you as a disappointment?'

Mrs Wickham shook her head. 'I was supposed to be a boy, which would have solved all of our family's problems at a stroke. My father's property is entailed, you see, in the event of his not having a son.'

'Then you might just as well say that the rest of your sisters are also disappointments. It is hardly your fault if you are the youngest. I dare say your parents lived in expectation of producing a boy four times before your own birth.'

She bit her lower lip. 'When you put it like that, my feelings do seem irrational, I suppose.'

'Besides, your sisters Jane and Elizabeth have made advantageous marriages so your family's future is secure.'

'Quite so.' She shook her head. 'Ignore me, Mr Shannon. I am not good company this evening and I shall happily excuse you if you wish to return to the drawing room.'

'Because you would prefer to walk in solitude?'

'Not in the least.'

He smiled. 'There's no need to be polite. I can tell you are keen to be rid of me.' Which would explain his determination to bear her company, he supposed. Patrick had always been a contrary devil.

'That is Georgie playing the piano now,' she said, cocking her head to one side. 'I recognise the piece. You will find her a great deal easier to listen to than... well, let's just say that Georgie is an exceptional musician.'

'Shall we have the pleasure of hearing you play?' he asked.

'Me!' She opened her eyes very wide, a smile playing about her lush lips. 'I do not play a note.'

'How very refreshing.'

'Now you're making fun of me.'

He stopped walking and smiled down at her. 'Do you have any idea how often I have been introduced to a young lady and told how accomplished her performance on the pianoforte or the harp, or more obscure instruments, happens to be? Or how well she sings?' He spread his hands. 'Then I am compelled to listen, usually to the most frightful performances.'

'Oh dear.' She stifled a smile.

She clearly considered smiling inappropriate, just as she inexplicably thought herself to be a disappointment to her family. Patrick wanted to tell her to release her smile and enjoy their frank exchange, but if he did that then her smile would not be spontaneous.

'Now you understand how I am forced to suffer,' he said with an exaggerated sigh.

'I don't play any instrument, nor am I trying to impress you.' She nodded. 'I can quite see now why I make you feel safe.'

'Then we are friends, I hope.' He proffered his arm and she hesitated for a fraction of a second before placing her gloved hand upon it.

'By all means, if you think it possible for a man and woman to be friends without... well, without—'

'Without our natural inclinations taking over?'

She bit her lip for a second time. 'Well, yes.'

'I dare say we shall be able to control ourselves. It will be an interesting experiment since I have never had a platonic friendship with a lady before.'

'Nor I with a gentleman, but since we are not attracted to one another that ought not to signify.' *Speak for yourself.* 'I shall look upon you as the brother I never had.'

'Then come, sister, let's walk a little more.'

They strolled along, the silence between them broken only by the swishing of her skirts. Patrick felt a great sense of achievement, as though he had crossed some sort of divide in his dealings with Mrs Wickham. Her lack of self-esteem ran contrary to everything Miss Bingley had spitefully allowed to slip about her previous conduct. Those revelations had had the opposite effect upon Patrick to the one she had probably intended, reinforcing his desire to get to know the young widow better.

'I hope Lizzy and I will be able to discover something to help you when we visit Mrs Bathgate tomorrow,' she said after several minutes had passed in companionable silence.

'I shall call to show Darcy my list and you will be able to tell me what luck you had.'

'I am sure Lizzy will be pleased to receive you.'

'But will you be, sister?'

'Are you flirting with me, Mr Shannon?' she asked tersely.

'Not if you would prefer me not to.'

'I would.'

He chuckled. 'Very well, I shall behave myself, hard as you make it for me to do so.'

'Me! What have I done?'

'You intrigue me. However, I can see that I have made you uncomfortable, so we shall talk of something else.' He smiled at her and could see that she was thoroughly confused by his behaviour, but probably not as confused as Patrick himself was at the manner in which she could so easily make him forget himself. 'I shall not be idle tomorrow morning either,' he said. 'Over port, Darcy mentioned the name of a man who lives in Lambton who might be able to set our enquiry on the right track.'

'Someone who worked for your father?'

'Evidently so, but not in a senior position so he might not know anything.'

They had done a tour of the garden and were now back at the steps leading up to the terrace. They ought to go back inside but Patrick was reluctant to let her go just yet. The music stopped and there was a smattering of polite applause. Then someone appeared on the terrace above them. Patrick observed a bronze-slippered foot on the steps and inwardly sighed. Miss Bingley was tenacious to the point of tedium.

'Oh, there you are, Mr Shannon,' she said, completely ignoring Mrs Wickham. 'I came out for some air and had not realised you'd had the same idea.'

Of course you did not.

Lydia Wickham removed her hand from his arm and commenced

climbing the steps at the same time as Miss Bingley started down to join him. Before she could get far, Patrick followed Mrs Wickham up and dredged up a brief smile for Miss Bingley.

'Shall we all go back inside?' he asked. 'Or would you like some solitude, Miss Bingley?'

'It is cooler than I anticipated and I did not bring a shawl.'

So saying, Miss Bingley placed her hand on the arm Mrs Wickham had just abandoned and swept back into the drawing room at Patrick's side.

11

'You see, it's as I predicted. You've spent the entire evening fretting for absolutely no reason,' Will said, squeezing Lizzy's hand as they crept down the stairs from the nursery.

'Are you telling me you weren't the tiniest bit concerned yourself?'

Will offered her a tender smile. 'We would not have left the children if we thought they were in the slightest danger.'

'Most gentlemen, I'm told, leave worrying about their children's health to their wives.'

'I, my love, am not most gentlemen.'

'For which I give daily thanks. No ordinary gentleman would satisfy me.'

Will opened the door to her chamber, ushering Lizzy through it ahead of him. 'I shall do my humble best to continue giving satisfaction.'

'It was a lovely evening,' Lizzy said, throwing aside her reticule. 'I enjoyed seeing Jane taking control of her own table without interference from her husband's sisters. At least Miss Bingley's treachery has opened Jane's eyes to her true character and she no longer allows the woman to act as though *she* still runs her brother's house.'

Will elevated both brows. 'Is that what she did after Jane and Bingley wed?'

'Oh, Will, you really are hopelessly inattentive sometimes!' Lizzy sighed. 'When Jane and Mr Bingley became engaged, my father predicted they would be so easy going that they would exceed their income and be shamelessly exploited. I think he meant to imply that their servants would cheat them, but it was Miss Bingley who tried to lord it over Jane. She suggested in all sorts of small ways that Jane wasn't running her household as efficiently as she ought, making poor Jane doubt herself.'

Will frowned. 'And Jane believed her?'

Lizzy seated herself at her dressing table and removed her jewellery. 'Caroline didn't take kindly to being usurped. I noticed what she was doing but Jane didn't ask for my advice so I decided not to interfere.'

'You did?' Will sent her a smouldering smile, his eyes coming alive with wicked humour. 'That cannot have been easy for you.'

Lizzy puffed out her cheeks. 'I hope you're not implying that I'm incapable of minding my own business.'

'I meant to pay you a compliment.' Will stood behind her and pulled the pins from her hair, running his fingers through her tresses as they fell free. 'I know how important your sister is to you.'

Lizzy sighed and pushed her head back against his hands, closing her eyes as his fingers massaged her scalp, sending shivers trickling down her spine. 'If I'd had to witness it first-hand, I doubt whether I would have been able to hold my tongue. But we were here in Derbyshire and Jane was still in Hertfordshire. All I knew was what Jane confided in letters... She had wanted to do something in particular, but Caroline had advised against it; that sort of thing.'

'Tonight went well for Jane.'

'Yes, the meal was exactly right, all her guests enjoyed themselves and it was nice to see Mr Shannon being so well received.'

Will flashed a devastating smile that turned Lizzy's insides to mulch. They were into the third year of their marriage, had three children and he could *still* make rational thought disintegrate into pure sensation, simply by smiling at her in a particular way.

'A lot of the young ladies present would agree with you,' he said.

'Mr Shannon is well able to...' She groaned when his hands drifted to her shoulders and started unknotting the tension in her muscles. 'Oh, keeping doing that.'

'I had no intention of stopping. I do so enjoy these rare moments when I have you at my complete mercy.'

'Rare!' Lizzy's eyes flew open. 'When did you last not sleep in my bed?'

'Are you giving me notice to quit, Mrs Darcy?'

'You are master of Pemberley, Mr Darcy. I would not presume to tell you what you can and cannot do.'

Will grunted, his eyes brimming with infectious good humour.

'Jane and I managed to exchange a few words about Lydia.' Lizzy frowned over her shoulder at her husband. 'She has taken to writing her journal with great enthusiasm yet seems determined to focus only on the bad things that she remembers.'

Will shrugged. 'Perhaps she needs to confront them?'

'It's as though she's determined to punish herself.'

Will bent his head, pushed Lizzy's hair aside and kissed the back of her neck. Then he rang the bell to summon Lizzy's maid. 'Stop worrying. Lydia will recover in her own time and in her own way.'

'Yes, I suppose she will, but I miss her vibrancy, even though it used to be so very annoying.' She turned to face Will, frowning as she attempted to articulate her thoughts. 'It is as though a part of her died with Wickham.'

'She and Shannon seem to get along well. Did you notice that they were both in the garden for a long time?'

'I noticed Miss Bingley hit a wrong note when she saw him follow her out there.' Lizzy shuddered. 'I hope to goodness she hasn't decided to pursue Mr Shannon. The last thing I need is Caroline Bingley as a permanent neighbour.'

'Good heavens! Do you think that's what she has in mind?'

'She probably feels in danger of being left on the shelf, and Mr Shannon *is* a very attractive man. She could do a lot worse.'

'But he has no intention of marrying. He said as much.'

'Miss Bingley is nothing if not tenacious.' Lizzy shuddered, unable to dispel the feeling that Caroline Bingley was still intent upon making trouble for her and Will.

'You worry too much.'

Will smiled as he disappeared through the connecting door to his own chamber when Jessie materialised to help Lizzy prepare for bed. As soon as she had completed her duties and left Lizzy alone, Will was back again. He slipped into bed beside Lizzy and pulled her into his arms.

'This investigation of Shannon's is good for Lydia. It will give her something to think about other than her own situation,' he said, resuming their conversation at the point where they had abandoned it. 'If you discover anything useful from Mrs Bathgate, let her take the credit for it and be the one to tell Shannon.'

'Why Mr Darcy, don't tell me you are matchmaking.' Lizzy lifted her head from his shoulder and permitted her astonishment to show.

'I think it will do Lydia good to feel she has achieved something in her own right.'

'How did you get to be so wise?' Lizzy demanded to know.

Will chuckled. 'The only wise thing I have ever done is marry you.'

'Well, I can hardly argue with that.'

Will's kisses distracted Lizzy momentarily, but her mind was still fixed upon Mr Shannon.

'Do you think Miss Bingley really does have designs upon Mr Shannon?' she asked when he allowed her up for air. 'I noticed the expression on her face when Lydia and Mr Shannon were outside for so long and it frightened me. It was as though she was fighting a tremendous rage just because the guest of honour had stepped outside for some air. It might have been impolite to leave the room while she was playing, but people do that all the time.'

'I think Caroline Bingley's inability to control her temper is indicative of her state of mind when she caused trouble for us.'

Lizzy's disquiet intensified. 'Now you are frightening me, Will.'

He stroked her hair. 'That was not my intention. Don't worry. She can't harm us. I simply will not allow it.'

'You think she might lose her wits again?'

Will shrugged. 'Is it possible to permanently recover from such a condition?'

'Poor Mr Shannon. If she has fixed her interest upon him and he spurns her, there's no way of saying how she will act in retaliation. She is used to having her way and in many respects is more selfish and self-centred than Lydia ever was. She's just better at hiding it, which makes her infinitely more dangerous.'

'Let it be, Lizzy. Bingley will keep control of his sister and Shannon can take care of himself.' He pulled her closer. 'For now, I would like to enjoy my wife's company and, being a simple soul, cannot think of anything else at the same time.'

Lizzy laughed as she snuggled into the safe circle of Will's arms. 'You are very simple, Mr Darcy. I have always suspected as much.'

'I am simply and comprehensively in love with my wife, which is probably a terrible thing to admit.'

'I promise not to tell her.'

* * *

Fury burned through Caroline like corrosive acid as she smiled and bade the last of her brother's guests adieu. She swallowed down her anger, doing her very best to appear composed, but the humiliation of her rejection continued to torment her thoughts. The dark despair that fogged her brain whenever she had one of her 'episodes' swamped rationality and left her floundering on the edge of an abyss. She remembered all the things she had been told to do to fight her despondency – breathe deeply and exhale slowly, think pleasurable thoughts, remain calm, count her blessings...

Nothing worked on this occasion.

Caroline wished her relations a curt goodnight and swept up the stairs to her chamber before the demons made her say something she would later regret. She was conscious of Charles and Louisa staring after her, of Jane looking worried and asking her if she was all right. Ha, what a foolish question! Of course she was not all right.

How dare someone as inconsequential as Patrick Shannon treat her with disrespect, she asked herself, almost tripping over her skirts in her haste to escape from her family's sympathetic concern. She slammed her door and threw herself into a chair, shooing her maid away when she dared to poke her head nervously around the door. She couldn't speak to anyone. Not until she had calmed down, and that enviable state, she knew from bitter experience, would take some time to achieve.

Caroline had been surprised to discover that she actually *liked* Mr Shannon. He was educated, well-travelled, possessed refined manners and was... attractive. She was not the only single lady in attendance to be impressed by the width of his shoulders and the impact of his persuasive charm. But she was the one who had enjoyed the majority of his attention, even if that was only because she had made Jane have him escort her to table. Caroline still planned to use him as a means to an end so she could rescue Mr Darcy from Eliza's grasping claws, but she was agreeably surprised to find herself looking forward to becoming his wife.

Caroline managed a brief smile when she thought how irritated Eliza would be to have her, Caroline, as such a close neighbour. She took considerable satisfaction from the prospect of finally getting the better of her rival. She reluctantly conceded that bringing that situation about would not be as easily achieved as she had at first supposed. She had pulled out all the stops to impress Mr Shannon, displaying herself at her most cultured and dignified best tonight, and yet... and yet he hadn't even had the courtesy to listen to her play. Worse, he had followed Lydia Wickham outside – and stayed there with her for a considerable amount of time. Caroline had thought her head might actually explode with rage when she watched him go. One of the savage headaches she had come to associate with her episodes hammered at her temple, making it hard for her to see the music and causing her to hit a few wrong notes. She had never gone to so much trouble to impress any gentleman other than Mr Darcy, and yet another member of the Bennet clan seemed set to snatch the prize from her clutches.

'Caroline, are you all right?'

Caroline sighed, wondering how Louisa could ask such a damned fool question. Her sister closed the door behind her, took the chair opposite Caroline's and reached over to take her hand.

'What is it, my dear? You seem quite out of sorts.'

'How would you feel if a gentleman preferred Lydia Wickham to you?' Caroline spat the words from between clenched teeth. 'I don't understand it. It's not as though she even tries to make an impression with her dowdy clothes and disinterested attitude.'

'She is not long widowed so can hardly behave in the manner that she once did.'

'So you're defending her now?' Caroline accused.

'I'm merely pointing out that she has lost her bloom. She's fragile. You, on the other hand, are as lovely as ever.'

'For all the good that did me tonight.' But Caroline was appeased by the compliment.

'Lydia is helping him to track down his father's former employees,' Louisa said. 'I expect that is what they had to talk about.'

'I could help him look for those people. I have more intelligence in my little finger than Lydia has in her entire head.'

'No, Caroline, you know very well that would show you in a bad light. Unmarried ladies simply don't gad about attending to men's business.'

Caroline bridled. 'I have never gadded about, as you so charmingly put it, in my entire life. Besides, Mr Shannon was flirting with her. I heard him most distinctly.'

Louisa shook her head. 'This obsession with the Bennets isn't healthy, Caro. Remember what Doctor Mayfield had to say on the subject. He stressed that you should not have fixations. You must strive to overcome this particular one or you will make yourself ill again.'

'I am not obsessed or fixated, or any such thing.' Louisa's eyes were full of doubt, which infuriated Caroline. 'But I am tired of tripping over the Bennet family at every turn.'

'Jane was a Bennet and is now married to our brother. Of course you're bound to see them, especially when we are in Derbyshire.'

'You hardly need to remind me of that fact,' Caroline said in a more moderate tone. 'I bear Jane no ill-will. It is not her fault Charles settled upon Hertfordshire. Had he not done so I am perfectly sure *I* would be mistress of Pemberley. I know Mr Darcy was on the point of making me an offer before Eliza came along and distracted him with her outspoken opinions and fine eyes.'

'It does no good to dwell upon the past.' Louisa spread her hands. 'And there is no avoiding Jane's family unless we return to London, which Mr Hurst is speaking of doing.'

'I have no interest in returning to London.'

'It would be for the best. You could speak with Doctor Mayfield and—'

'I have no need of doctors, thank you, Louisa,' Caroline said stiffly.

'Then I shall stay here with you, even if Mr Hurst decides to leave.'

'Do not put yourself out on my account. I am sure you must be anxious for Mr Henley's society.'

'I am more concerned about you.'

Caroline closed her eyes and nodded. She knew it was true and that she was acting unreasonably. Her headache endured and when agitation gripped her she couldn't think coherently. But there was no escaping the fact that the glittering future Mr Darcy had led her to suppose would be hers, even if he hadn't actually declared himself, had been snatched away from her by an inconsequential nobody. It would not have mattered quite so much if she hadn't been so passionately in love with him.

No, leaving Derbyshire was out of the question.

'I shall be fine,' she said, staring at the opposite wall. 'Whether Mr Shannon likes it or not, I shall find a way to discover what happened to destroy his father's business and earn his gratitude as a consequence.' Caroline thrust her shoulders back and elevated her chin. 'You just see if I do not.'

Louisa sighed. 'As you wish, my dear.'

12

'Are the children well this morning?' Lydia asked. 'If you have concerns I can easily see Mrs Bathgate alone.'

'They are very well.' Lizzy's smile was imbued with equal quantities of affection and relief. 'Besides, Nanny would not thank me if I interfered with her routine.' Lydia stood in the doorway to Lizzy's elegant chamber, watching as her sister picked up her bonnet and fitted it on top of her curls. 'I shall certainly come with you. I am as curious as you are about Mr Shannon's situation. Besides, Mrs Bathgate is a curmudgeonly old lady and won't say a word unless she takes a liking to you.' Lizzy picked up her gloves, stood up and grinned. 'Fortunately she happens to like me.'

'Nothing to do with your being mistress of Pemberley?' Lydia asked playfully.

'Mrs Bathgate is not the type to be swayed by such considerations, which is probably why we get along so well,' Lizzy replied, linking her arm through Lydia's, and they descended the stairs together.

'I admire you, Lizzy. It must have been terrifying for you, coming here and assuming responsibility for this vast house. And yet all the servants appear to respect you, as do the local gentry and villagers.'

'Why thank you, Lydia. What a very nice thing to say. I *was* apprehensive to begin with, but in the end I simply decided to be myself and so far it has all worked out for the best.'

'In spite of Miss Bingley's efforts to cause trouble for you.' Lydia wrinkled her nose. 'To say nothing of Wickham's.'

Lizzy patted her hand. 'But you and I are closer as a consequence.'

Lydia was conscious of tears pricking her eyes. Years of trying to make amends would never atone for the trouble she had caused. Yet Lizzy was willing to forgive so readily, and her generosity of spirit only increased Lydia's guilt.

Mr Darcy was in the vestibule when they reached it.

'Good fortune with your investigation, ladies,' he said as he handed each of them into the waiting curricle. 'Drive on,' he told the coachman, raising a hand in farewell.

'Did you enjoy Jane's party?' Lizzy asked as the carriage made its way down Pemberley's long drive.

Lydia managed a half smile. 'You and Jane have come a long way since we were all at Longbourn, squabbling between ourselves.'

'As have you.'

Lydia twisted her lips. 'That is undeniable.'

'For what it's worth, I have long been of the opinion that our futures are preordained and things happen for a reason. Regretting things we can't change is futile. It's better to learn from our mistakes and live the best lives we possibly can.'

'In other words, I have everything I could possibly want and nothing to complain about.'

'You have more reason than most to harbour regrets, my dear. All that your family care about is that you recover your spirit and find happiness again. Being widowed at such a young age must be a terrible ordeal and I suspect you blame yourself for the way things turned out.'

Lydia widened her eyes. 'Whatever makes you say that?'

'It is human nature to feel culpable when something truly terrible happens, but you will come to see you are not at fault, and with the passage of time you will start to like yourself again.' Lizzy grinned. 'Then perhaps we shall have the pleasure of seeing the vibrant, impulsive Lydia again; the young sister who drove us all demented.'

Lydia, in emotional turmoil because Lizzy appeared to understand her better than she understood herself, smiled through another onset of tears. 'Beware what you wish for.'

'You were outside for a long time with Mr Shannon last night,' Lizzy remarked after a short pause.

'No, Lizzy, I was outside for a long time on my own. Mr Shannon joined me much later.' Her lips twitched. 'I don't think he appreciates music very much.'

Lizzy's smile was far less circumspect. 'And Miss Bingley didn't appreciate him walking out when she was at the instrument.'

'I don't give two figs for Miss Bingley's feelings and nor should you. Not after what she tried to do to you.'

'Just be careful around her, Lydia. She is spiteful and vindictive.'

Lydia allowed her surprise to show. 'I have done nothing to deserve her spite.'

'We both know her mind is not rational and she probably thinks you lured Mr Shannon into the garden just to annoy her.'

'Mr Shannon would not have walked out on her performance if he had feelings for her.' Lydia sighed. 'I wonder how Jane tolerates her.'

'Jane loves her husband too much to ask him to ignore his sister and has a far more forgiving nature than you or me. Even so, she is no longer taken in by Caroline and won't tolerate her interference in her household affairs.'

'Good for Jane!' Lydia sat a little straighter as the carriage approached the village. 'Now, tell me about Mrs Bathgate and how you came to know her.'

'I think you will like her. She doesn't suffer fools gladly but if she takes a liking to you then nothing will be too much trouble. She is a herbalist, amongst her other talents. Dominic drew her to my attention. He knew her when he was a child and isn't too inured to modern medicine to dismiss her older remedies.'

'She worked for old Mr Shannon?'

'Apparently so. And now you know as much as I do about that aspect of her history.'

The carriage made its way into Lambton where everyone it passed tipped their hats to Mrs Darcy. Lizzy had the coachman stop on several occasions so she could greet them by name and ask after their families. Clear of the main street, the conveyance turned into a smaller lane and the carriage rattled to a halt outside a well-kept cottage, the garden in full bloom. Lizzy and then Lydia accepted the coachman's hand to help them alight and stepped up to the cottage. There was no answer when they knocked at the door.

'She is a little hard of hearing,' Lizzy said. 'Either she hasn't heard us or more likely she's working in the garden. Come on.'

They rounded the side of the cottage to be confronted by an extensive herb garden. An old lady was bent over, cutting off stems, muttering to herself as she raised each one to her nose before placing it carefully in a different section of a wicker trug.

'Mrs Bathgate,' Lizzy said, raising her voice. 'Are we interrupting?'

'I were expecting you,' she replied, picking up the basket and heading towards the cottage with a heavy tread. 'You'd best come in. This would be your sister, I suppose. The one who married young Wickham.'

'Yes,' Lizzy replied, flashing a wry smile at Lydia. 'This is Mrs Wickham.'

Mrs Bathgate subjected Lydia to a discerning scrutiny and nodded. 'You'll do,' she said.

From which Lydia assumed she had passed muster.

'Why were you expecting us?' Lizzy asked as they stepped into an extremely neat, spotlessly clean cottage.

'I heard young Shannon were back.' She shrugged her hunched shoulders. 'Reckoned he'd want some answers. Heard you'd already been askin',' she added, nodding towards Lydia.

'Well yes, that is why we came,' Lizzy replied. 'I believe you worked for his father.'

Mrs Bathgate placed her herb basket on a shelf and lowered her bulk onto a stool, motioning Lizzy and Lydia into the only two chairs in front of the fire. 'Bathgate and I both did, right until the last. Then old Mr Shannon insisted we take this cottage for life as a reward for long service.'

'I hear he was very generous,' Lydia said.

'That he was and I'll give an argument to anyone who says a word against him. If that son of his turns out to be half the man he was, the world will be a better place with him in it.'

'He seems like a good man,' Lizzy said. 'He went to America and made a fortune. Now he plans to settle back in Derbyshire.'

Mrs Bathgate nodded, looking pleased. 'It's where he belongs. A man of conscience don't just abandon his responsibilities.'

'Did you work in the mill?' Lydia asked.

'Heavens, no. Bathgate and I ran the house where the apprentices lived.' She gathered her assortment of shawls more closely about her shoulders. 'He looked after the boys. I had charge of the girls. Made sure they were properly fed, had their lessons and attended church.'

'Oh, I see.' Lydia was discouraged, unsure how that would help their investigation. If Mrs Bathgate had not been at the mill, she wasn't in a position to know why the business had failed.

'Mr Shannon had the first water-driven mill in the locality, I understand,' Lizzy said after a short pause.

'Lord no, not a bit of it.' Mrs Bathgate shook her head, causing her multiple chins to wobble. 'I can see you know nothing about it.'

Lydia suppressed a smile. Mrs Bathgate definitely didn't pander to Lizzy just because she was mistress of Pemberley.

'I suppose I'll have to educate you.' She muttered to herself for a few minutes, causing Lydia to wonder if she was the full shilling. But in spite of her advanced years and decrepit body, there was a brightness to her eye that suggested she still had her wits about her. 'The Lombe brothers had the first mill on the Derwent that opened back in '21. John Lombe copied the design for machines that spun large quantities of silk while working in the industry in Italy.'

'He stole their secrets?' Lizzy suggested.

'Aye, you're most likely right about that. It caused a right to-do, an' all.' Mrs Bathgate sniffed disdainfully. 'Before them horrible machines, spinning wheels were used to produce small quantities of silk thread in local spinsters' homes. The work didn't pay much but it helped put bread on tables. Then them machines came along and could produce more thread a heck of a lot quicker. It were a disaster for the local women, so it were.'

'Because they reduced the need for their services,' Lydia surmised. 'I can quite see why that would cause resentment.'

'And competition for Italian imports, too. It were bound to cause trouble.'

'How did the mill work?' Lizzy asked.

'It looked complicated but it weren't, not really. An undershot water wheel turned by the mill drove the spinning machines.'

'Oh,' Lydia said, unsure if she could picture it.

Mrs Bathgate settled her bulk more comfortably on her stool. 'It was successful, until John Lombe died in mysterious circumstances before his time.' Lydia sat a little straighter. Mr Shannon's father had died before his time too, although as far as she was aware there was nothing mysterious about his death. Anyway, it happened years after Lombe's demise and could have no connection to it. But still... it was an odd coincidence. 'There was talk he was poisoned by an Italian assassin to pay him back for stealing trade secrets.'

'Good heavens,' Lizzy said. 'How extraordinary.'

'Not really,' Mrs Bathgate replied. 'The Italian silk trade really did lose a lot of orders from England and blamed the Lombes for that.'

'Yes, perhaps...' Lizzy spread her hands. 'But poison?'

Mrs Bathgate shrugged. 'There was a lot of money involved, to say nothing of good names and pride at stake. Nothing would surprise me.'

'What was the mill like to work in?' Lydia asked.

'Huge noisy place, it was. Five storeys high, housing more than twenty winding engines that made a hell of a din spinning the raw silk. They were on the upper three floors and the lower two had spinning mills producing thread.'

'Were Mr Shannon's ancestors involved in the silk trade?' Lizzy asked.

'No, they were just landed gentry, far as I know. It was the current Mr Shannon's father who took an interest in it. I heard tell that his own father was a bit of a gamester and the family fortune had dwindled.'

'So a new means of income was needed?' Lizzy suggested.

'If what I hear is right. Old Mr Shannon went to Italy on one of 'em Grand Tours young men of quality seem to think essential.' She sniffed. 'By all accounts, he took an interest in the Italian silk trade while in that country, knowing something about the success the Lombes had had with it in Derbyshire. They'd gone out of business by then. When Lombes died his brother took over until his own death, at which point the widow advertised the lease for sale. The new people didn't prosper, and Shannon saw an opportunity and persuaded his father to invest his dwindling resources in their own mill.'

'With success, I gather,' Lizzy said.

'He were clever. He knew the big machines were a cause for unrest but also appreciated the value of the handloom weavers. Local women who'd got the knack of twisting silk into thread. The quality was grand and couldn't be copied by machine.'

'And with the Lombes out of business and no unrest from the independent weavers, success was all but guaranteed,' Lydia suggested.

Mrs Bathgate tapped the side of her nose. 'Hardly. There was another mill going in the locality by then and they didn't appreciate the competition. Gunther's did everything by machine, you see, didn't treat their workers nearly as well as Shannon did, and so when Shannon opened his doors they paid the price in lost business and deserting workers.'

'It sounds as though they deserved to,' Lydia said.

'You'll get no argument from me on that score,' Mrs Bathgate replied. 'Right old bullies, their overseers were, as we came to discover for ourselves before too long. We were doing that well but all of a sudden profits started to fall for no apparent reason. Machines broke down, key workers left without giving notice, orders were cancelled and given to the competition—'

'Treachery?' Lizzy asked.

'Some of us thought so, but it couldn't be proved.' She screwed up her eyes. 'Everyone thought Mr Shannon were too soft, that people took advantage of his good nature, but in actual fact, he was a hard-headed businessman. He just didn't happen to think you got the best out of people by threats and bullying.'

'What did he do when things started to go wrong?'

'We all feared for our futures. Rumours went round that he was out of funds and would need to close down. But he called us all together and brightened us up. He had a partner who would see us through the hard times, so he said.'

'The American,' Lydia said.

'Wouldn't know about that, but all was well again for a while. Then out of the blue he brought that devil Jessup in.'

'Did he need a new manager?' Lizzy asked.

'None of us thought so. Heston, the man he had in place, knew the trade backwards. He was liked and respected. Then he was gone and we were stuck with Jessup. Nothing was the same after that.'

Lydia sat forward. 'Why him? Where did he come from?'

'That I couldn't say.' The old lady wiped her mouth with the back of her hand. 'I always thought he had something on Mr Shannon. They certainly argued enough and Jessup didn't show him an ounce of respect. We all hated the man. Usually Mr Shannon listened to me. I passed on any just complaints I picked up from the girls but all tales of Jessup's mean ways fell on deaf ears.'

Lydia and Lizzy shared a glance. 'How peculiar.'

'What happened to Mr Heston?' Lydia asked.

'He moved to Denton and wouldn't speak a word to anyone about what happened. Right tight-lipped about it, so he was. I thought someone had threatened him but it weren't none of my business so I let the poor man be.'

Lydia nodded, fairly sure that was the man Mr Shannon planned to call upon today.

'Do you remember a spinner by the name of Elsie Fletcher?' Lydia asked.

'Oh, aye. Married one of your husband's keepers, so she did, Mrs Darcy.'

'Do you know how that match came about?' Lizzy asked. 'It would have been a beneficial one for Miss Fletcher.'

Mrs Bathgate harrumphed and scratched her chin. 'Elsie Fletcher wasn't much to look at and Hobson was a right moody sod. We all thought he was a confirmed bachelor. Elsie made no secret of the fact that she had her eye on the miserable cove but none of us thought she stood a hope of snaring him. Then blow me, out of the blue they were man and wife and she went off to live on the Pemberley estate.'

'How very peculiar,' Lizzy said.

'Aye, that it was.' Mrs Bathgate leaned her elbows on her knees. 'I'll tell you something that's even more peculiar,' she said, scowling. 'If Mr Shannon died of "digestive complications" then I'm a Chinaman.'

Lizzy and Lydia both inhaled sharply.

'What do you mean?' Lydia asked.

'What I say. I've forgotten more about herbs than most people will ever know. I saw Mr Shannon practically every day. He was a strapping man in the best of health. Then he started having all those problems with Gunther's, but kept finding money to keep the business going and refused to buckle to pressure. I reckon the rows with Samuel Gunther turned into fisticuffs at times and threats were made... You know how men can be.'

'Oh, we know, Mrs Bathgate,' Lizzy assured her, looking as intrigued as Lydia felt. 'But why do you suspect his death was from anything other than natural causes?'

'Because he was strong as an ox. Then he started getting headaches, got all confused and had stomach problems an' all. His hair fell out in handfuls. I know 'cause he asked me if I could help him with my herbs. He had all the signs of arsenic poisoning but by the time he came to me it was too late to do 'owt about it.'

The sisters exchanged a glance. 'You think he was deliberately poisoned?' Lydia asked breathlessly.

13

Patrick asked directions at the inn and found Heston's cottage on the edge of Denton village without difficulty. It was larger than those that surrounded it and appeared to be well maintained. He dismounted, tied Gladiator's reins to a stout gatepost and adjured his horse not to eat any of the thriving shrubs that he appeared to be eyeing with speculative interest. He then walked up a neatly raked path edged by crowded flower borders, his boots crunching on the gravel, and rapped at the door with his crop. He wondered if he would recognize Heston after all these years. But when the door was opened by the cottage's owner and his weathered face lit up with pleasure at the sight of his visitor, those years fell away and Patrick would have known his father's old manager anywhere.

'Mr Shannon, it's a pleasure to see you again, sir.'

'It's good of you to say so, Heston.'

'I heard you'd returned and hoped you would honour me with a visit,' he said, standing back to afford Patrick admittance.

Patrick shook the man's hand warmly. His stance was still rigidly upright and he had maintained the full head of unruly hair Patrick remembered so well, even if it was snow white nowadays. Intelligence gleamed as bright as always from grey eyes that regarded Patrick with genuine-seeming affection.

'I'm happy to see you looking so fit, Heston.'

'Oh, I believe in keeping myself active; that's the key to good health.'

Patrick stepped over the threshold and came face to face with a woman hovering in the background, obviously Heston's wife. Patrick didn't remember her but then he had been away at school for the majority of the time when Heston had worked for his father and wouldn't have had occasion to meet the man's wife. Heston made the introduction and Patrick exchanged a few pleasantries with her as she led them into a neat sitting room and invited Patrick to take the chair beside the fire. She served them with refreshments and then excused herself, her expression apprehensive as she closed the door behind her.

'How have you been, Heston?' Patrick asked, stretching his legs out in front of him and crossing them at the ankles. 'You look to be thriving.'

'Well, like I say, I'm a man who doesn't take naturally to idleness.'

'The garden is your work, I imagine,' Patrick remarked, glancing out of the window and admiring the orderly riot of colour.

'That it is.' He shifted his backside in his chair and fixed Patrick with a probing gaze. 'I'm mighty glad to see you, sir. I've waited a long time for this day.'

That assertion surprised Patrick. 'You knew I would have questions about the doomed silk mill when I returned?'

'And my abrupt departure from that enterprise.' The older man nodded. 'That I did, and I've been waiting ten years to tell my story. Plenty have asked but you're the only one who has a right to know.'

'You intrigue me, Heston. Nothing will persuade me that you were anything other than completely loyal to the pater and you would not have left him in the lurch just because the business was going through a lean spell.'

'I hope I knew my duty and did my very best for your father.'

'Just tell me what happened, Heston.' Patrick's anxiety made him sound more acerbic than had been his intention.

The older man sighed. 'Your father ruffled a lot of feathers with what others saw as a lenient attitude towards his workforce.'

Patrick raised both brows. 'I'm well aware of that but I don't see how his treatment of his workforce was anyone's business other than his own.'

'Perhaps that's because you are an honourable man.' Heston screwed his features into an expression of disapproval. 'That's a great deal more than can be said for Percival Gunther.'

Patrick grunted. 'I knew they disagreed about working methods but I had no idea feelings ran so deep.'

'Your father wanted you kept out of it. He insisted you be allowed to go to university and, as he put it, sow your wild oats before joining the business. Unfortunately, that also wasn't to be.' Heston chuckled. 'Well, as to the wild oats, I couldn't possibly say, but the sorry state of the business came to light when your father died, before you even went up to Cambridge.' He leaned back in his chair and closed his eyes. 'Matters ran out of our control long before your father's passing, you see. Our best workers were intimidated into leaving, although we couldn't prove it. It was done gradually and by the time we realised there might be a conspiracy it was too far out of control to stop the rot.'

'Gunther, I suppose.'

'Right. And it got worse. Machines were damaged, customers tempted away, and money was fast running out. My suggestion was to reduce the workforce until we recovered our position, but your father wouldn't hear of it.'

Patrick felt anger welling at his father's stubbornness, albeit fuelled by the best of intentions. 'He could be hopelessly impractical at times.'

Heston paused to sip at his coffee, his weathered features compressed with worry. Patrick waited him out, a sense of foreboding gripping him as he sensed they'd reached the crux of the matter. 'Your father had a better idea. His old butler Jenson had made a fortune in America and your father put a proposition to him.'

'No, you've got that wrong,' Patrick said, shaking his head. 'My half-brother, Edward Makepeace, was the one who aided the pater. He told me so himself.'

'Ah, that's where you've been all this time, I take it.'

'Yes, but—'

'It was definitely Jenson who entered into partnership with your father.'

Patrick absorbed that disquieting information and assimilated the implications. 'He wanted revenge because my father and... well, his daughter—'

'Quite. But, of course, your father didn't know it at the time and thinking the best of everyone worked to his disadvantage. Jenson knew that's how he would be and played him like a fiddle. They had kept in touch over the years and when Jenson heard of your father's problems he offered to give him the loan he required to save his business. But, of course, he had conditions of his own which he insisted upon implementing. The main one was that Jessup took my position.'

'Good God!'

'Quite. Your father and I were friends, even though I was his employee. We were of a similar age, if not of the same social class, but of course such considerations didn't deter him from treating me as an equal and confiding in me.'

Patrick managed a ghost of a smile. 'Certainly they would not.'

'I was one of the few people who knew of your father's affair with Jenson's daughter and its catastrophic consequences. She was the love of his life, you know,' he added philosophically. 'And I could well understand why. She was quite the most beautiful, sweetest-natured creature I had ever met, before or since.'

'I have met her myself,' Patrick said. 'And she is still beautiful, even today.'

'Aye, well, that doesn't surprise me.' Heston again shifted his position, as though raking up the past made him uncomfortable. 'Your father was conflicted about Jenson's demands. It was I who persuaded him that he had no choice, even though I didn't entirely trust Jenson's motives.' Heston sighed. 'But there was no alternative other than closing our doors and putting all of those people out of work. That's what happened in the end, but at least your father did everything within his power to prevent it and didn't live to see the consequences of his failure.'

'I suppose one must be grateful he was spared that agony.'

'Your father was a good man who made mistakes,' Heston said

assertively. 'He had his back to the wall and really had no choice but to do as Jenson asked.'

'And you were the sacrificial lamb,' Patrick surmised, his anger erupting when he thought how comprehensively he had been duped by Edward Makepeace, a man whom he had considered a friend. A man who *had* been his friend and helped him to earn a fortune in his own right, but had deliberately misled him regarding Jenson's business with his father.

'Jessup was Gunther's man, although we didn't know that at the time. Jenson had married the rich widow who employed him in New York as her butler and used his new wealth to keep tabs on your father's business. When he got wind of his dispute with Gunther, he approached Gunther with his plan.'

Patrick shook his head. 'It defies belief.'

'Of course, if I had known that Gunther was being manipulated by Jenson I would not have agreed to step aside.'

'Your loyalty isn't in question, Heston,' Patrick said with sincerity. 'My father was lucky to have you. How did you survive once you were put out of work?'

Heston smiled. 'Your father gifted me this cottage. He insisted upon it.'

'I'm glad he looked after you and that you kept his secret all these years. At least now I know what happened. I have been wondering for too long.'

'Unfortunately you don't know it all.' Heston's heartfelt sigh and wary expression set warning bells ringing in Patrick's head.

'Let me guess. Gunther didn't think there was room for two mills in this part of Derbyshire and conspired with Jenson to drive the pater out of business.'

'Not only that.' Heston drilled Patrick with a bitter look. 'He was also killed.'

Patrick's entire body jerked forward. 'What the devil are you talking about? There was nothing suspicious about the pater's death. It was unexpected, I'll grant you, but... Damn it, Heston, what aren't you telling me?'

'I have no proof,' Heston replied, flexing his jaw and sucking in a trembling breath, 'but no one will persuade me that your father wasn't poisoned.'

Patrick let forth with a string of vitriolic oaths. 'And no one noticed?' He fixed Heston with a probing look, desperately wanting him to be wrong. Already suspecting that he might not be. His father had been in the rudest of health and had barely suffered a day's illness in his entire life. Patrick had been too grief-stricken by his untimely death, too devastated when he learned of the loss of his inheritance, too concerned about his own survival to think more deeply about the mystery illness that had taken his father. But he was more than ready to think about it now. Heston had been his father's closest friend and would not have mentioned his suspicions without evidence to back them up. 'If there were any signs of foul play there would have been an inquest.'

'Your father was as fit as a flea almost up until the last,' Heston reminded Patrick.

'So there definitely should have been an inquest.'

Heston's expression showed disgust. 'Only if that fool of a doctor treating him suspected foul play, which he did not.'

'The pater's gastric problems could have been brought on by having to go cap in hand to Jenson.'

'No, sir. You weren't here. You didn't see the rapid deterioration in him.'

Patrick listened, slack-jawed, as Heston described his father's decline. 'Mrs Bathgate came to me not long before his passing, telling me she suspected someone was poisoning him.'

'The herbalist?' Heston nodded. 'Mrs Darcy and her sister are speaking with her today. I never would have asked them to get involved if I'd even suspected...'

'It was one thing suspecting that someone had poisoned your father, but who could we tell and who would listen if we did speak out? I was a former manager who could be accused of having an axe to grind and Mrs Bathgate was a mother hen to the girls in the mill who might soon be out of work. We could both be dismissed as being out to cause trouble. I tried to speak to your father about it but it was beyond his capabilities to accept that anyone would deliberately harm him.' Heston rubbed his chin. 'If he *was* being poisoned, he would be ingesting that poison through his food, which meant someone in his household whom he trusted was administering it.'

Patrick shook his head. 'He would never have accepted that possibility.'

A humourless smile graced Heston's lips. 'Quite so. Anyway, before Mrs Bathgate or I could decide what we ought to do, your father was beyond help.'

'And his doctor really didn't suspect foul play?'

Heston grunted. 'Old Pardrew wouldn't recognise a case of poisoning if the poisoner left a note telling him what he'd administered. Worse than useless, he was. Thank the good lord that Sanford has set up in the area. At least now there *is* a forward-thinking medical man in this part of Derbyshire.'

'Why did you not say anything about your suspicions to the magistrate?' Patrick asked, disappointed that Heston's loyalty had not endured beyond his father's death. 'Or to me when I came back from school?'

'I planned to do so but was persuaded to keep my suspicions to myself.'

'Persuaded?' Patrick leaned towards Heston, hands planted on his thighs as he felt a tingling of unease filter down his spine. 'Persuaded by whom?'

'I never knew the man's name, never even saw his face. He accosted me one dark night in the village. He told me where my married daughter lived and the names of her children. He promised me that if I breathed a word of my suspicions—'

'How did he know you *had* suspicions?'

'I've often wondered about that myself. Mrs Bathgate and I spoke about it a lot and I asked a few discreet questions of the servants at Shannon House.' He shrugged. 'Stupid of me. I wasn't thinking straight. You know how servants gossip, and if word got back to the person responsible, well...'

He spread his hands and Patrick nodded his understanding.

'Anyway, the oaf who accosted me told me my daughter's family would suffer and so would I. My cottage would burn to the ground with my wife and me asleep in our bed.' Heston shuddered. 'I don't scare easily, sir, but I believed the man. If whoever he worked for had resorted to poisoning a well-respected gentleman like your father then they were capable of anything. Your father was gone, there was nothing I could do to bring him back and I didn't want to spend the rest of my days looking over my shoulder.' He shook his head in disgust. 'I was a coward and have had to live with that disquieting knowledge ever since.' He sat a little straighter, his expression almost defiant. 'But I did what I thought best for the sake of my family.'

Patrick nodded. 'Of course you had to put your own interests first. I quite understand that and know the pater would have, too.' He sighed. 'I am sorry if I spoke out of turn.'

'You did not say a word I don't richly deserve. I was mighty glad to see you here today so I could finally share what I knew.'

'Mrs Bathgate, was she threatened?'

'I have no idea but neither of us has raised the subject since your father died so I reckon she must have been.'

'Let me see if I've got this straight,' Patrick said. 'Percival Gunther and my father were in competition and at odds with one another. Jenson, my grandfather's old butler, emigrated to America with his daughter and my father's illegitimate child. He married his rich employer but never recovered from the grudge he bore the pater. He kept in touch with his activities and knew when his silk mill was in financial trouble. He also knew of the rivalry between my father and Gunther and used it to exact revenge, putting Gunther's man in charge of the pater's mill to expedite its demise.'

Heston nodded. 'That's about the size of it.'

'All right, I can understand what motivated both men. But, Heston, why poison my father?'

'That is a question I've been asking myself these past ten years.' Heston shook his head. 'It makes absolutely no sense. Anyone who understood your father's character would know it would be more of a torment for him to live and see his enterprise being run into the ground, to say nothing of his workforce having no means of support.'

'That is undeniable.'

Patrick stood, aware that Heston had told him everything he knew, and offered him his hand. Heston took it with a firm grip.

'Thank you for being so frank,' Patrick said, clasping his shoulder. 'And I am truly sorry for all you have been forced to endure.'

'It was less than I deserved for not having the courage of my convictions.'

'Oh, before I go,' Patrick said, turning with his hand on the door handle. 'Why have you told me all this now? Is there not still a threat to your family?'

'After all this time, no one can prove anything. Pardrew is long since dead and I doubt the people who wanted your father dead are still in the area.'

'Gunther's Mill still operates.'

'Yes, but Gunther died and his son took over, but he too is dead now. His widow sold the lease to someone who is not a native of Derbyshire. Everything has changed.'

Heston walked Patrick to the front door and opened it for him. 'Good day to you, sir. I am very glad to see you back in Derbyshire and only sorry the circumstances could not have been different.'

'No more than I am, Heston. No more than I am.'

Patrick reclaimed Gladiator, who fortuitously didn't appear to have destroyed any of Heston's garden, and swung up into the saddle. His head was still reeling from the enormity of Heston's revelations, but he couldn't decide what he intended to do about them quite yet. First he needed to go to Pemberley and make sure that in their effort to assist him, Mrs Darcy and Mrs Wickham hadn't put themselves in danger.

* * *

Caroline Bingley had Charles's coachman wait for her at the inn in Denton. She strolled down the village street awash with people taking in the pleasures of market day. There were stalls offering every type of fresh produce imaginable, as well as travelling merchants hawking anything from medicinal compounds to shoe repairs. There was a carnival atmosphere, competing taverns were doing a roaring trade and someone was playing a lively jig on a fiddle. It was all very rural, very parochial, not at all to Caroline's taste.

Most of the customers appeared to be servants or villagers, but there were ladies of quality also taking interest in ribbons, lace and buttons. Grubby children ran everywhere, irritating Caroline, who kept a tighter hold on her reticule. She looked through the throng of people, attempting to get her bearings, not having been to the village very often since Charles had moved to the area. Besides, it looked very different on market day.

Her difficulty was that she had no idea where Mr Shannon planned to be. All she had managed to overhear of his conversation with Charles was that he would be in Denton this morning, and Caroline intended to run into him by accident. He would surely offer to buy her refreshments – indeed, it would be the height of bad manners if he did not – and she would finally have him to herself. Caroline firmed her jaw, quietly determined. Half an hour in her refined company and he would forget all about the widow shrouded in grey.

But first she needed to find that distinctive horse of his so she would know where he actually was. The beast wasn't stabled at the inn's mews; she had surreptitiously looked for it, grateful that its near-white coat made it so easily distinguishable. So where could he be? There were no large houses in the village itself and so she could only conclude that his destination was one of the bigger cottages. A gentleman would hardly have urgent business in one of the hovels occupied by the villagers, she thought with distaste.

Having come to that conclusion, she walked down several of the better-looking roads without success but on her third attempt was rewarded by the sight of his horse, tethered to the gatepost of a cottage that had a lovely garden. Whose garden? Women liked flowers. Caroline went cold inside when the possibility of his visiting a mistress occurred to her. But no, if that was the case he would hardly have discussed it with Charles; especially not when there were ladies in the room who might accidentally overhear.

As luck would have it there was a haberdasher's on the corner of the street in which the cottage in question was situated. Caroline put up her parasol and lingered at the window, pretending an interest in the dreary display. It was a good vantage point, especially when so many people were around, and she would not seem out of place.

Perdition, what is he doing? she wondered after ten long minutes passed with no sign of him. The woman running the shop kept peering out at her, sensing a customer, and it wouldn't be long before she tried to entice Caroline inside. She couldn't allow that sort of distraction. A rough-looking oaf brushed past her, nudging her aside without bothering to apologise. Caroline's first instinct was to take him to task. She took one look at the set of his features and changed her mind. She was here alone, with no maid or footman to protect her, and so allowed the incident to pass unchallenged. But inside she was hot with anger at his impertinence.

The rational part of her brain told her she was wasting her energy. Then she thought of Mr Shannon shamelessly flirting with Lydia Wickham. Familiar dots danced in front of her eyes and pain launched a brutal assault inside her head, heralding the onset of one of her episodes. The only way to overcome them, she knew from experience, was to have the final word. And that meant securing Mr Shannon's affections, no matter what it took to bring herself to his notice.

She turned from the shop window and strolled slowly away from it, making it appear as though she was waiting for someone. Ladies of quality did not arrange meetings in the middle of public streets, but she hoped no one would take enough notice of her to think anything of it. She walked a few hundred yards, turned back to cover the same area and was finally rewarded by the sight of Mr Shannon on the back of his prancing horse, wending his way through the congested street. She waved a hand in acknowledgement.

'Mr Shannon, what a coincidence. I—'

To her utter dismay and disbelief, he either didn't see her or chose to ignore her. He cleared the last of the stalls, pushed his horse into a trot and disappeared from view. Caroline watched him go, surprised her head didn't explode with rage. She turned towards the inn, quietly seething. If he thought to discourage her then he didn't know her at all.

The more inaccessible he made himself, the more determined she would become. That was simply the way she was. More importantly, she needed to know what pressing business could possibly have taken him to that cottage.

Knowledge was power.

She returned to the inn and gave Charles's coachman instructions. She waited in the conveyance while he went inside the establishment and discharged her instructions. A short time later, he returned and she was in possession of the information she sought. The cottage was owned by a man who had once managed Mr Shannon's father's silk mill. Caroline breathed a relieved sigh, not having completely dismissed the possibility of a woman's involvement. She had the coachman take her home, mulling matters over as they made the short journey. Presumably the investigation Lydia Wickham was helping him with had to do with his father's old business. But why?

Caroline knew next to nothing about the man she planned to marry. But that situation was about to change.

14

After luncheon, Lydia left Lizzy to play with Marcus and wandered around Pemberley's rose garden. Clarence, Lizzy's marmalade cat, darted in and out of bushes to ensure the rodent population knew its place but mostly strolled along beside her, tail erect, brushing his big body against her skirts. Lydia liked cats and accepted his company.

'What do you make of it all, Clarence?' she asked him, reaching down to run her hand down his sleek back and tug gently at his tail. 'Shall we tell Mr Shannon about Mrs Bathgate's suspicions? I don't suppose anything can be proven one way or the other after all this time, so upsetting him by repeating her speculations would be needlessly cruel.'

Clarence's ears twitched and his body went rigid beneath Lydia's hand. Lydia saw a thrush on the other side of the garden, industriously digging for worms beneath a rose bush. She smiled as the big cat slunk along on his belly in a futile attempt to creep up on the bird. The thrush saw him before he could get anywhere near and took to the wing in a graceful arc, dipping low over the cat's head, taunting him.

'You're hardly inconspicuous, Clarence,' Lydia told him when he returned to her side with a disgruntled meow.

Lydia told herself there was nothing more she could do for Mr Shannon. As far as she was aware, there was no one left for her to interrogate. A small part of her would welcome the excuse to find someone else to talk to about the mill. It would give her a legitimate excuse to see him again, but she simply refused to give way to the impulsive side of her character that had already had too much to answer for. There was no denying that whenever she was in Mr Shannon's company it was as though she had awakened from a long sleep and the emotions she had kept under close guard these past fifteen months sprang spontaneously back to life. Her mind, on the other hand, kept warning her not to follow her misguided instincts, and she was mature enough nowadays to heed that warning.

Desire? Her surprise was genuine when it occurred to her that she actually desired Mr Shannon. Their new neighbour was undeniably attractive, but Lydia couldn't afford to think of him in that way. She was *a* 'disappointment', she reminded herself, and bad things happened to anyone she allowed herself to feel affection for. She wasn't wallowing in self-pity. She was simply facing up to the unpalatable truth, something she should have done before carelessly causing havoc with so many lives.

In an effort to reinforce her dwindling resolve, Lydia reminded herself of the half-hour she had spent on her journal today. She had written of the time when she was about twelve and had deliberately destroyed one of Kitty's sketches because she was jealous of her talent. Lydia had no recognisable accomplishments and couldn't permit the only sister over whom she exerted any control to find an occupation that excluded her.

Kitty had cried for several days afterwards, wondering who could have done anything so spiteful. Lydia had consoled her and suggested diversions more suited to her own pleasures to take Kitty's mind off her ruined sketch. Kitty eventually recovered her spirit but didn't pick up her charcoal again until she came to live at Pemberley with Lizzy. It was a talent she shared with her major – now her husband – and had helped to bring them together. A talent that might have blossomed much earlier if Lydia hadn't been so vindictive.

'It's a penance, Clarence,' she told the cat, sighing. 'I like Mr

Shannon very much. There, I have admitted it, but I know my secret's safe with you. Even if he returned my regard, which is far from likely, what right does such a wicked person as I have to happiness? Besides, happiness is unreliable. I thought I would be happy with Wickham and yet I was miserable most of the time.

'Miss Bingley seems to like Mr Shannon, too,' she added, seating herself in an arbour with roses in full bloom arching over her head, giving off a sweet perfume that caressed her senses. Clarence leapt onto her lap and settled there, his big body rattling with purrs. Lydia absently ran a hand over his head. 'I dislike Miss Bingley but even she has a better character than I do. I know she was horrid to Lizzy, but everyone agrees she temporarily lost her wits so I don't suppose she could help herself.' Lydia puffed out a breath. 'Anyway, I shall think of Mr Shannon in that manner no more. He's perfectly safe with me. What do you say, Clarence? Shall I stick to my resolve?'

'Talking to yourself, Mrs Wickham?'

Lydia almost leapt out of her skin at the sound of Mr Shannon's deep, arresting voice, briefly wondering if she had conjured it up in her imagination. It seemed odd that she had been thinking about him and that he should suddenly appear. But she looked up and there he was, as large as life and just as handsome as she recalled, standing in front of her with an amused smile playing about his lips. Clarence took exception to the intrusion, howled with indignation and jumped from her lap.

'Mr Shannon!' Lydia clapped a hand over her heart. 'You scared me half to death.'

'I apologise. I assumed you would have heard me approaching.'

Lydia felt her cheeks redden, wondering how long he had been there and how much of her embarrassing monologue he had overheard. She gathered up her scattered wits, returned her chin to its correct location and smiled up at him.

'I was *not* talking to myself but to Clarence.'

'Ah, that would explain it.'

'Certainly it would. He's a very good listener and never contradicts me.'

'I can see the advantages in that,' he replied, nodding towards the vacant part of the seat beside her, asking permission to seat himself. She was unsure how she felt about having him sit so close to her so soon after the inappropriate thoughts she had just voiced to Clarence, but could think of no reason to refuse. He swished the tails of his coat aside with the practised flip of one wrist and there he was, far too close, far too masculine, far too tempting... Far too every wretched thing. 'But the beauty of conversing with another human is that there *is* a possibility of contradiction, thereby forcing one to consider the validity of one's arguments before getting carried away with them.' He sent her a teasing smile that had a most disconcerting effect upon Lydia's resolve not to be affected by him. 'Unless, of course, one has secrets to impart and doesn't wish to be dissuaded from one's intransigent point of view.'

Perdition, he *had* overheard her!

'I had forgotten you were calling today,' she said.

'I came to show Darcy my list of names but he is not here.'

'No, there was some emergency on the estate that required his attention, I believe. I am sorry you have had a wasted journey.'

'How can it be wasted when I have the pleasure of your company?'

Stop being nice to me. I don't deserve it. 'How gallant,' she said, an edge to her voice.

Mr Shannon shot her a bemused look but had the good sense not to comment upon her curmudgeonly mood.

'Simpson suggested I wait,' he said in a composed tone. 'He does not think Darcy will be that long. Mrs Darcy is in the nursery. So I am afraid you're stuck with me for now, Mrs Wickham.'

She bit back a smile. 'How tiresome.'

'Would it make matters easier for you if I promised to be more like Clarence and never disagree with a word you say?'

Lydia's determination to remain immune to his charm was already showing signs of strain, for which she held him entirely responsible. She was doing her very best to remain politely aloof and yet he seemed determined to... To what, precisely? He was merely making conversation. Yet there was something more fundamental in the way he focused his full attention upon her that gave her pause. And the elusive light in his dark eyes, so very disconcerting, set her mind running off in all the directions she had expressly forbidden it to take.

'You ought not to make promises you are not in a position to keep. You are an intelligent man and intelligence breeds curiosity and... well, argumentativeness. It's not your fault, Mr Shannon,' she said kindly. 'You simply cannot help yourself.'

'I'm just an idle fellow,' he replied, stretching his legs out in front of him, offering Lydia a close view of his muscular thighs whenever her gaze drifted from his face. But focusing on his face wasn't much safer because she was confronted instead with seductive brown eyes gleaming with amusement, his very attractive mouth, the cleft in his chin that she found so appealing... and, God's beard, this simply wouldn't do! 'I cannot imagine why you should think me intelligent.'

She canted her head and tried to look severe, ashamed to admit that she was enjoying this exchange a little too much. It occurred to her then that she had never been an adequate flirt, not really. Her sisters had rightly accused her of being a little too ready to flaunt herself, but she had been too young to realise that flirting was actually an art. It was important, she now knew, to give as little as possible away about one's own feelings whilst encouraging the subject of one's flirting – the flirtee? – to surrender his own aspirations. Well, Mr Shannon had set the tone. *He* was the one to start flirting, and Lydia would not be the first to back down.

'Are you fishing for compliments, Mr Shannon?' Lydia resisted telling him that he ought to call upon Miss Bingley if that was the case.

'Not in the least, ma'am. I merely wish to know why you imagine I'm clever.'

'Well, let me see. I know you were orphaned unexpectedly at the age of seventeen, deprived of the inheritance you had grown up expecting to come your way and yet managed, by dint of your own wits, to restore your lost fortune in the space of ten short years.' She turned to partially face him. 'I very much doubt if you would have achieved that ambition if you were not very clever indeed.'

'It goes against every gentlemanly instinct I possess to tell a lady she is wrong and so I shall thank you for the compliment and we shall agree to differ.'

Lydia sobered. What was she thinking of, bandying words with this elegant man when she had tidings to impart that would cause him pain. And she would have to tell him, she decided. If she did not, it could only be a matter of time before he asked her what she had learned from Mrs Bathgate and Lydia couldn't bring herself to be untruthful.

'Mr Shannon—'

'Mrs Wickham,' he said at the same time. Then he laughed. 'Please, you go first.'

'I wanted to tell you about our visit to Mrs Bathgate.'

'Ah, about that.' The laughter left his eyes and he suddenly seemed severe, unreachable. 'Yes, I suppose we must speak of it. Tell me what you learned.'

Lydia did so. He listened intently and she could see that nothing she imparted came as any great surprise to him. But, of course, she had not yet revealed Mrs Bathgate's suspicions about poisoning. When she hesitated, Mr Shannon's deep voice filled the silence.

'You are trying, I suppose,' he said, 'to find an easy way to tell me that Mrs Bathgate suspects my father was poisoned.'

Lydia widened her eyes. 'You already know about that?'

'I visited Heston this morning. He told me something similar, and sprang a few other surprises.'

Lydia listened as he related the particulars of his interview with Heston, expressing surprise and anger at Jenson's involvement from America.

'I wonder what made him act so spitefully,' Lydia mused. 'He married his employer, became a rich man in his own right and was accepted by America's elite. I doubt whether English society would have been so quick to embrace a former butler, even if he did manage to pull off such an advantageous match on these shores.' Lydia wrinkled her brow. 'It seems to me that crossing the Atlantic was the best thing that he could have done to advance his ambitions. His daughter was happy in her marriage and her son prospered.' She lifted her shoulders. 'I simply don't understand why his resentment towards your father endured.'

* * *

Patrick watched a gamut of conflicting emotions filter across Mrs Wickham's pretty face as she considered the matter. On each of the occasions they met she fascinated him more and yet made no special effort to garner his attention. She had seemed annoyed when he flirted with her earlier – as though her determination to remain in half-mourning should have deterred such behaviour.

It should have.

And yet she responded because she couldn't seem to help herself. She was an intriguing mixture of decorum and melancholy warring with a quick wit and lively spirit that she couldn't completely suppress. Patrick had met his share of widows, many of whom had made their availability as mistress material readily apparent. Lydia Wickham had not given him any reason to suppose that was her purpose. It was clear that she was still trying to untangle her emotions following Wickham's demise, and he ought to respect her desire for privacy.

Why he did not do so, what he actually wanted from her, he could not have said. He was as adamantly opposed as he had ever been to the prospect of matrimony and, despite what he had told her once before, shared her view that a man and woman could not be friends without sexual attraction intruding. He really ought to run a mile before he did something he would live to regret.

He remained precisely where he was since there was nowhere else he wanted to be. He had come to Pemberley straight from Denton to keep his engagement with Darcy, partly in the hope of seeing her.

'We shall never know,' Patrick said in answer to her earlier question. 'Edward deliberately misled me regarding his business arrangement with the pater and then took me under his wing and ensured I prospered.' He managed a brief smile. 'You can take it from me that, intelligence or lack thereof notwithstanding, I would not have done nearly so well without his patronage.'

She tilted her head to one side as she contemplated matters. 'You imagine, I suppose, that he promised his grandfather he would not tell you the truth if the two of you ever met?'

'Yes, I do think that. Jenson wanted his daughter to shine within English society and probably looked upon America as second best.'

'I thought you told us it was his decision to leave England.'

'I think he lived to regret doing so. England was where he really wanted to be and, paradoxically, his resentment grew with the upturn in his fortunes.' Patrick ran his arm along the back of the seat they shared, his fingers inches away from the enticing, creamy skin of Mrs Wickham's neck. 'Jenson was a bitter man who manipulated his daughter and grandson into doing things his way. Edward kept his word but eased his conscience by helping me to restore my fortune.'

'You could write to him and ask him to confirm your suspicions.'

'I could, but I probably shall not.' He shrugged. 'It would place Edward in a difficult position. He need not have had anything to do with me when I arrived in America if he preferred not to and yet he couldn't have been kinder or more welcoming.'

'What about your father's death?' she asked after a short pause.

Patrick expelled a prolonged sigh. 'What *can* I do about that? Nothing can be proved after all this time. The doctor who attended him is dead and... well, I doubt whoever did it is likely to confess, even if they are still in the district.'

'No, you're probably right about that.'

'What is it, Mrs Wickham?' Patrick removed his arm from the back of the seat and sat forward, looking at her intently. 'What is it that you are not telling me?'

'I have been thinking about your father's death,' she replied pensively. 'If he was poisoned, I am not convinced it had anything to do with Gunther or Jenson.'

'Good heavens!' Patrick elevated both brows. 'You think someone else bore him a strong enough grudge to have him killed?'

She hesitated. 'When you put it like that, it *does* sound rather unlikely.'

'But you must have reasons for having mentioned the possibility. I should like to hear what they are.'

'Firstly, the young man I saw outside of Mrs Hobson's cottage was loitering in the street when we left Mrs Bathgate's today,' she said bluntly.

Patrick tensed. 'Are you absolutely sure?'

'Oh yes. He was looking directly at us, quite deliberately. I recognised him at once.'

'When I accepted your offer of help, I didn't mean to put you in danger, Mrs Wickham. Please accept my most sincere apologies for having done so.'

'Oh, we were not in any danger.' She waved the suggestion aside with the careless flip of one wrist. 'We had our coachman and a footman with us.'

'Even so...' Patrick was appalled. 'The youth must have followed you.'

'Or anticipated that my next call would be upon Mrs Bathgate.' She turned sideways and fixed Patrick with a probing look. 'That is why I think whoever killed your father must still be in the locality. Gunther is dead, so is his son, and whoever owns the mill now cannot be culpable. They have no reason to be. So, whoever is following me must be concerned that we might uncover evidence of poisoning.'

'But how?' Patrick was furious with himself for putting her in danger. And she had been in danger, no matter how light she made of the situation. People did not follow ladies of quality for recreational purposes. 'Even if we suspect foul play, we have no way of proving it.'

'Someone in your household would have had to administer the poison to your father in his food. Gradually. You could do worse than ask Mrs Mason about the servants in your employ at that time.'

'That I will, but—'

'And Mrs Hobson definitely knows more than she was willing to tell me.' Mrs Wickham absently plucked at her lower lip with her index finger; a compelling gesture that briefly distracted Patrick, sending his mind off in all sorts of inappropriate directions. Her lips were plump and full and highly kissable and he would wager half his fortune that he could dispel the bruised look that permanently resided in her eyes with a passionate kiss. 'Her sudden and very advantageous marriage to a man she had set a cap at but who wanted nothing to do with her keeps niggling at the back of my mind.'

'She worked in the mill and had nothing to do with serving my father's meals.'

'As far as we are aware.'

Patrick looked upon her with a combination of admiration and respect. 'Yes, you are right. We have taken everything people tell us as gospel and need to verify our facts.' He paused. 'No, *I* need to verify the facts. I am very grateful for your help, Mrs Wickham, but you must leave matters to me from now on. If there is the slightest risk to your safety, then I cannot ask you to involve yourself.'

'But I am involved and you can hardly expect me to stand back now my curiosity is piqued. Mr Darcy is trying to gain more particulars about Hobson's family. Let's wait and see if that points us in any particular direction and then decide upon how best to proceed.'

'I still won't have you involving yourself.'

'As you wish,' she replied stiffly, turning away from him.

Blazes, now he'd overset her. Patrick placed a finger beneath her chin and used it to turn her head until she was compelled to meet his gaze again. 'I cannot allow you ladies to fight my battles for me,' he said softly.

Her eyes flared as she met his gaze and held it. Patrick suspected she was aware that he wanted her and sensed her waging war with her own emotions.

'Because we might discover things that elude your own investigation.' She found her voice, albeit huskier than usual, and raised a challenging brow. 'Really, Mr Shannon, I did not think you quite so unenlightened.'

'Enlightenment has nothing to do with the matter.' He fixed her with a determined look and firmed up his voice. 'Your safety is my only concern. If you are right, if my father was murdered and the people who committed the deed are still around, then they will do whatever is necessary to ensure their crime goes unpunished. And that includes using anyone I care about to deter me from my purpose.'

Mrs Wickham swallowed. 'No one would harm me in order to deter you.' She gave a nervous little laugh. 'We are mere acquaintances.'

He caressed her with his eyes, much as he had been fighting the urge to do the same thing with his hands for the entire time they had been together. 'Are we?'

'What is it that you want of me?' she asked, turning away from him, her voice so low that he barely caught the words.

'Since you ask, forgive me but I want you to be yourself.' He indicated her grey gown with a wave of one hand. 'Until you can face up to what it was you felt or did not feel for Wickham, you will be stuck in a cycle of discontent.'

She gasped. 'I don't understand.'

'I think you understand me perfectly, Lydia.'

Using her name when they were having such an intimate discussion, a discussion he had not come here with any conscious intention of instigating, seemed natural and right. She made no objection, perhaps because she thought he had no right to speak to her so intimately – which, in truth, he did not – and was busy formulating a reprimand.

'You are confusing me.'

'Then let me speak plain. From my observations, you don't feel Wickham's loss nearly as acutely as you think you should and so you believe there must be something wrong with you.'

She gasped, her eyes round with surprise. 'How could you possibly know that?'

'I am right,' he said, feeling vindicated. 'I thought as much.'

'Go on,' she said, neither confirming nor denying his assertion.

'I don't pretend to know anything about your marriage but I do know something of Wickham's character and, excuse me, none of it is to his advantage. For instance, are you aware that as children he once tried to drown Darcy in the lake here?'

Lydia gasped. 'No! He would not go that far.'

'It was generally considered to be an accident but Darcy was a strong swimmer, it was a calm day and there was speculation here amongst the servants that Wickham was the one at fault. With Darcy out of the way, he would have been old Mr Darcy's obvious heir apparent because Wickham made it his business to flatter and charm the old man.'

Lydia shook her head, clearly too shocked to reply.

'I can see you believe me,' he said. 'I am sorry to cause you pain but I am simply trying to point out in my clumsy way that if you don't regret Wickham's demise or are even secretly glad to be rid of him then there is no reason to feel guilty about it.'

'Wickham was obsessed with Pemberley. At first I shared his outrage because I believed he had been unfairly treated.' She emitted an unlady-like snort. 'Now I know better. So much better. Even so, I would never have imagined him capable of wilful murder.'

'Old Darcy must bear some of the blame. He favoured Wickham, gave him a gentleman's education and encouraged him to have expecta-tions that would never be fulfilled, at least while Darcy's son lived.'

'Even so, I was as bad as him.' She fixed Patrick with a focused look. 'I eloped with Wickham, if you want to know the truth. I thought nothing of the disgrace my actions would visit upon my family, but only of myself.'

'How old were you?' Patrick asked, careful to show no surprise at this astonishing revelation.

'Just sixteen.'

Patrick chuckled. 'Then you were hardly to blame. Wickham was a charming rogue, I'll grant him that. At such a young age you would not have seen through his artifice.'

'I was persuaded he loved me and intended to marry me as soon as it could be arranged, but of course, he was not thinking of marriage.'

'He was running from debts?'

'Yes.' Lydia sighed. 'Mr Darcy forced him to marry me. Only imagine how distasteful that must have been for him – Mr Darcy, I mean. And through my selfish actions I almost ruined my sisters' chances of happiness.'

'And yet three of them have made advantageous marriages.'

'Yes, but even so.' She plucked at the fabric of her skirt. 'Everyone must atone for their sins at some point and that is what I'm doing now.'

'Because you are a disappointment?'

'You see. You understand and agree with me. I am a lost cause. You are wasting your time with me, Mr Shannon.'

'Patrick,' he replied softly. 'And I most certainly do not agree with you.' He stood, reached for her hand and pulled her to her feet. He placed her hand on his sleeve and they strolled together through the lovely rose garden. 'I am trying to make you see that it is perfectly all right to be glad you are rid of Wickham.'

'I am every bit as wicked as he was. Lizzy suggesting that I start a journal has brought that fact home to me.'

'You told me before that all you can remember are the bad things you did.' He looked down at her. 'But has it occurred to you there might be just as many acts of kindness in your past?'

'No!' She stopped walking and gaped up at him. 'I cannot accept that. If they exist, not a single one has occurred to me thus far.'

'Because you are determined to punish yourself by remembering all the outrageous things you did to draw attention to yourself. Your mother and father must take some of the blame for indulging you.' Patrick smiled at her astonishment. 'The youngest in any family is almost always indulged.'

'Yes, I was spoiled, I will admit that much, but I was also not a nice person.'

'Then prove it.'

'How?'

'When you next sit down to your journal, try to think of some of the good things that you did. You have blocked them out in your determination to paint yourself in a bad light.'

'I am perfectly willing to try.'

'And you will succeed.'

She wrinkled her brow. 'How can you be so sure?'

'There are not so many differences between you and my father.'

'But... but he was a good man, whereas I—'

'My father was riddled with guilt about what happened with Jenson's daughter and for producing a son he could have no contact with. He felt he had ruined their lives and, I suspect, continued to love Miss Jenson a little too passionately even after he married my mother. So he overcompensated by being generously inclined towards everyone he subsequently had dealings with.' He smiled at her. 'You, on the other hand, are turning your self-imposed guilt inwards and finding fault with yourself when there is probably no fault to be found.' His hand cut through the air in a dismissive downward motion. 'I dare say you were a wilful child but I challenge you to think of anything wicked or spiteful that you have done since growing up.'

She elevated a brow. 'Other than eloping?'

He chuckled, enjoying her company a little too much. 'Other than that.'

'When did you become such a philosopher?'

'I'm not a philosopher, I'm a self-confessed cynic.'

'Because you feel your own childhood was based on a lie?'

He nodded, unsurprised by her perception. 'Perhaps.'

'You do not like the way supposedly loving families conduct themselves.' She grinned. 'All those dark secrets grow into glowing monsters and so you have decided to avoid becoming a family man yourself.'

'Good heavens, whatever gave you that idea?'

She sent him a teasing smile. 'You are not without charm—'

He chuckled. 'Why, thank you, ma'am.'

'I was being objective rather than trying to pay you a compliment. Now do stop interrupting and allow me to finish my thought.'

He bit back a smile and inclined his head. 'By all means.'

'As I was saying, you are not without charm but you are also a man of fortune. It stands to reason that ambitious ladies will have thrown themselves at you at every turn. Indeed, I believe you told my sister that was one of the reasons why you left America. It seems naïve to imagine you will have any greater success in avoiding the match-making mamas on this side of the Atlantic but the fact that you have so far managed to do so indicates that you have dissuaded them by adopting the cynical attitude you just now referred to.'

'Bravo, Lydia,' he said softly. 'A very astute observation of my character.'

'I would be the first to admit that I made the most dreadful mistake. That is why I am determined not to risk embracing matrimony for a second time. My sisters will doubtless put up with me if I don't give any trouble. But Lizzy and Jane *are* both blissfully happy in their unions as, I believe, my sister Kitty is also. And that rather defeats your view of the institution, and mine.'

'Perhaps.'

Patrick smiled at her, aware that he was on dangerous ground. She might be a widow but she was still little more than a child and would almost certainly change her mind about marrying again. He must absolutely not give her reason to look towards him when she had learned to like herself and was ready to move on.

'I must ask for your word that you will start recording all the acts of kindness you carried out as a child,' Patrick said.

'I have already said I will do so, but such recollections won't fill many pages in my journal. There really is no hope for me.'

'I disagree.' They strolled on for a little longer. 'And I will know when you have reached the same conclusion.'

'How?'

He chuckled. 'You will no longer feel the need to drape yourself in grey. I have a great desire to see you wearing bright colours to suit the personality you seem determined to keep hidden.' He canted his head and subjected her person to close scrutiny; no great hardship since she had a neat, enticing figure concealed beneath all that dreary fabric. 'Hmm, pink, I think. Vibrant pink would suit you.' He plucked a bud from a bush they passed and handed it to her. 'This exact colour. Make sure your modiste matches it exactly.'

Lydia twirled the rosebud between the fingers of her free hand, looking a little lost and unsure of herself. 'You can have no idea what you are saying.'

'We shall see.' He glanced up and saw Darcy walking towards them, which he thought to be just as well. He had allowed himself to become too involved with Lydia's personal demons and had enjoyed their flirtatious exchanges a little too much. Not that *she* had done any of the flirting, he belatedly realised, but still... 'Let's see what news Mr Darcy brings, shall we?' he suggested, steering her in that direction.

15

Marcus squealed and stretched out his arms to be picked up. Will swept him from the floor and tossed him in the air, producing more squeals.

'More, Papa! More!'

Will obliged.

'I so admire the resilience of children,' he said as he placed his son back on the floor and tousled his unruly mop of curls. 'A few days ago he seemed to be at death's door.'

'I am relieved at the speed of his recovery.' Lizzy bent to kiss her precious son's forehead. She loved all her children equally, but Marcus, who had given her so much trouble when he attempted to enter the world upside down, would always hold a special place in her heart. 'However, Nanny will not thank us for overexciting Marcus.'

'Shannon is here,' Will said as they left the nursery together. 'Simpson informed me of his arrival when I got back just now. I thought you might like to join us and hear what he has to say.'

'I already knew he was here.' They paused on the landing and Lizzy nodded towards the spot in the rose garden where Lydia and Shannon were engaged in animated conversation. 'I've been watching them for a while. He makes Lydia laugh, so I decided to leave them alone for a little longer. Mr Shannon is good for her. He is a relative stranger who knows nothing about her history with Wickham and won't seem as though he is judging her conduct.'

'We none of us judge her, do we?' Will asked, looking surprised.

'Lydia thinks we do.' She shrugged. 'Still, whatever she and Shannon find to talk about, it seems to have rejuvenated her and *that* is what pleases me.'

Will wrapped an arm around Lizzy's waist as Lydia and Mr Shannon walked out of their line of sight. 'Well then, to please you, I shall just have to find something to occupy us so they can enjoy one another's company for a little longer,' he said in a throaty drawl that sent anticipatory shivers down Lizzy's spine.

Lizzy expelled a reckless little laugh. 'It's the middle of the day, when we have a houseful of servants. I think you had better behave yourself, Mr Darcy, or you will shock them into giving notice.'

'My house and my servants.'

Lizzy rolled her eyes, loving the way she and Will could so easily *talk* one another into a state of heightened awareness. Once Will introduced his hands into the equation Lizzy knew that her token resistance would evaporate. They entered the drawing room and Will pulled Lizzy into his lap, proving his determination to behave as he pleased in his own house. She still had difficulty accepting that her reserved husband had become so openly demonstrative since the dreadful business with Miss Bingley. In the early days of their marriage Lizzy had accused Will of keeping his feelings too closely guarded, giving someone as determined as Miss Bingley reason to think he regretted his choice of wife. No sane person who saw them together now could possibly make the same mistake.

'I suppose you ought to send someone to summon Mr Shannon,' Lizzy said somewhat breathlessly when Will finally stopped kissing her.

'Since you have had enough of me, I shall go and fetch him myself.'

'And I shall ring the bell for tea,' Lizzy replied as she straightened her gown and patted her curls back into place.

A short time later the tea in question was being consumed by the four of them. Lydia seemed preoccupied but Mr Shannon was his usual charming self as he told them about his meeting with Mr Heston.

'So, it's most likely true,' Lizzy said, sighing. 'About the poison, I mean. But why go to such lengths?'

'Mrs Wickham thinks it might have been someone other than Gunther or Jenson who ordered it,' Mr Shannon replied. 'At first I thought it unlikely, but the idea is growing on me. The pater truly was a decent man but still collected his share of enemies along the way.'

'A natural consequence of making a success of his business,' Will said. 'Some people's feathers would have been ruffled; especially if your father treated his workers better than his competitors did theirs. But still, I agree with Lizzy. Poison seems extreme. It's also very personal and a dangerous thing to attempt.'

'Poison is supposed to be a woman's weapon, I think,' Lydia remarked speculatively.

'Heavens, I hope there are no more disappointed females in the pater's past,' Mr Shannon said, making them all smile with his theatrical shudder.

'Even if there are, they would have to be in a position to administer it,' Lizzy pointed out. 'It would have to be done gradually, would it not?' She shared a glance between Will and Mr Shannon. Both gentlemen nodded. 'Otherwise, the symptoms would be obvious, even to a doctor as idle as the one who attended your father.'

'I plan to quiz Mrs Mason about the servants in our employ at the time,' Mr Shannon said.

'I still think Mrs Hobson knows more than she told me,' Lydia insisted. 'Did you learn anything of interest about Hobson's family, Mr Darcy?'

'As a matter of fact, I did.' Will paused, his expression pensive. 'I wrongfully assumed that Hobson's father had been a keeper on the estate before Hobson himself, occupations of that nature tending to run in families. However, my steward tells me otherwise.' He directed his gaze towards Mr Shannon. 'His father was an overseer at your father's mill.'

'Really?' Mr Shannon's eyebrows shot up. 'His name didn't appear on the list Fenton supplied me with.'

'I said "was",' Will replied. 'He defected to Gunther a year or so before your father died.'

'And so wouldn't have been able to poison him.'

'Ah, but here's the interesting part. Hobson's son, the one who married Elsie Fletcher, has a sister named Agnes. And Agnes was a maid at Shannon House.'

'Good heavens!' Mr Shannon and Lydia looked equally astounded.

'I told you this had to do with Mrs Hobson's advantageous marriage,' Lydia said, setting her chin in a stubborn line that had once sent a warning to her entire family since it usually preceded a tantrum. Nowadays, Lizzy knew, it simply implied determination. 'Elsie Fletcher was a senior weaver at your father's mill, Mr Shannon. She would have had more freedom than the junior workers and probably knew more about grievances, real or perceived, held against your father. Hobson, as far as we know, gave loyal service to your father until he defected to Gunther's.'

'We need to try and establish why he left,' Lizzy said. 'Is he still alive?'

Will shook his head. 'No, I am told he died about five years ago.'

'Everyone who could have helped us is dead,' Mr Shannon remarked. 'How very disobliging of them.'

Lydia smiled. 'Elsie set her cap at Hobson's son, but he had no interest in her or any other woman as far as we know. He wanted nothing to do with the silk business and preferred to work his way up to a position as keeper here at Pemberley.'

'Go on,' Mr Shannon said when Lydia paused to assemble her thoughts.

'What if Elsie knew Hobson was somehow involved in ruining your father's business and used that information to get the man she wanted?' Lydia bit her lip. 'And then there is Hobson's sister, a maid in your father's house, to consider. All paths lead back to that family.' She sent Mr Shannon an impassioned look. 'I've hit upon something. I just know I have.'

'Steady, Lydia,' Will said. 'I agree it seems suspicious, but you cannot simply barge into Mrs Hobson's cottage demanding answers when you have no proof that she knows anything.'

'I agree,' Mr Shannon said succinctly. 'Besides, it is too dangerous.'

'Mrs Hobson lives here at Pemberley,' Lydia replied indignantly. 'I have every right to ask her questions.'

'Actually, you don't, Lydia,' Will said. 'This has nothing to do with her tenure at Pemberley and she is entitled to her privacy.'

'And don't forget about the youth who has been watching you on both occasions when you asked questions,' Mr Shannon said.

'What!' Lizzy and Will cried together.

Lydia sent Mr Shannon a look of deep betrayal. He smiled an apology but stood his ground.

'There is nothing more that Mrs Wickham can do; at least, until we know what we are up against and we can plan our strategy together, the four of us. I shall speak with Mrs Mason, see what she remembers about Agnes Hobson and come and tell you what I find out.'

'You must do as you think best,' Lydia replied acidly.

'I agree,' Will said, standing when Mr Shannon did and shaking his hand. 'Let me know as soon as you need anything more from me.'

'You are very kind.'

He took his leave of Lizzy first and then Lydia, lingering over her hand and treating her to a somnolent smile that piqued Lizzy's curiosity. Unless she mistook the matter, Mr Shannon was more interested in Lydia than he realised.

* * *

Lydia returned to her chamber and watched from her window as Mr Shannon rode down the drive on his grey horse, thinking over their rather strange conversation in the rose garden. A conversation that would have seen him beat a very hasty retreat had he been aware of the inappropriate emotions it had stirred within her. Dormant emotions that she hadn't expected to experience ever again. Pleasurable emotions she had no right to entertain. He had taken her by surprise with his insightful suggestions, frank manner of address and infectiously wicked smile. Still, she had his measure now and wouldn't permit his lazy, persuasive charm to penetrate her defences in future.

Lydia had not lost sight of the fact that she was *a* 'disappointment', *a* dangerous person to know. However, in the spirit of friendly co-operation, she would keep her promise to Mr Shannon and try to think of acts of kindness she had perpetrated during her adolescence. She nibbled at the end of her quill and stared at a blank sheet of paper. Mr Shannon's determination to protect her when she was perfectly capable of taking care of herself rankled. It was not as though she was a green miss fresh from the schoolroom. She might still be young but she had been married and knew a great deal about the ways of the world; an inevitable consequence of being married to a man of Wickham's ilk, pursued at every turn by debt collectors and persons of exceedingly dubious character.

Lydia had formed an embryonic bond with Mrs Hobson because she had managed to coax a word or two from Maisie. A gentleman couldn't be expected to understand the strength of a woman's maternal instincts. Lydia understood far too well and felt a momentary pang for the loss of the baby she had been carrying shortly before Wickham's demise. She pushed it aside. That tragedy was still too raw, too painful, for her to think about without breaking down. Wickham's death, on the other hand, she could contemplate with comparative composure.

Thinking about Mr Shannon's masculine qualities was probably not the best manner in which to tamp down her interest in him. He enjoyed her society because he felt safe with her. Even so, she was depressed, not dead, so felt vindicated in admiring him from the vantage point of recent widowhood. He had joined her in the rose garden because he wanted to know what progress she had made with Mrs Bathgate. Quite how he had gone on to draw her out on her 'disappointing' qualities, or the redeeming features he seemed adamant about her possessing, she couldn't have said. He had this manner about him that made him an easy person to confide in; someone who did not judge and couldn't be shocked.

'Enough!' she cried, disturbing Clarence, who had followed her into her room and was curled up in a patch of sun on the window seat. 'Sorry, Clarence, but I cannot help feeling just a little disappointed. Mr Shannon put into my head the possibility of my wearing a pink gown.

He couldn't possibly know that I really like the colour. Anyway, I shall not follow his advice because I haven't earned the right. I have been sitting here this full half-hour, staring at this page and racking my brains for something to write that will highlight at least one redeeming feature in my character. And yet the page remains blank.' She threw aside her quill, rested her chin on her clenched fists and pouted. 'It's quite hopeless. One simply cannot redeem the irredeemable.'

As she stared at Clarence, inspiration struck. She had just thought of an incident that occurred when she had been about ten years old, and she started to write it down, her pen struggling to keep pace with her thoughts.

Perhaps there was a glimmer of hope for her after all.

* * *

'What can you tell me about a maid who worked here during my father's day, Mrs Mason? Her name was Agnes Hobson.'

'Agnes?' Mrs Mason nodded. 'Oh, I remember her right enough. Pretty little thing, so she was, but a hard worker. Well, she was to start with.'

'What changed?'

'I'm not entirely sure. Her father worked as an overseer in your father's mill, I seem to recall, which is how Agnes came to work here in the house. The master told Mrs Longhurst, the housekeeper here at the time, that Hobson's girl needed a position but had a weak chest and so couldn't work in the mill. It was all moonshine,' she added with a disapproving huff. 'The moment I clapped eyes on her I knew she was as fit as a flea. But it wasn't my place to say.'

'You think she was set against the mill?'

'She thought herself above such work.' Mrs Mason sniffed. 'She had ideas of being a lady's maid but soon had her eyes opened. Mrs Longhurst set her to work in the scullery. Agnes wasn't too happy about that but learned quickly enough that batting her lashes at Mrs Longhurst would get her precisely nowhere.'

'She tried to flirt her way into the position she wanted?'

Mrs Mason grunted. 'Much good it did her. The male servants were more than willing to fight her corner, but Mrs Longhurst told the girl she had to start at the bottom, just like everyone else. And she did, I'll give her that. She knuckled down and got promoted to kitchen maid, then upstairs maid.'

'So she had full knowledge of the workings of the kitchen?'

'Aye, she did that.'

And access to the bedchambers when they weren't occupied. Poison could have been added to the pater's glass of water on his nightstand. Patrick was fairly certain that arsenic was virtually tasteless. But what possible reason could Hobson's daughter have for wanting to poison the pater?

'Do you know what became of her?' Patrick asked.

'Yes, she married. A most advantageous match but, like I say, she was a comely lass; spirited, very clever and easy on the eye. I was head parlour maid when she joined the household. She never did anything to harm me but... Oh, there was something about her I never did take to. It's hard to describe why. It was just a feeling.' Mrs Mason nodded, apparently satisfied with that explanation. 'She was ambitious, knew what she wanted. Nothing wrong with that. But she was calculating, too. She hid it well and the men would never look far enough beyond her physical charms to notice what lay beneath, but I did.'

'Who did she marry, Mrs Mason, and when?'

'Oh, it were right after your father died. She married Gunther's son and heir. He died several years back and she sold on the lease. Left her well off, it did.'

Good God in heaven, Patrick thought. What the devil had he uncovered, and more to the point, by stirring up this hornet's nest, in what danger had he unwittingly placed Mrs Bathgate, Heston and most importantly, Mrs Wickham?

'Do you know where she resides now?'

'In a large house on the outskirts of Derby, sir. That's all I know, and all I want to.'

16

By asking questions of Charles's servants, Caroline learned that Mr Heston had once been one of old Mr Shannon's most trusted employees. All fine and good, but why had Mr Shannon felt such a burning need to visit a retired servant so soon after his return to the district? Caroline imagined it must have something to do with the investigation that Lydia Wickham was deemed worthy of assisting him with and Caroline was firmly excluded from.

She ambled around Charles's garden, seething at the thought. There had to be something she could do to make herself indispensable to the man she fully intended to marry. She needed an excuse to put herself more frequently in Mr Shannon's path; then he would soon see she had ten times more breeding and a great deal more sophistication and style than her rival. She was five or six years older than Lydia but it would be frowned upon if she spent too much – or any – time alone with a single gentleman. Tongues would wag and aspersions would be cast upon her character. Lydia, on the other hand, had the freedom of widowhood to lend her behaviour respectability.

The injustice caused familiar black dots to dance in front of Caroline's eyes. She was still determined to ingratiate herself with Mr Darcy but, oddly, now that Mr Shannon had shown little interest in her, she was equally determined to make him fall in love with her, if only to prevent Lydia from having him. Winning Mr Shannon's love had not previously been part of her plan, but she had developed a degree of affection for him that changed matters. Her heart was large enough to encompass two and she would be an exemplary wife to Patrick Shannon in all respects, other than one.

She could not be faithful.

She was only planning to marry Mr Shannon in order to make herself available to Mr Darcy, but she would also be discreet and ensure that her husband didn't learn of her infidelity. Married people had affairs all the time – there was nothing so very shocking about Caroline's intentions. The mist cleared from her brain and with it came clarity of thought. At such moments, Caroline was unable to hold back niggling doubts that Mr Darcy may not want her in any capacity. But her hatred for the Bennet women and her firm conviction that she was ten times Eliza's equal strengthened her resolve. If she did fail with Mr Darcy then her union with Mr Shannon would be her consolation. She would be close enough to Pemberley to be a permanent thorn in Eliza's side *and* she would have saved Mr Shannon from Lydia Wickham's grasp.

Caroline felt rather pleased with her selflessness.

The sound of a curricle being driven at speed up the driveway caught Caroline's attention. Interested to know who had such urgent business with her brother, she rounded the side of the house and re-entered it just in time to see Doctor Sanford alight from the vehicle.

'Doctor Sanford.' Caroline joined him in the drawing room just after he had been shown into it. 'What a pleasant surprise.'

'Miss Bingley.' The doctor ran a distracted hand through his hair. 'I apologise for the intrusion.'

'You are always welcome at Campton Park. My brother is not at home, if it is him you have come to see, but I am sure he won't be long. I shall ring for refreshments.'

'Please don't do so on my account. I cannot stay. I came in the hope of prevailing upon your brother to run an errand for me but if he is not here it will just have to wait. I am sure it cannot be that urgent.'

'In which case you would not have come,' Caroline replied, her

senses on high alert. 'Perhaps I can help. I am here, with nothing particular to occupy me, and I would be happy to make myself useful.' Caroline clapped a hand over her mouth as a thought occurred to her.
'Georgiana, has something...'

'She is in the best of health. I would not be here if it was otherwise.'

'No, of course you would not.' She smiled at her visitor. 'Then what is
so very urgent that you have come so far out of your way?'

'One of my patients in Denton has had a nasty accident. He's quite
agitated and asked me to deliver a message to Mr Shannon on his
behalf—'

'Mr Shannon?' Caroline sat on the edge of her chair and leaned
forward. Some premonition must have alerted her to his involvement in
Dr Sanford's business and she sensed an opportunity. 'Who is your
patient?'

'A man called Heston. He used to work for Shannon's father and...
well, I was happy to act as messenger but now I have to attend another
patient. I have just received word that a woman in Kympton has gone
into labour. There might be complications and I must... Well, Heston's
message will just have to wait.'

'It must be important,' Caroline replied. 'And it so happens I was
about to order up the carriage. I could easily stop at Shannon House and
deliver the message for you.'

'Are you absolutely sure? I don't like to impose.'

'It is no imposition.' Caroline stood, implying that the matter was
settled. 'It's on my way and would be my pleasure.' *You have no idea how
much pleasure it will give me.* She held out a hand for the message. 'Please,
don't let me detain you. I can see you are anxious to attend your next
patient and I am very happy to provide this trifling service.'

Doctor Sanford smiled with evident relief. 'That is really most kind
of you, Miss Bingley.' He withdrew a sealed letter from his coat pocket
addressed to Shannon and handed it to her. 'I am very much obliged to
you.'

'You are entirely welcome.'

Caroline smiled as she rang the bell for Charles's butler to show their
visitor out. She watched him go, aware that providence had provided her

with an opportunity, and she fully intended to exploit it. Finally the gods were smiling upon her.

'Have the curricle brought round at once,' she said to the butler as she ran up to her chamber to don her bonnet and pelisse.

* * *

'Lizzy, do you remember when the sow on Papa's farm had all those babies and that horrible boy threw stones at the dear little runt?'

'And you chased him away with a pitchfork.' Lizzy smiled. 'You couldn't have been more than eight years old; a ball of fury and indignation. But then, you have always loved animals, especially cats,' she added, laughing as Clarence spilled over the edges of Lydia's lap and lifted his chin so she could tickle beneath it. 'Whatever made you think of that?'

'Oh, it was something Mr Shannon suggested yesterday. I told him I was trying to write a journal but couldn't think of anything that showed me in a good light.' Lizzy elevated a brow, clearly surprised that she had discussed her project with a relative stranger. 'He refused to believe that I am a bad person. He said I was suppressing all of the goodness and I couldn't convince him otherwise.' Lydia shook her head and managed a wry smile. 'Obviously, he did not know me when I was a child.'

'Sometimes strangers have better perception. I only said to Will the other day that I regretted suggesting the journal since you were concentrating upon all the negative aspects of your character.'

Lydia pursed her lips. 'It's impossible for me not to since the exercise calls for brutal honesty. And in the spirit of honesty, you cannot deny that I was the most disagreeable child on God's earth.'

'And yet you have already started to remember some of your acts of kindness.'

Lydia wrinkled her nose. 'That won't take very long.'

Lizzy put her sewing aside and fixed Lydia with a disbelieving smile. 'Don't tell me the incident with the piglets is the only recollection you have come up with because I simply refuse to believe it. Your difficulty is that you feel too deeply, either very strongly for or against a particular person or thing. There is no middle ground with you. Anyway, what other good deeds have you recalled?'

'Well, there was one other thing. Do you remember Mary playing a dreadful dirge on the piano?'

Lizzy rolled her eyes. 'Mary's playing was almost always dreadful. However, I think I recall the occasion you refer to. We had visitors one afternoon and Miss Philpot made some disparaging remark about Mary's performance. You sprang to your sister's defence and told Miss Philpot that if we had access to a tutor as talented as hers then everyone would be able to play as well as she thought she could.' Lizzy laughed. 'You really put her in her place.'

'I did, didn't I?' Lydia bit her lip, unsure if she ought to smile at the memory, even though Lizzy had no compunction about so doing. 'And yet I was beastly to Mary most of the time.'

'You were allowed to criticise her but anyone outside of the family was not.'

'Yes, I suppose that was what I thought; if I bothered to think about it at all.'

'Well, it was very kind of you to defend Mary. Our sister brought criticism upon herself. She is not nearly as clever as she thinks she is and has an inflated opinion of her own worth.' Lizzy fixed Lydia with a capricious look. 'You see, you are not the only one of us capable of uncharitable thoughts.'

Will entered the room and smiled at them both. 'I have business in Lambton,' he said, 'and since it is market day, I wondered if either of you ladies would like to come along.'

'I shall not, thank you,' Lizzy replied. 'Mrs Reynolds and I are to consult about the linen later this morning.'

Lydia thought quickly. Mr Shannon's problems were never far from her mind. She had promised that she wouldn't actively seek Mrs Hobson out but she happened to know she had a stall at Lambton market where she sold the vegetables she grew in her garden. If Lydia chanced upon her and they fell into conversation, she couldn't be accused of reneging upon her promise, and it would make her feel as though she was doing something to be of service to Mr Shannon. She wanted to repay him in some small way for forcing her to approach her journal from a different perspective. She would not admit it to Lizzy, but she *was* feeling just a little bit better about herself already and the future no longer seemed quite so bleak.

'I would like to come, if I won't be in the way,' she said.

'Not in the least. Can you be ready to leave in ten minutes?'

Lydia could and a very short time thereafter she sat beside Mr Darcy as he drove the curricle himself. She was surprised how comfortable she felt to be alone with a gentleman who had once terrified her. She was even more astonished that after all the trouble she had caused him he went out of his way to be kind to her. Her family was very forgiving; more so than she deserved.

'Here we are.' Mr Darcy turned the conveyance into the mews at Lambton Inn where two grooms came running up to take charge of it. Mr Darcy jumped down and helped Lydia to alight. 'I shall be about an hour. Will you be able to entertain yourself for that long?'

'Very easily.' Lydia glanced at the bustling street and smiled. 'I shall see you back here in an hour.'

Lydia joined the cheerful throng of people from all classes of society as they browsed the different stalls and listened to a traveller on the back of a wagon extolling the virtues of his cure-all medication – anything from headaches to swollen joints would be a thing of the past apparently, all for the princely sum of one penny. Lydia smiled to herself, surprised to see just how many people were foolish or desperate enough to give it a try. A juggler had drawn a small crowd as he effortlessly kept four balls at once in the air, his hands moving so fast that they were a blur. She wandered on, stopping to look at a stall selling lace and another with a selection of pretty buttons that would once have enthralled her. But not today.

Today she was here for a purpose.

And that purpose became evident as she neared the end of the street and came upon Mrs Hobson's stall, brimming with fresh garden produce. Two lads who looked so much like her that they could only be her sons were keeping the stall stocked from baskets placed on the ground while several customers waited in an orderly line for Mrs

Hobson's attention. Her little girl was dancing about in the middle of the crowd, singing to herself, in a world of her own as she twirled the yellow ribbon that Lydia had given her. Lydia stopped to watch her and felt a fresh jolt of regret for the baby she had lost.

She blinked tears from her eyes and was jerked back to the present when a rider approached at speed, yelling that his horse was spooked and that he couldn't stop him. It was obvious that he had absolutely no control over the animal as he cut a dangerous swathe through the crowd. People jumped out of his way, shaking fists at him and shouting insults.

All except the little girl.

Lydia gasped. The child was so self-absorbed that she hadn't heard him. Several people called out to her. She didn't respond. Lydia wanted to snatch her to safety but felt as though her feet were glued in place as a combination of fear and inertia gripped her. The horse was almost upon the oblivious child but its rider couldn't stop. Lydia prayed Maisie would realise the danger and run for cover, or that someone would snatch her away. There were people standing closer than she was. Why were they all gawping and not helping?

Someone screamed. Someone else cried that the horse was bolting. A third person darted forward and snatched the child from beneath flailing hooves seconds before they struck her delicate head. Lydia's shoulder hit the ground with a crushing blow and pain shot through it.

Only then did she realise it was she who was the child's saviour.

* * *

Patrick couldn't decide what to do about Agnes Gunther, as she now was. Lydia had been right to suggest the Hobsons were somehow involved, but if Agnes did poison Patrick's father she would hardly admit it. Patrick sighed. Knowing his father might have been murdered, knowing the identity of the murderer and not being able to do anything about it was almost worse than having been blissfully unaware.

He sat behind his father's old desk, booted feet propped on its edge, in the now fully restored library with its book-lined walls and assortment of artefacts collected over the years by his forebearers. The French doors were open, letting in a warm summer breeze and the peaty smell of freshly dug earth from gardens that were in the process of being reclaimed from the weeds that had taken them over.

Speaking directly to Agnes was out of the question, Patrick decided, aware he would never be able to let the matter rest, even if producing proof was next to impossible. Old Hobson, Patrick's father's former overseer, was dead and his son had never worked in the mill, preferring to become a keeper at Pemberley. But he was looked upon as a confirmed bachelor until he unexpectedly married Elsie Fletcher, who *was* involved in the mill. What did he know about the past, what pressure had been put upon him to wed Elsie and how much would he be prepared to reveal in order to retain his position? Patrick shook his head, deciding that blackmail was unworthy of him. Besides, he was Darcy's keeper, not Patrick's, and Patrick couldn't threaten the livelihood of another man's servant.

The only other option was Mrs Hobson, a curmudgeonly individual by all accounts, with whom Lydia appeared to have formed a tenuous connection. But involving Lydia more deeply in this farrago was out of the question. He flashed a smile as he thought about his conversation with her the previous day and wondered if she had yet changed direction with her journal. Why it should matter to him he could not have said. He had already determined he would not follow his father's example and take up the cause of every lost soul who crossed his path. He had worked hard to develop a cynical edge and suspicious nature, but the alluring little minx had somehow slipped past all his defences.

All the more reason not to involve her further with his affairs, Patrick reminded himself.

What would she look like dressed for me in pink silk?

Patrick shook his head to dispel such an intrusive speculation. He would visit Darcy again and ask his opinion about putting gentle pressure on Hobson. It was the only alternative he was prepared to consider.

'There's a Miss Bingley here to see you, sir,' Mrs Mason said, striding into the library. 'She says it's urgent.'

'Miss Bingley?' Patrick's feet hit the floor. What the devil was she doing calling upon him? There was something peculiar about that woman. If he was any judge he would say she was the victim of violent mood swings and sulked if she didn't get her way. He had no particular wish to see her, especially if she was alone, but she was here and in spite of his misgivings, good manners prevailed. 'Show her in, Mrs Mason, if you please, and leave the door open.'

Mrs Mason nodded her understanding. 'That I will, sir.'

Patrick was in shirtsleeves and had no time to alter that situation before Miss Bingley entered the room. She irked Patrick by looking about it with a proprietary air. Her gaze lingered for a little too long on his torso, covered only by the thin linen of his shirt, and he regretted not taking a moment to reclaim his coat.

'Please excuse my attire,' he said, standing to receive her. 'I was not expecting visitors.'

'I would not have come ordinarily. I am on a mission for Doctor Sanford.'

'Sanford? Has someone been taken unwell?'

'One of his patients in Denton, a Mr Heston, I believe—'

'Heston?' Patrick's stomach lurched. 'What happened? I saw him only yesterday. He was in fine fettle.'

'He was involved in an accident and wanted Doctor Sanford to deliver a message to you. Unfortunately the doctor was needed elsewhere and so called to see if Charles could act as courier. Since Charles was not at home I offered my services.'

'That was good of you,' Patrick said absently. This had to be his fault. Someone must have heard he was asking questions and was trying to halt his enquiry. He *had* been toying with letting the matter rest but that was now out of the question. 'May I have the message, please?'

'Of course.'

Patrick took the missive from Miss Bingley with a steady hand and broke the seal.

Shannon. I was called to Heston this morning since he had taken what he initially insisted was a fall and hit his head. He is shaken up, has a nasty cut, but as far as I can tell, no permanent damage has been done. He became very agitated and insisted that he needed to speak with you. Of course, I forbade him to move and his wife will ensure those instructions are adhered to. Instead I offered to deliver a message. I cannot make head nor tail of it, but presumably it will mean something to you.

He claims to have seen someone loitering outside of his cottage when you left him yesterday. The same person appeared again today, standing outside, watching his door. Heston confronted the fellow, an altercation ensued and Heston was thrown to the ground. The person who did the throwing told Heston to remember what was at stake if he didn't keep his mouth closed. And so, you see, it was no fall but an unprovoked assault. Heston would not hear of calling the constable but insisted you needed to be made aware.

Be assured that Heston has not incurred a lasting injury, but his concern was for Mrs Bathgate. He said you would understand. I hope you do since I don't have the first idea what he was talking about.

Yours, etc.

'Mrs Bathgate,' Patrick muttered as he read the note twice before throwing it aside. 'Of course!'

'Is everything all right?'

Patrick's head jerked up at the sound of Miss Bingley's voice. He had forgotten she was there and had no time for her. He needed to see Mrs Bathgate for himself, warn her of the danger, and there was no time to lose.

'You must excuse me, Miss Bingley. I must go out on urgent business.'

'Is Mrs Bathgate the woman who dabbles with herbs?' she asked in a derisive tone. 'I believe I have heard tales about her... shall we say, methods.'

'Yes, but you must—'

'Would you like me to come with you, just in case a woman's influence is required?'

'Thank you, but no. I really don't have any time to spare at present.' Patrick didn't try to disguise his impatience. 'Thank you so very much for coming. Mrs Mason,' he called through the open door. 'Please show Miss Bingley out and have Mason saddle Gladiator.'

'My curricle is outside. Let me drive you there.'

'It will be quicker if I go on horseback.'

He glanced at Miss Bingley's countenance as he all but bundled her out of the door and noticed thunderheads sweeping through her eyes. One of her mood swings, he thought absently. Patrick didn't have time to deal with her wounded pride and made do with thanking her again, belatedly adding that he hoped to have the pleasure of seeing her again soon. Still in shirtsleeves, he strode out to the stables and swung into Gladiator's saddle. He left the yard at a canter and cut across his park, raising a hand to Miss Bingley as he overtook her curricle and gave Gladiator his head.

Mrs Bathgate received him with lack of ceremony and even less surprise. She tutted when he told her about Heston.

'A damned rum business,' she said, rubbing her whiskery chin. 'I thought it was settled long since.'

'I'm concerned for you, Mrs Bathgate. So is Heston. I apologise for stirring feelings up again. It is my fault and so the very least I can do is protect you.'

'Don't you worry none about me; forewarned is forearmed. I have two strapping grandsons who live with me and half the village would rise up against anyone who tried to do me harm.' She folded her arms defiantly. 'I was glad when I heard you was back. I don't hold with folks taking matters into their own hands as a general rule, but if this ain't your business then I don't know whose it is, and I dare say you'll get to the bottom of it.'

Patrick spent another five minutes trying to persuade her to let him employ extra protection for her.

'I will not have your being harmed on my conscience.'

'God bless you, sir, get away with you now. No one will raise a hand to an old woman like me.'

And with that, Patrick was forced to be content. He rode back into the centre of Lambton, cursing when he found the main street clogged with market day traffic. He gaped when a man passed him on a runaway horse, the wild-eyed, obviously frightened young beast foaming at the mouth and heading not away from the human traffic but straight for it.

He called out a warning to a little girl who seemed oblivious to the danger as she twirled a yellow ribbon above her head. She paid no heed and Patrick was convinced she would be struck down by several tons of horse flesh. He was too far away to help. Damn it, why was everyone simply standing and staring?

At the very last second a woman darted forward and pulled the child to safety, taking a nasty tumble herself as she dived for safety mere seconds before the horse's hooves pounded on the spot where she had been standing. Dear God, not just any woman! Patrick's heart lurched. He would know that figure, that enveloping silver-grey gown, anywhere.

It was Lydia Wickham. She was now lying on the ground, cradling the child protectively against her, and not moving.

17

The sound of someone repeatedly calling her name slowly penetrated Lydia's befuddled brain, but it seemed like too much effort to open her eyes. The familiar-sounding voice persisted. It felt as though a crowd was pressing down on her, their murmurs of concern growing louder. Something squirmed in her arms. Reluctantly she forced her eyelids upwards and found herself looking directly into Patrick's rich brown eyes, clouded with worry.

'What happened...?'

'Lydia, are you all right?' he asked at the same time, crouching beside her. 'Can you move?'

The bundle Lydia was clutching started to bawl. She tried to move but a searing pain shot through her shoulder, and she fell back to the ground with a startled cry.

'Hush, it's all right now.'

Lydia was unsure if Patrick was addressing her or the grubby little girl he extracted from her arms. It was Maisie Hobson, she realised. Vague recollections trickled through Lydia's mind. She didn't remember snatching the child from the path of the runaway horse, thinking that someone else would, but if she was crumpled on the ground, holding the child, it must have been she who saved her.

'Can you move your arms and legs?'

Mrs Hobson lumbered into the periphery of Lydia's view and snatched up her little girl, alternately cuddling and then berating her for daydreaming, so Lydia assumed Patrick had to be addressing her this time. She obediently tried wiggling her limbs and found them to be in working order.

'It's my shoulder,' she said, gritting her teeth through the pain.

'What's going on? Let me through.' Lydia recognised Mr Darcy's voice. 'Lydia, what the devil—'

'Right brave, she were, sir,' someone said.

'Saved that little girl from getting trampled, so she did.'

'Never did see the like.'

'Stand back.' The authority in Mr Darcy's voice saw people shuffle out of the way.

'She isn't seriously injured,' Patrick said. 'Is your carriage in the mews?'

'Yes.'

'Have it ready and I will bring her. It will never get to her here.'

'Are you sure?'

'Absolutely.' Lydia noticed the firm set to Patrick's jaw which, she suspected, was what persuaded Mr Darcy to cede responsibility to him.

'We ought to take Mrs Hobson back with us,' Lydia said, thinking quickly. 'She will tell us what she knows now, I expect. I saved her child and her husband dotes on that little girl.'

'Very well,' Mr Darcy replied.

Lydia sat up and waited for her head to stop spinning, biting her lip against the pain that ripped through her shoulder if she moved too quickly. Mr Darcy strode across to Mrs Hobson, who was still cradling Maisie in her arms and exchanged a few words with her.

'Pack up our things and take them home,' Mrs Hobson said to her sons, who were hovering in the background, looking frightened. 'Give me the baby. He comes with me.'

Mr Darcy took the basket with the baby in it and led Mrs Hobson, still clutching Maisie, in the direction of the mews. Now that the excitement was over, the crowd began to disperse. Lydia was still feeling woozy and was unsure if she could walk even as far as the mews. She was saved from the inconvenience when a pair of strong arms swooped her from the ground and cradled her against a rock-solid chest. Patrick's chest. He wasn't wearing a coat and she could feel hard muscles at work as he carried her effortlessly towards the mews, her injured shoulder held away from his body.

'About you being a disappointment,' he said softly. 'Selfish people do not risk their lives for the sake of insignificant little girls.'

'I... I don't remember actually deciding to do anything,' she said hesitantly.

'But you did. I was too far away to help and no one else seemed willing to.'

'I must have acted instinctively.'

'And saved the child's life.'

'Perhaps the horse would not have hit her.'

Patrick harrumphed. 'In that packed street, the child would not have stood a chance.' He brushed the hair away from her face which was most likely smudged with dirt. She must look a fright. 'Like it or not, Lydia, you are a heroine. How does it feel?'

'Like everyone is making too much fuss.'

By the time they reached the inn, Mr Darcy's curricle had been drawn up at the entrance to the mews. Patrick lifted Lydia onto the seat, placing her in between Mrs Hobson and Mr Darcy. It was quite a squash, with Maisie still clinging to her mother but seemingly oblivious to the nature of her narrow escape. The baby's basket was placed on the floor, its occupant fast asleep.

'Can you manage, Darcy?' Patrick asked. 'I could take the child up with me.' Maisie's eyes widened and her fingers curled more tightly into her mother's bodice. 'Or perhaps not.'

'It isn't far,' Darcy replied. 'Ride ahead and warn my wife that her sister has been injured. Sanford should be sent for.'

Lydia closed her eyes against the pain as the curricle moved off, jolting her bruised body. Some instinct, the impression of a cold, hard stare being directed her way, caused her to open her eyes again, only to regret it. Caroline Bingley stood beneath the overhang of the stable roof, the fires of hell burning in her eyes as she held Lydia in a death glare. Lydia shuddered, afraid suddenly of the woman's unpredictability. She sensed Caroline was working up to another bout of irrational behaviour and that for some obscure reason Lydia was now the object of her antipathy.

* * *

Patrick reclaimed Gladiator and made his way back to Pemberley at a flat out gallop. He was proud that Lydia had found the courage to save the little girl when others ought to have interceded ahead of her. His reaction was dangerously close to admiration. All well and good, he thought. There was much to admire in Lydia Wickham but she was still trying to come to terms with the bittersweet nature of her marriage to Wickham. She didn't like herself very much at present and the last thing she needed was him making a nuisance of himself. After all, she had made it abundantly clear that her only purpose was friendship.

As was his, even if inappropriate thoughts wormed their way past his defences whenever he was in Lydia's company. The type of thoughts he had spent years avoiding without difficulty. Why now? Why her? He had been introduced to a dozen more attractive females, even during the few short weeks he had been back in England. Females who were not consumed by guilt and self-doubt. Females who had not warmed another man's bed. Females who were infinitely less interesting than Lydia.

He arrived at Pemberley and had just had time to tell Mrs Darcy what had happened in Lambton before Darcy drew the curricle up to the entrance portico. They both ran out to greet it. Patrick wanted to lift Lydia down himself but he had enjoyed carrying her through Lambton a little too much and it wasn't his place do so again. Reluctantly he allowed Darcy to do the honours but as soon as she was clear of the carriage, Lydia insisted upon walking into the house unaided, other than taking her sister's arm for support.

'You have given us the most frightful scare,' Mrs Darcy told her, 'but we are all very proud of you. And now you are shaking all over.'

'Delayed shock,' Patrick said. 'A little brandy should set her straight.'

Lydia wrinkled her nose. 'It would probably make me fall over again.'

'Go on up,' Mrs Darcy said. 'I shall send Nora to you and have Dominic summoned.'

'I believe he is attending a lady who is giving birth,' Patrick told them.

'I am not in need of his services, Lizzy,' Lydia insisted. 'I shall clean myself up and then come straight back down. I have a great curiosity to hear what Mrs Hobson has to tell us.'

All eyes turned in that lady's direction. She was standing in the hallway, mouth gaping open as she took in the opulent vestibule.

'Come through to the morning room, Mrs Hobson,' Mrs Darcy said, taking the baby's basket from her and carrying it herself. 'This must be Maisie,' she added, ruffling the little girl's hair. 'What a very pretty ribbon,' she added, referring to the grubby yellow string the child was clutching with both hands. 'I expect we have some more colours here that you could have if you like.'

The child stared at Mrs Darcy through wide eyes but didn't open her mouth.

'Simpson,' Darcy said. 'Send someone to find Hobson and have him brought to the house.'

'No need,' Mrs Hobson said, her voice sounding tired and defeated. 'I'll tell you everything.'

'He needs to be here,' Darcy insisted.

Simpson took himself off to carry out his master's instructions. Patrick thought the child might be better off in the nursery. She seemed withdrawn but he suspected she understood a great deal more than people realised, and the conversation they were about to have with her parents was not for her ears. But her accident had unsettled her and she screamed when anyone tried to detach her from her mother's arms.

After twenty minutes or so, Lydia returned to the room, looking pale yet composed. Patrick stood to greet her. She was wearing a fresh gown –

grey, of course – and had cleaned the grime from her limbs. She had scratches on the back of one hand and also on the side of her face – the only visible signs of her ordeal.

'How do you feel?' Patrick asked, conducting her to a chair.

'My maid tells me I shall have a colourful bruise on my shoulder.' She wrinkled her nose. 'Apart from that I just feel a little shaken.'

She smiled at Maisie, still snuggled on her mother's lap, and held out a strand of pink ribbon. The child's eyes grew round as saucers as she slid from Mrs Hobson's lap and trotted across to Lydia. Patrick was dangerously close to falling in love with the conflicted chit at that moment. She had just avoided death by a whisker, was clearly more affected by the experience than she implied, definitely suffered some discomfort and yet her first thought had been to give the child a gift. *A disappointment, Mrs Wickham? I think not.*

'Yes, it's for you, sweetheart,' Lydia assured her.

'Be careful, Mrs Wickham,' Patrick said, amusement in his tone. 'You are in danger of ruining your reputation.'

'If I can make Maisie smile then it will be worth it.'

Simpson entered the room with a large man dressed in working clothes in his wake. He clutched his cap in his hand, looking awkward and out of place, but when Maisie saw him and squealed with delight his entire face lit up.

'Papa!'

She threw herself at him and Hobson swept the child he clearly idolised into his arms. 'I hear you've been getting into trouble, little 'un,' he said in a gruffly affectionate tone.

'Papa, look.' She held up the pink ribbon Lydia had just given her for inspection.

Hobson stood in front of Lydia, the child still in his arms, and bowed his head, but not so quickly that Patrick didn't notice his eyes were glassy with tears. 'We'll never be able to thank you enough, ma'am.'

'That we won't,' Mrs Hobson added, holding a grubby handkerchief to her eyes.

'We'll talk of this later,' Hobson said, fixing his wife with an accusatory glare.

'Don't look at me like that. I don't have eyes in the back of my head.'

'It happened very fast,' Lydia said. 'No one could have anticipated a runaway horse.'

'How many times have I told you to keep her by you at all times?' Hobson growled.

'It weren't my fault.'

'If you want to show your gratitude,' Lydia hastily interceded, 'then you can tell Mr Shannon everything you know about the failure of his father's silk mill.'

Hobson glowered at his wife. 'Go on then,' he said. 'The telling's long overdue.'

'It don't show your family in a good light,' Mrs Hobson said in a warning tone.

'It don't show you in a good light, is more to the point,' Hobson replied, sniffing.

'Have it your way.' Mrs Hobson squared her shoulders and gamely met Patrick's gaze. 'I had a good job with yer dad but I wanted to be married, with a family of me own. I just couldn't find a fella who liked me and were good enough.'

'You wanted to better yourself,' Mrs Darcy suggested. 'There is nothing wrong with ambition.'

Hobson sniffed. 'Begging your pardon, ma'am, it depends how you go about it.'

Mrs Hobson elevated her chin. 'I wanted to get away from the noise and choking dust of the mill. Hobson here,' she said, waving a hand at her husband, 'was a good-looking brute back in them days.' She gave a brittle little laugh. 'Aye, hard to credit that now, ain't it? All the lasses had their eye on him but he didn't want to know any of us.'

'What changed?' Patrick asked.

'I happened to be at the inn in Lambton one night. That was where all of us gals out of indenture went occasionally of an evening. I er... well, pardon my frankness, but I went outside to relieve myself and heard two men talking in whispers down the side of the inn. One of them was his father,' she said, jerking a thumb towards Hobson. 'He were talking with

Gunther, who was enticing him to leave Mr Shannon's employ with all sorts of wild promises.'

'Tell it all,' Hobson said, grim-faced, when his wife paused.

'We all knew Jenson, old Mr Shannon's butler, and his daughter had suddenly taken off for America and rumours was rife as to their reasons. I was astounded when I heard Gunther confiding that Jenson's daughter had been carrying Shannon's child and that they'd been paid to go away for good.'

Mrs Hobson fell silent and found something to admire on the patterned rug beneath her feet.

'Go on,' Patrick encouraged.

'Jenson had plans for his daughter that didn't involve hiding her away in America. Still, he was a handsome man himself, which is where his gal got her looks from. Rumour has it that he traded on his appearance to marry well and make a fortune. But, according to Gunther, who kept in touch with him, Jenson felt his life had been ruined by Mr Shannon's unwillingness to marry his daughter.'

'Ah, now I start to see,' Patrick said, nodding slowly. 'He bore a grudge all those years because he thought his daughter was the pater's equal and that they ought to wed.'

'His resentment ran deep.' Mrs Hobson swallowed. 'He didn't want to just ruin your pa, sir, he wanted him dead an' all.'

There were several audible intakes of breath.

'Just a moment, Hobson,' Darcy said. 'Your father had given years of loyal service to Shannon and was well rewarded for it. Why would he even consider defecting to Gunther's establishment and why would Gunther risk entrusting him with such sensitive information?'

'Agnes Hobson?' Patrick said, his voice a sibilant hiss. 'I'll wager a fortune that she's behind all of this.'

Mrs Hobson nodded. 'She and Gunther's son were in love. Gunther senior had forbidden the match but said it could go ahead if Hobson danced to his tune. It was essential to have him out of the way so they could put Jessup in his place, yer see. Jessup was more than willing to cook the books, deliberately lose customers and all the other stuff done to make the mill fail.'

'But Heston was in charge and the duties you refer to were his,' Patrick said. 'Now his being removed makes sense. Jenson's arm had a long reach.'

'How despicable,' Lydia said indignantly.

'Those weren't Hobson's duties, it's true, but they needed him out of the way so Jessup could destroy the business without anyone loyal to your father interfering. So they found Hobson's weak spot. Rather like my dear husband dotes on Maisie, so his pa doted on Agnes.' Mrs Hobson sniffed. 'It would have been hard for Hobson to deny her anything, especially marriage to the man she adored who would one day be a mill owner. Besides, everyone knew Shannon's mill was doomed by that stage and it was every man for himself.'

'And you finished up married to the man you adored as well,' Darcy said scathingly. 'I hardly dare ask how that came about.'

'It weren't my finest hour but, like I say, everyone has to look out for themselves in this world,' Mrs Hobson said defensively. 'Basically I told Hobson what I'd overheard and the price of my silence was marriage to his son.'

'Wasn't that taking a chance?' Mrs Darcy asked. 'These people sound ruthless. Besides, your husband had nothing to do with the plot. Why should he agree?'

'My father and sister were involved in a murder.' Hobson glowered at his wife. 'I couldn't risk that coming out and ruining everything I'd worked to achieve for myself. I had no choice.'

'You could have gone to my father and told him the truth,' Patrick said scathingly.

'By the time I knew what had happened, it were too late. Your pa were dead.'

'And I've had to live all these years facing his resentment for forcing him into a marriage he didn't want in the first place,' Mrs Hobson said. 'Serves me right, an' all.'

Patrick couldn't disagree with that.

'And your sister now lives the life of a wealthy widow,' Lydia said, condemnation in her voice.

'I have nothing to do with her,' Hobson replied. 'I cut off all relations with me pa an' all. I did what I had to do for their sake but I wanted nothing to do with any of the scheming so-an'-sos after that.'

'That's unfortunate,' Patrick said, flexing his jaw, 'because I would very much like to have a conversation with your sister.'

'Funny you should say that, sir,' Hobson said. 'She sent word to me yesterday saying she'd heard you were back.' He paused. 'And she wants to see you.'

18

'Excuse me,' Patrick said to the Hobsons, turning away from them and speaking in a low tone to his host. 'What do you make of that, Darcy?'

'I have not the slightest notion.'

'Agnes must know we have been asking questions,' Lydia said. 'I wager the lad who's been watching us was sent by her.'

'And probably the oaf who hurt Heston also,' Patrick added, an angry scowl darkening his countenance. 'But it hasn't stopped us from digging and so she plans to invent an alternative explanation. She must assume that we know about her advantageous marriage and have also recalled she was once a maid in my father's house. We would be bound to wonder about that, but she cannot know her estranged brother has told us the truth about how her marriage was contrived. He has kept it to himself all these years. Why would he break his silence now?'

'She has probably heard that you and I are friends,' Mr Darcy reasoned. 'Hobson relies upon me for his livelihood. There is no love lost between him and his sister so she probably imagines it will only be a matter of time before he tells the truth.'

'She will try to convince you of her innocence first,' Lydia warned.

Lizzy nodded. 'And attempt to manipulate you in some way, since bullying and intimidation have not stopped you. She can only be a year or two older than you are, Mr Shannon, and probably plans to beguile you with her feminine wiles.'

'Much good that will do her,' Patrick replied with determination.

Lydia snorted. 'Nevertheless, she sounds very conniving and we already know she will do anything necessary to protect her own interests.'

'I will not be taken in by her, Mrs Wickham,' Patrick replied, the smile he sent her way so intimate that it almost broke through Lydia's determination not to be influenced by his charm – or any man's charm ever again.

'Are you able to make contact with your sister?' Patrick asked, turning back to Hobson.

'Aye, I know where she is.'

'Write a note inviting her to come and see you, Shannon,' Mr Darcy said. 'I shall feel happier if you see her on your own ground. Once it is written I'll arrange for it to be delivered.'

'Thank you,' Patrick replied. 'I shall see to it at once.'

Lydia was curious to know what Agnes had to say for herself and would have liked the encounter to take place at Pemberley where she could be a party to it. It seemed unfair to be excluded, just when things were getting interesting. But, she conceded, the woman would not be forthcoming if others were present. She wouldn't be foolish enough to hang herself with her own words and so Patrick would have to see her alone.

Patrick wrote his note and Mr Darcy had Simpson arrange for its immediate delivery. Lizzy busied herself with seeing Mrs Hobson off while Mr Darcy had a private word with Hobson, leaving Lydia and Patrick alone.

'Are you really all right?' he asked, gently touching the uninjured side of her face. 'You took a very hard fall. I would feel happier if Sanford had a look at you.'

'Don't worry about me.'

'Ah, but that is precisely my difficulty. I *do* worry about you.'

'Then I wish you would not.' Lydia felt warmth spreading through her. 'I am perfectly safe here at Pemberley. You, on the other hand, are about to receive a woman of dubious character and even more dubious intent in your own home. Perhaps *I* should worry about *you*.'

His laughter was soft and sinfully tempting. Lydia was doing her very best to show the world in general and herself in particular that she was a changed character. But the manner in which his eyes glowed with an unholy light when he focused them upon her didn't make it easy for her to stick to that resolve.

'Your concern for *my* welfare is touching, but you have no occasion to fear for me.'

'I do not recall saying I feared for you,' she replied, tossing her curls at the arrogance of the assumption. 'I simply meant to imply that a woman of Mrs Gunther's alleged beauty probably knows how to manipulate a gentleman to the point where he doubts his own opinions and forgets what is important.'

'You overlook the fact that she poisoned my father,' he replied softly.

'I have not forgotten that, but it wouldn't surprise me if Agnes makes you doubt it.'

Patrick raised a challenging brow. 'Jealous, Mrs Wickham?'

Was she? 'Don't be ridiculous! Stronger men than you have succumbed to such women. She went from being a housemaid to a mill owner's wife. No matter how beautiful she happens to be, I very much doubt whether she achieved that improvement in her circumstances without being ruthlessly determined. And *that* is what makes her dangerous.'

Patrick grasped her hand, lifted it to his lips and slowly, very slowly, kissed the back of it. Lydia momentarily abandoned her struggle to resist his allure. The maelstrom of conflicting emotions he stirred up inside of her was simply too violent to overcome. She would be quite herself again just as soon as he released her hand and stopped looking at her with such reckless sensuality in his expression.

Lizzy re-entered the room, Patrick dropped her hand and Lydia turned away from them until she had better control over her tangled emotions.

'Please tell us when you hear from Agnes,' Lizzy said. 'And you must promise to call immediately she leaves and tell us everything she said.'

'That I shall most assuredly do,' he replied, taking his leave.

Lydia and Lizzy watched through the window as he headed towards the stables, his long strides eating up the ground.

'Very curious,' Lizzy said musingly.

'I think it could be dangerous,' Lydia replied, unable to keep a note of apprehension out of her voice. 'I wish he had agreed to meet her here at Pemberley, where there would be more people available to protect him.'

Lizzy smiled. 'She's hardly likely to physically attack Mr Shannon, and even if she tries it, he will easily overpower her.'

'Then why suggest meeting him at all?' Lydia shook her head. 'She has nothing to gain from it and everything to lose.'

'It does seem that way but I expect she has her reasons.'

That was what concerned Lydia.

Lizzy took Lydia's arm and guided her to a settee. 'Now come and sit down and tell me every detail about your heroics today. I want to know it all.'

* * *

Patrick rode the short distance home and found plenty of occupations to fill the rest of the day, determined not to dwell upon his increasing attraction towards Lydia Wickham. Resisting her charms was daily becoming more challenging. Despite her best efforts to keep it suppressed, each time he encountered her, she revealed a little more of her spirited character and gave him a few tantalising glimpses of the vivacious young lady she was supposed to be. Her enforced state of self-hatred was rather like keeping a hot house flower in total darkness, he thought, depriving it of the sunshine it required to blossom and beguile.

Guilt was motivating Lydia to turn herself into something she was not. Given time, her naturally vibrant personality would shine through, only this time it would be tempered by experience – too much experience for one as young as she was. Patrick, in the spirit of neighbourly co-operation, decided that he would make it his business to convince her she had absolutely nothing to feel guilty about.

Patrick turned his thoughts to Agnes Gunther. He was deeply suspicious of her motives, but rejecting her request for an interview had not occurred to him. It saved him a ride to Derby since had she not agreed to come to him then he would have eventually gone in search of her.

Late in the day, Darcy's messenger returned with a reply from the woman in question agreeing to be at Shannon House at eleven the following morning.

Patrick spent a restless evening and he was glad when the morning came around. He watched from a window as his visitor's smart curricle made its way up the driveway. He felt anxious yet composed when he heard voices in the hall as Mrs Mason admitted her to the house. A short time later, a strikingly attractive woman was shown into his library and he stood to receive her. She was short in stature and had a profusion of blonde curls spilling from beneath a bonnet that barely contained them. Her features were perfectly symmetrical, her lips rosy and plump, her eyes a most unusual sea-green. Her body was trim, encased in a smart walking gown that perfectly matched the colour of her eyes. Patrick suspected she was well aware of that fact and of the effect she had on men generally. He himself was all but gaping at her, his defences already lowered, which simply wouldn't do.

'Mrs Gunther,' he said.

'Mr Shannon. Thank you for agreeing to see me.' Her cultured tone belied her humble origins. He suspected she had received lessons in elocution.

He indicated one of the chairs arranged in front of the fireplace. 'Please take a seat.'

'It's a long time since I set foot in this house. I never thought to do so again.' She canted her head and regarded him quizzically. 'You resemble your father. You did not look much like him when you were younger but you are his image now.'

That she would initiate the conversation and speak of such matters so brazenly astounded Patrick. 'You have the advantage of me,' he said brusquely. 'I don't remember you at all.'

She winced, obviously not accustomed to going unnoticed, even when she had been a servant. 'Yes, well, you were away at school for most of the time when I worked here.'

Patrick observed her closely but said nothing, doing all in his power to make her feel uncomfortable. Having already decided that she was unaccustomed to being ignored, he decided to make reserve work to his advantage. Sure enough, her fingers fiddled restlessly with her reticule. She puffed out her cheeks and was the one who broke the brittle silence.

'I can see you are going to make this difficult for me,' she said, sounding offended.

He fixed her with a disinterested look. 'You asked to see *me*.'

'When I heard you had returned, I suspected you would want to know why your father's mill failed.'

'I am rather more interested in the reasons for his death.'

She flinched but there was no sign of guilt or shame in her expression. Nor had she so far attempted to flirt her way into his good graces. Upon reflection, he decided it would have been optimistic of him to expect a display of remorse. Women of her ilk were always able to square their actions with their consciences by laying the blame for them elsewhere.

'You could not have known it but your father and I were friends.'

Sarcasm shaped the arch of Patrick's brow. 'Friends?'

'I know what you are thinking, but nothing of an inappropriate nature occurred between us. Your father was one of the best, the kindest men I have ever had the good fortune to meet. However, you do not need me to tell you that.'

Patrick refused to be drawn in by her sham sincerity. 'What has this to do with his death?'

'You were not aware that he had been unwell for some considerable time because he forbade anyone to tell you. His illness explains why he didn't keep on top of his business affairs as well as he once had.'

'If he *was* unwell why would he not tell me, his only son?'

She shrugged. 'He thought he would recover and didn't want to put you off your education. However, although he was kind-hearted he was also a good businessman. That being the case, have you stopped to consider how the silk mill started to fail? He would never permit sentiment to get in the way of turning a profit.'

No, Patrick thought, he most likely would not. 'What are you suggesting?'

'He wasn't well enough to keep proper control and when control slips, people get ideas about exploiting weak management.' She shook her head. 'Men of your father's ilk, who see the best in everyone, are the easiest to dupe.'

Patrick frowned. 'How do you know so much about his supposed illness?'

'I was an upstairs maid. It often fell to my lot to take him medicine when he stayed a-bed. He used to ask for me.'

Patrick curled his upper lip disdainfully. 'I am perfectly sure he did.'

'It's not what you think.' Patrick wanted to stop her. He had no interest in hearing about the way she had manipulated his father in his own bedchamber, but something in her expression prevented him from cutting off that line of conversation. 'He used to ask me to sit and talk to him. He told me I reminded him of Maryellen.' Patrick inhaled sharply. 'Oh yes, I know all about his first and only true love.'

'Of course you do,' Patrick replied acerbically, well aware she would have received that information from her father who, in turn, had learned it from Gunther who was in contact with Jenson in America.

'He told me himself,' she said, fixing Patrick with a look that, if he hadn't known better, would have fooled him into thinking she was sincere. But, of course, he knew a great deal better. 'He said I reminded him of her. We became very close.'

Patrick was dangerously close to losing his temper, mainly because her melodious voice, sincerity, lack of flirtatiousness and... yes, her beauty, combined to influence him; a circumstance he had promised himself he would not permit.

'Your account is all very touching,' he said, 'but I don't have time to waste with this moonshine. Your brother and his wife told me the truth yesterday.' He fixed her with a probing glare of unmitigated dislike. 'I know what you did, and I know why you did it.' He leaned back in his chair, one foot balanced on his opposite knee, in command of his emotions again and wanting, through his stance, for her to be aware of it. 'So why are you here? What is it that you want from me?' His tone was scathing. 'Absolution? In which case you have had a wasted journey. You got what you wanted from this sorry business. I cannot prove what you did but I do have the satisfaction of knowing that you must live with your conscience.' He paused. 'Always assuming you have one, which is far from certain.'

'You think I poisoned your father?'

He fixed her with an icy look of contempt. 'I *know* that you did.'

She shook her head. 'You are quite wrong.'

Patrick tutted. 'Well, of course you would say that.'

'I was in love with the man who subsequently became my husband,' she said after a short pause.

'Ah, and love conquers all,' Patrick said scathingly. 'No matter the criminal means you employed to bring that situation about. No matter what lives were ruined or lost along the way.'

'It sounds conceited,' she replied, lowering her gaze but not directly addressing his accusations, 'but I knew from an early age that I was attractive to the opposite sex, and not unnaturally I wanted to trade upon that fact to better myself. We must all work with what God gives us, especially when as lowly born as I was. There is nothing wrong with that.'

'It depends upon what you trade in order to achieve your ambitions.'

'Gunther refused his son Samuel permission to marry me *unless* I agreed to... well, to poison your father.'

Patrick's feet hit the floor and he sat bolt upright, no longer caring that he allowed his loss of composure to show. 'Ah, so you admit it.'

'I admit it was asked of me and I also admit I was tempted. But I liked and respected your father. He was my friend.' She shook her head. 'I said I would think about it, but I couldn't bring myself to actually do it. Not even for Samuel's sake.'

Perdition, she was so convincing that Patrick almost believed her. Almost.

'And yet my father died of what I have subsequently learned were symptoms very akin to arsenic poisoning, you were able to marry Gunther, and Jenson, through Gunther, ruined the pater's business and achieved his ultimate revenge.' Patrick twisted his lips into an expression of distaste. 'And you expect me to believe that's all a happy coincidence.'

'Oh no, I am not quite that naive.'

'Then what—'

'Your father smoked a great deal of opium in his last months. It helped to ease the pain. I don't know what the signs of arsenic poisoning actually are but I know the opium made him delusional at times.' She sent Patrick a shamed look. 'He died very soon after I was asked to poison him and... well, when Gunther assumed I had done it, there seemed little point in pretending I had not when by admitting my failure it would mean Samuel and I could not wed.' She waved a hand. 'Not very moral of me, I know, but your father was dead and he had told me many times how much he regretted not standing up to his own father and marrying his Maryellen. He never got over the loss of her.'

'I don't believe you,' Patrick said, no conviction in his tone.

'That your father loved Maryellen?' That wasn't what Patrick had meant, but his mind was still mulling over all she had said and so he did not set her straight. 'Oh, he adored her. He was fond of your mother and he loved you without reservation, but Maryellen owned his heart. He said there were a lot of similarities between my own situation and his and that I should take every opportunity to grasp happiness because second chances were so rare.' She lifted one shoulder. 'And so when the fates conspired to give me the opportunity, I didn't hesitate.'

'Very touching.'

'My time with Samuel was too short. He died in a freak accident at the mill just a few years into our marriage and we had no children. I have always thought that was retribution for my not having told the truth.'

'It is very convenient that all the people who could authenticate your story are now dead.'

'Do you imagine I would have come here if I couldn't prove it?'

'I am still at a loss to understand why you did come. You have set people to watch me and those helping me *and* you had someone attack Heston. Even if I was inclined to believe you, that circumstance would give me pause.'

'It was that circumstance that made me decide to talk to you myself.' She fiddled absently with the cuff of her glove. 'As soon as I heard you had returned to the district, I had to decide whether or not to tell you the truth. That all depended upon how much curiosity you displayed about the past. Telling the truth does not reflect well upon me and will destroy the good reputation I have sought to acquire if you speak out. That is why I had people watching the most obvious places. Heston saw my man outside his cottage and confronted him. The man stupidly tried to intimidate him, Heston was pushed to the ground and I regret that he was injured. I gave no such orders and the man is no longer in my employ.'

'But I still cannot accept what you say without independent corroboration.'

She looked down at her hands. 'There is one thing in this whole sorry affair that I especially blame myself for.'

She extracted a letter from her reticule and handed it to Patrick. The seal looked old but was unbroken. It was also immediately recognisable as his own family's seal. Patrick smothered an oath when he recognised the hand that had addressed the letter to him. It was his father's.

'I should have given this to you ten years ago,' she said softly. 'I am so very sorry.'

19

Patrick had kept his promise and called at Pemberley immediately after luncheon to relate particulars of his astonishing interview with Agnes Gunther. Lydia was still reeling from those revelations as she and Patrick strolled together in the grounds.

'I find it hard to comprehend,' Lydia said, shaking her head as she erected her parasol against the fierce sun. 'There is no question, I suppose, that your father did write that letter.'

'None,' Patrick replied. 'His handwriting is untidy, due I suppose to his debilitated health. He wrote it over the course of several days, dating each new page, which was typical of his methodical mind. No, there is no doubt whatsoever.' He slapped his thigh with the flat of his hand. 'I just wish he had told me he was living on borrowed time. I deserved the opportunity to say goodbye.'

'He didn't want you to see him like that, I suppose,' Lydia replied.

Patrick expelled a deep sigh. 'Think of all the difficulties his not telling me caused.'

'But he thought he had told you by explaining everything in that letter. He wasn't to know that you wouldn't receive it for another ten years. If you want to direct your anger anywhere then Agnes Gunther is

the one who deserves it. If she had not withheld that letter from you...'
Lydia blinked. 'Why *did* she do that?'

'My father was dead and no one knew she hadn't poisoned him. If she admitted that she had not, she would not have achieved her heart's desire. The pater strongly encouraged her to put her all into the pursuit of happiness and so—'

'If you had received the letter, you would have known the truth and Gunther senior wouldn't have let her marry his son.'

'Yes, I would have known but it would still have been too late to save the mill. I most likely would not have gone to America seeking answers, would not have met Edward and would not have made enough money to return to England and restore my property.' He shrugged. 'If I had remained in England I would probably have had to sell Shannon House.'

'You sound as though you're making excuses for Agnes.' Lydia sent him a censorious smile. 'You liked her, I think. I knew you would be influenced by a pretty face and a little flattery.'

'She is attractive but she didn't try to use those wiles of hers on me that so concerned you. I think she was happy to finally have the truth revealed. She did love her husband. He died far too soon and they had no children. She could marry again but I don't think she will and now she is the one who suffers.'

'Then I am very sorry for her,' Lydia replied softly. 'But I also cannot help thinking about the other lives that were affected by her selfishness.'

'Hobson?'

'Yes, he married against his will to save his sister from being branded a murderess. And the woman he was forced to marry was his sister's accuser. No wonder Hobson is so curmudgeonly. How could Elsie have thought that a congenial marriage could be based on such a foundation?' Lydia shook her head. 'Although, what makes me qualified to speak about the *right* manner in which to approach matrimony is questionable.'

Patrick took her hand, placed it on his sleeve and squeezed her fingers. 'The loss of her brother's respect is one of the crosses Agnes has been forced to bear this past decade.'

Lydia stopped walking and fixed him with a wide-eyed look of condemnation. 'You defend her?'

'I didn't expect to like her and I wouldn't have you think that I was influenced by her pretty face.' Patrick shook his head. 'There was nothing in her nature that revealed the calculating, conniving character I anticipated being confronted with. Quite the reverse. There was a quiet dignity about her. She made mistakes and is tormented by them. I think she was pleased to finally relieve her conscience, but that doesn't mean I approve of what she did.' He shrugged. 'Still, she is far from the only person involved in this business who has been keeping guilty secrets.'

Lydia expelled a deep sigh. 'She was young and young people do foolish things. I speak from bitter experience.'

'Agnes has gone to see Hobson this afternoon. I insisted that she tell him the truth and she is more than ready to do so. Whether it's too late to heal that particular breach is anyone's guess, but she plans to try. And as to Hobson being forced into matrimony, at least he has Maisie to give him comfort.'

'Very true.'

They strolled on for a while, lost in their individual thoughts and, in Lydia's case, awareness engendered by the close proximity of a man she held in increasing affection. More than that. A gentleman who, had her circumstances been different, she might easily have fallen in love with. But Lydia simply wouldn't permit that to happen. The destruction of Patrick's family had been brought about by inappropriate love and a burning desire for revenge, and she simply refused to risk having history repeat itself.

She stole a glance at his handsome profile and was filled with a desire to smooth away the deep furrows etched in his forehead. She briefly considered reminding him that he was now free to search for his own heart's desire, but the words stuck in her throat. She might be able to ignore her own burgeoning feelings for him but wasn't quite that charitably minded.

'All I know,' he said a short time later, 'is that this entire business has confirmed my already strongly held belief that it would be safer to avoid the perils of matrimony altogether.'

'Quite so.' His words echoed her own thoughts. They absolutely did, even if hearing him voice them made her heart feel like a leaden weight inside her chest.

'This whole sorry business came about because my father carelessly impregnated a woman who was not his social equal. Admittedly, he was in love with her and did not stop loving her until his dying day. He said as much in his letter to me.'

'Perhaps that is why he didn't send for you. Telling you something like that to your face would have been a lot harder than committing it to paper.'

'Cowardice?' Patrick shrugged. 'The same thought had occurred to me.'

Lydia covered her mouth with her hand. 'I did not mean to imply that your papa was a coward.'

'We shall never know if he was afraid, ashamed or what his motives for telling Agnes but not me were. Still, I can't help feeling he should not have abandoned Jenson's daughter no matter what his father said. Jenson never got over his disappointment or desire for revenge. In a sense, his life was ruined too.'

'What did your father say in his letter about Edward Makepeace?'

'Oh, that was Jenson's final stipulation when making the loan that would supposedly save Shannon's Mill,' Patrick replied, bitterness in his tone. 'Edward, my father's first-born son, was to become his equal partner in the enterprise.'

'So that, if by some miracle your father had managed to rescue the failing business, you would not be the sole beneficiary.' Lydia shook her head. 'Such vindictiveness. Your only crime was to be your father's legitimate heir, and that was hardly your fault.'

'Jenson succeeded in his destructive purpose and I was left with a house I couldn't afford to maintain. I was probably supposed to be put in the ignominious position of selling a home that had been in my family for generations.'

'Reversing your roles. Jenson, the butler, was now the man of consequence.'

'I don't believe achieving his revenge gave him any peace of mind.'

Patrick's chuckle owed little to humour. 'If he knew that his own grandson was the cause of my salvation he would turn in his grave.'

'He has no business resting in peace.' Lydia inverted her chin. 'I fail to understand why it is perfectly acceptable to consider a person dislikeable in life but the moment he passes he is generally regarded as the finest fellow to have walked this earth.'

'Your candour is refreshing,' he replied with an amused chuckle.

'Oh bother. I so wanted to shock you.'

Patrick threw back his head and laughed. Lydia realised with a jolt that she was flirting with him. Old habits were clearly harder to break than she had previously realised.

'Who was it that threatened your Mr Heston and Mrs Bathgate?'

'I asked Agnes the same question. She said her husband, who knew the truth, heard of their suspicions and needed to keep them quiet.'

'I don't see why. They were married by then and nothing could change that.'

'Other than people taking the gossip seriously and looking upon Agnes as a murderess. Her own family believed that she was, a lot of people resented her for the way she improved her circumstances and I suppose her husband was trying to protect her.'

'He had a very unpleasant way of going about it.' Lydia paused. 'And Jessup, going from overseer to mill owner in his own right?'

Patrick shrugged. 'Money siphoned from my own father's mill, I should imagine, and payment from Gunther for doing his bidding. But I refuse to think about that since there is absolutely nothing I can do about it.'

'We were right in our supposition that Edward had sworn not to reveal the particulars of the arrangement to you and kept his word, even after his grandfather's death,' she said pensively. 'But he compensated by helping you to recoup your fortune.'

'He inherited my father's goodness of character.'

Lydia laughed. 'And you did not?'

'Certainly I did not. When Edward meets a person for the first time, he sees all their finer qualities whereas I, cynic that I am, always assume they want something from me.'

'Perhaps *you* should be the one to record all your acts of kindness in a journal.'

'Speaking of which.' He conducted her to a bench in a peaceful spot that overlooked the lake, seated himself beside her and offered her a smile that enhanced the richness of his brown eyes and further tested Lydia's resolve not to acknowledge her growing attraction towards him. 'I have not had an opportunity to ask you how you feel after your experience yesterday.'

'No lasting effects, other than a bruise on my shoulder and a few scrapes that will soon heal.'

'What you did was incredibly brave.'

She looked down at her lap, undeserving of his praise. 'Anyone would have—'

'But they did not.' He placed his index finger beneath her chin and forced her to meet his gaze. 'And do you know what moved me most about the entire affair?' She shook her head, dislodging his finger. He grasped her hand instead, lacing his fingers with hers and making it ten times harder for her to ignore the delicious shivers that invaded her body at the simple contact. 'When we got back here yesterday, I expected you to be overcome with delayed shock. But instead your only thought was to supply Maisie with another ribbon to add to her collection.' He framed her face with the fingers of the hand not holding hers. 'Putting the welfare of an insignificant child first is a sign of true goodness.' His smile widened as he lowered his voice to a gravelly purr. 'But fear not, your secret is safe with me.'

Lydia simply didn't know how to respond, how to convince him he was quite wrong about her character. 'You don't understand. Wickham, the things I...'

Her words trailed off and she was mortified when a fat tear slid down her cheek. He arrested its progress with his forefinger and seemed disturbed to have made her cry. Well, that was probably just as well. Gentlemen never knew how to behave when a lady cried in their presence. Wickham frequently made her cry and then fled the aftermath.

'Hush,' he said, brushing a curl back from her injured cheek with infinite gentleness and tucking it behind her ear. 'You have shed more than enough tears over the loss of your husband. If you honestly meant what you said a moment ago about not necessarily speaking well of the dead, then Wickham certainly doesn't qualify for fond recollections.' Her tears intensified. 'There, now I've made matters worse by insulting the memory of the man you loved and obviously still do. That was insensitive of me.'

'No, you don't understand.'

'Perhaps not, but I had no right to say such things.'

'What I meant is...' She paused to swallow back more tears. 'I haven't shed a single tear for Wickham up until now.'

'What!'

'I know.' She shrugged, wishing she had a handkerchief. Patrick anticipated her difficulty and handed her his. She thanked him and mopped her eyes. 'But the brutal truth is that I didn't love him.' She sent him a defiant look. 'There, I've said it. Now I give you leave to think as badly of me as I deserve.' She lowered her voice. 'You cannot possibly despise me more than I despise myself.'

'Ah, now I think I understand. Wickham charmed you into eloping and you justified such action by convincing yourself you were in love with him. But you soon discovered that was not the case because you saw his true character. Then you started to feel the terrible burden of guilt for the damage you might have caused to your family.'

'I *did* cause it, but since we are speaking frankly, my tears are not for Wickham but for the baby I lost when... Well, it doesn't matter.' Fresh tears spilled from the corners of her eyes. 'Every time I see a child such as Maisie, I think... I wonder if my baby might have been anything like her and if a stranger might have shown her some kindness at a time when she needed it the most. I am absolutely convinced it would have been a girl, you see.'

'Oh, my poor love.' Patrick enfolded her in his arms. 'You have held all this hurt inside of you for over a year and not discussed it with anyone?'

Lydia nodded against his chest, too choked with emotion to move away from his comforting presence, as she knew she ought. Instead, the tears that she had refused to shed since losing her husband and child streamed down her face. She sobbed against that broad shoulder of his while his large, capable hands swept across her back, soothing her, allowing her to lay the ghost of her regret. Gradually her sobs became intermittent hiccups but she kept her face buried, too embarrassed to meet his gaze and apologise for her breakdown. Instead she examined how she felt, and to her utter astonishment, it was as though a huge weight had been lifted from her shoulders.

'Better?' he asked softly.

'Actually, yes. Wickham was a wastrel. Everyone else could see that before I could but I was the one who had to live with his philandering and pretend everything was fine. Well, it was not fine. Constantly running from broken promises and growing debts is not my idea of fine. I'm not glad that he's dead but I don't regret his passing either.' Lydia sniffed rather inelegantly. 'But I do regret the loss of my baby, more than anyone could ever know.'

'I know it doesn't compensate, but you are young. You can have other children.'

'No, Patrick.' She set her chin in a stubborn line. 'I shall not marry again. I can't take that chance.'

'Because you were convinced you loved Wickham but quickly discovered he did not love you?'

'Well, yes, partly for that reason.'

Patrick chuckled. 'You are older and wiser and have learned from your youthful mistakes,' he said softly. 'Don't condemn yourself to a lonely life simply because you were taken in by an unprincipled cove.'

She sighed. 'You make it all sound so straightforward.'

'It doesn't need to be complicated.'

Finally Lydia lifted her head from his shoulder and found the courage to meet his gaze. His eyes burned with an unfathomable emotion that made it impossible for her to look away again. She didn't want to look away. She wanted to drown in the seductive depths of his glowing eyes and forget, just for a moment, all the reasons why it would be so unwise to relax her guard.

'Lydia.'

He spoke her name like a gentle caress and then he was kissing her.

As his lips firmed against hers, she realised that all their interactions had been leading up to this moment. She had known on a visceral level that he would kiss her and that she would want him to. Beyond that, she simply refused to think. Her eyes fluttered to a close as she forgot all the compelling reasons why she shouldn't kiss him back.

* * *

Caroline sat in her brother's carriage, watching Charles and Jane playing with their young daughter Emma, making the child giggle. They were on their way to Pemberley. Jane had been a jumble of anxiety since receiving Eliza's note about Lydia's exploits in Lambton the previous day and would not be happy until she had seen her sister with her own eyes and satisfied herself that she was not severely harmed.

Severely harmed? Caroline wanted to laugh at the absurdity, aware that she could never be that fortunate. She had been in Lambton, watching Mr Shannon from a discreet distance, more determined than ever to discover the secrets that he shared with Lydia but kept from her. Secrets that involved an old lady who grew herbs. She had seen Lydia throw herself into the path of that horse and, just for one blissful moment, had been sure she would not survive those flailing hooves.

Naturally, Lydia Wickham had come through with barely a scratch, saved the child and had been hailed a heroine by everyone who witnessed the event. Mortifyingly, Mr Shannon had then carried her through the village as though making some sort of declaration of intent. It was shocking. It was insupportable. It simply could not be permitted. Jealousy and rage had ricocheted through Caroline as she was forced to stand impotently by and watch as the man she intended to marry displayed public concern for another woman.

And not just any other woman. But a Bennet.

Mr Darcy was there. Caroline reluctantly conceded that he *was* related to Lydia. If she required carrying, and Caroline was perfectly sure that she did not and was merely using her exploits to draw attention to herself, then Mr Darcy ought to have carried her. Caroline wouldn't have minded that quite so much. He must feel nothing for Lydia other

than brotherly concern and tolerated her only because he had been
misguided enough to marry her sister.

The question that had plagued Caroline's mind ever since witnessing
Lydia's theatrics was whether her claims upon Mr Shannon's affections
were real. It would be very fast work, even by Bennet standards, if they
were, but Caroline couldn't take that chance. Finding out and doing
something to stop her was a priority. All her plans hinged upon Mr
Shannon proposing to her, and she would not have those plans over-
turned by another Bennet.

Not this time.

She had returned to Campton Park in a foul temper, anxious to be at
Pemberley where she would find the answers. Never had the restrictions
placed upon her, an unmarried female, been more irksome. Caroline
couldn't mention what she had seen in Lambton without answering
awkward questions about her own presence in a place she had no reason
to be. But she consoled herself with the knowledge that Eliza would
waste no time in apprising Jane of their sister's adventures.

Sure enough, Eliza's note had arrived in the morning post and Jane
had been in a fever of anxiety ever since, insisting that they go to
Pemberley so she could see Lydia with her own eyes. Caroline was
scarcely less anxious to be there, albeit for different reasons. She forced
herself to express concern and asked to be included in the party. Jane
didn't look especially pleased but agreed to it. Charles however had business with his steward and persuaded his wife to wait until after
luncheon, at which time he would be able to accompany her. For some
reason, Emma's presence was also deemed essential. Caroline failed to
understand why.

And now, at last, they were driving through Pemberley Park. Jane and
Charles were still occupied with their daughter, leaving Caroline to
watch the passing scenery. She glanced to her left, where the lake shim-
mered in the afternoon sunshine. Someone was sitting on a bench on its
opposite side. A very familiar someone. Caroline's heart lifted. Mr
Shannon was here! Delighted for this unexpected opportunity to further
her acquaintance with him, glad that she had worn her most flattering

afternoon gown, she wondered why he was sitting alone beside Mr Darcy's lake and how she could contrive to join him there.

Then she noticed he was not alone.

Lydia!

A familiar black blaze of anger blurred Caroline's vision as they drew closer and she could see that Mr Shannon was actually kissing her.

20

The sound of a carriage making its way up the driveway brought Patrick to his senses. He released Lydia, blood pounding through his head, and lower. What in the name of Hades had caused him to act so impulsively? Permitting instinct to trump willpower could easily excite the sort of expectations he had spent the past decade assiduously avoiding.

Fool!

Patrick fought to control his ragged breathing, adjuring himself to back away from her, but the devil of it was that he didn't want to. He smiled into grey eyes rendered hazy with passion, reinforcing his conviction that the usual rules did not apply in Lydia's case. She looked so touchingly vulnerable that the desire to finish what he had started, to offer reassurance in its basest form, was almost impossible to resist. But resist it he absolutely must. He probably ought to apologise as well but couldn't find the right words. Apologising for something that felt so utterly right was quite simply beyond him.

'That is Mr Bingley's carriage,' Lydia said, glancing towards the vehicle in question, her voice a husky, intoxicating whisper.

'I dare say your sister heard about your heroics and is anxious about you.'

She looked confused, embarrassed, and was unable to meet his gaze.

Staying here with her until she recovered her composure when he no longer knew his own mind would be sheer folly.

'Lydia, I—'

'Jane will want to see me,' she said, abruptly getting to her feet.

Patrick stood too, offered her his arm and they crossed the manicured lawns together in tense silence. They slipped through the open doors to the drawing room just as the new arrivals were shown into it. Mrs Bingley flew across the room to Lydia and embraced her.

'I was beside myself when I received Lizzy's note. Are you sure you are unharmed?'

'Perfectly sure, Jane. Just a few scrapes and bruises. There was no need for you to dash all the way here on my account.'

'Your poor cheek.'

'You were incredibly brave, by all accounts,' Bingley said, sending Lydia a warm smile. 'The heroine of the hour.'

'Hardly that.'

Lydia flashed a modest smile as she took a seat beside Mrs Darcy and accepted a cup of tea from her. Patrick could see that she was still distracted and that it was costing her a supreme effort of will to appear normal.

Caroline Bingley was there and had yet to say a word to Lydia, contenting herself with sending Patrick speaking looks from beneath lowered lashes. Patrick had been the recipient of such looks from determined females too often in the past to mistake the signs. Those females had driven him from America, but he was damned if Miss Bingley would drive him from his home here in Derbyshire. He acknowledged her presence with the minimum of civility. She was too self-aware for his tastes, too ready to treat those whom she considered to be her social inferiors with aloof indifference, and Patrick found her lack of empathy unattractive. He moved as far away from her as possible and stood beside Bingley on the other side of the room.

'I am glad you are unharmed, Mrs Wickham,' Miss Bingley finally remarked with patent insincerity.

'Thank you,' Lydia replied succinctly, her tone sweetly sarcastic.

Childish laughter broke the tension when Marcus Darcy was

brought down to become reacquainted with his cousin. The babies were permitted to play on the rug under the watchful eye of Marcus's nanny and the indulgent gazes of two sets of doting parents. Patrick's own gaze confined itself to Lydia. She had fallen to her knees and was joining in the children's game, handing them bricks with which to build a rickety tower and laughing with them when they smote it to the ground again. He imagined she must be thinking of her lost child.

The conversation became more general when the children were taken away again and Patrick started to think about returning home. Before he could do so, Mrs Darcy issued an invitation for him to remain for dinner. He ought to refuse. He was becoming far too engrossed with Mrs Wickham. One glance at the destructive artillery of that lady's eyes, and he accepted with thanks. As did the Bingleys.

* * *

When the children were taken back to the nursery, Lydia excused herself and slipped back out into the garden, anxious for solitude in which to untangle her jumbled emotions. Patrick had made her understand that it was all right to have negative feelings about her disastrous marriage, removing a healthy wedge of the guilt she had been harbouring. She walked across the lawns with a lighter step than she had managed since Wickham's passing. One kiss, spontaneously delivered, had temporarily made her forget the heartrending agony she had experienced when love and fidelity did not coalesce. That kiss had probably meant nothing to him, she reminded herself. It had been intended to soothe and reassure and so Lydia would treat it equally casually and consider herself to have been duly soothed and reassured by it.

Eventually.

She wandered without conscious thought of walking in that direction towards the bench on the banks of the lake – the exact same bench that she and Patrick had occupied a short time ago. She touched lips that still burned from the intense passion of his kiss and fell victim to the renewed desire that spun its delicate thread through her body.

She wanted him. There, she had admitted it, albeit to herself. An air of expectancy sprang up between them whenever they were in the same room; she just hadn't been ready to acknowledge the fact before now. Hadn't felt worthy of his regard. She waited for guilt to outweigh desire, but to her astonishment it did not. It was as though her mind was giving her body permission to follow its instincts.

She knew what she would have to do. Patrick wasn't interested in matrimony. Nor was she, but she would willingly become his mistress. She felt her cheeks warm, a little shocked by her brazenness but still convinced she had hit upon the ideal solution. They would have to be very discreet, of course. Lizzy would not approve, but she didn't need to know, not if they were very careful. And when she was not with him, she could occupy her time writing the novel she had promised herself she would attempt. The idea had lodged in her brain and her enthusiasm for the project endured, but she would keep it to herself, at least for the time being. She would probably fail miserably and would prefer for people not to know she had been unsuccessful at something so ambitious.

She looked across the lake, tranquil in all its summer glory, barely a breath of wind to agitate its glassy, torpid surface. Perhaps the role of mistress had always been her destiny. She would play it well, be carefree and not cling. But most importantly of all, she would give the performance of her life and not frighten Patrick away by ever letting him see that she had fallen desperately in love with him.

She had been honest with herself, admitted to her feelings, and the experience was liberating. Now, all she had to do was put her plan into practice. When she heard footsteps approaching, she felt absolutely sure it must be Patrick, coming to look for her.

She swallowed down her disappointment when she glanced up and saw that it was not.

* * *

Caroline thought her head would explode if she heard one more word about Lydia's heroics. Really, such a fuss. But worse, far worse, was Patrick Shannon's apparent fixation with the woman. She was well aware that Lydia's moral conduct could charitably be described as loose and that she made a convincingly fragile widow. Really, men were so easily manipulated when their protective instincts were called into play. In such situations, what they actually needed was protecting from themselves.

Never more so than in Mr Shannon's case since it seemed he was falling for Lydia's questionable charms and rather obvious attempts to... to what precisely? She recalled the kiss she witnessed them sharing but failed to convince herself there could be any innocent explanation for it. The question remained: did Mr Shannon plan to take her for a mistress, or did he have something more permanent in mind?

Caroline's head buzzed, signalling the onset of one of her episodes. Dear God, not now! If ever a situation called for a clear head and sound reasoning, this was it. She struggled to appear calm as the conversation continued to centre upon Lydia Wickham, even though she had slipped out into the grounds and was no longer there to enjoy the accolades heaped upon her. Patrick Shannon, she noticed, kept glancing at the door through which she had left, as though he planned to follow her.

Enough!

If she remained here she would say or do something she might later regret. Better to follow Lydia herself and put her straight on one or two matters. Having the odious child spoil her carefully laid plans was quite simply out of the question.

The part of Caroline's brain still capable of rational thought balked at following Lydia when on the point of an 'episode'. She recalled the advice she had been given by the doctors in London after she tried to rescue her beloved Darcy from his travesty of a marriage. She was supposed to breathe deeply and find a soothing occupation that concentrated her mind away from the cause of her agitation. Pursuing Lydia would be flying in the face of that advice, but for the fact that the doctors didn't know what they were talking about. She had fooled them all, aware that if she was declared temporarily out of her wits, she would be absolved of blame for what she had been drawn into and eventually readmitted to Pemberley and Darcy's precious company.

That was precisely how matters had turned out. If she still occasionally felt like two different people, she had learned to live with both aspects of her character. She was sane and rational, perfectly capable of ridding herself of Lydia Wickham's interference once and for all.

No one appeared to notice her slipping out onto the terrace. She breathed deeply, in perfect control, but for the continued buzzing and descending fog inside her head. She didn't allow such trivialities to deter her, reminding herself that she had learned to manage her 'episodes'. She walked towards the lake, where Lydia sat on the same bench she had occupied with Mr Shannon a little earlier, a remote expression on her face. Really, the child had no shame.

'Oh, hello,' Lydia said with minimum civility, looking up as Caroline approached.

'I thought I would find you here.'

'Really? Is there something I can do for you?'

'You can leave Mr Shannon alone.'

Lydia widened her eyes. 'I beg your pardon?'

'I believe I spoke in plain English. Mr Shannon is a respectable gentleman and does not need his reputation sullied by association with the likes of you.'

Lydia waved a hand in casual dismissal. 'If you have come out here to insult me then you can save your breath. I don't respond well to threats.'

Lud, this was not going the way Caroline had hoped. The child dared to sneer at her, causing Caroline's grip on her emotions to slip and for darkness to take a tighter hold on her brain. 'Don't imagine I am not aware of the particulars of your hastily arranged marriage to Wickham. You cannot expect a man of Mr Shannon's morality to take on such a person.'

'Ah, now I understand. You think I have hopes of marrying Mr Shannon. Even supposing that I do, why that should be any concern of yours is beyond me.'

'Is that your intention?'

Lydia shrugged. 'We are friends.'

'Then you will be aware that he and I have an understanding.'

Lydia gaped at her, then had the audacity to actually laugh. Caroline cursed the blackness, the buzzing and ringing that had caused her to overplay her hand. Why on earth had she made such an assertion? It made her sound desperate and jealous and could easily be disproven if Lydia and Mr Shannon really were on friendly terms.

'If you have an understanding, I fail to imagine why you think Mr Shannon has an interest in me.' She flapped a hand, sounding disinterested. 'I'll thank you to leave me be. We have nothing more to say to one another.'

'Mr Shannon didn't take his eyes off you in the drawing room just now.'

Lydia shrugged. 'Then perhaps you ought to renegotiate your understanding.'

Rage and resentment joined forces with the darkness. Caroline knew she was losing her grasp on rationality and struggled to hold back the words that sprang to her lips. She fought the demons, bit her tongue so hard that she tasted blood trickling down her throat. She ought to return to the house before she made an even bigger fool of herself. But it was too late to retreat because the darkness had won its battle with rationality.

'You are a disgrace!' she screamed, spittle dribbling down her chin. 'Your sister stole Mr Darcy from me and now you seek to take Mr Shannon.'

'Are you quite well, Miss Bingley?' Lydia asked. She stood, her nonchalant expression replaced with one of genuine-seeming concern that infuriated Caroline. She didn't need pity, especially not from Lydia Wickham. She reached out and slapped the injured side of Lydia's face with considerable force, causing her to reel backwards, teetering for balance on the bank of the lake. Lydia windmilled her arms in an effort to retain her balance. 'Help me!' she cried, holding out a hand. 'I'm going to fall.'

'With pleasure.'

With a malicious smirk, Caroline placed a hand in the centre of Lydia's chest and pushed. Lydia fell into the lake with a cry and a loud splash. It was immediately apparent from the way she panicked that she couldn't swim.

'Help me, for pity's sake!' she yelled, pulling weed from her mouth and pushing sodden hair from her eyes.

Caroline finally held out a hand and Lydia reached for it. But instead of pulling her from the water, Caroline placed her other hand on top of Lydia's head, released the hand she had been holding and held her under the surface. Lydia was stronger than she looked and fought like the devil. But Caroline knew for a certainty that when it came to demons they were firmly on her side. They were her closest friends and they were urging her to do this. She laughed manically when Lydia opened her mouth and it filled with water.

Then Lydia abruptly stopped struggling.

* * *

The drawing room seemed dull without Lydia in it. Patrick was concerned to see Miss Bingley follow her outside and had a bad feeling about her intentions. He excused himself and slipped back into the garden, scanning the wide expanse to see where Lydia might be, wanting to reassure himself that she was safe.

He saw movement down by the lake. It lifted his spirits to think she might have deliberately returned to that spot where he had recently kissed her, and he headed in the same direction himself. As he got closer he heard a splash, then shouting. Then nothing. Something was terribly wrong! He sprinted the rest of the distance and his heart turned to stone when he observed Miss Bingley holding something beneath the water. Something that struggled against her but didn't succeed in breaking the surface.

Blazes, the woman was trying to drown Lydia!

In two strides he reached the mad female, unrecognisable at that moment as the sophisticated Miss Bingley. Patrick physically dragged her away from Lydia and threw her to the ground, protesting.

'I was trying to pull her out! You must help her. She can't swim.'

Patrick didn't believe a word of it. He knew what he had seen but the time for recriminations would come later. Patrick waded into the shallows, reached for Lydia and pulled her from the water. She was deathly pale and he couldn't be sure she was breathing. His heart stalled. If she was dead, if Miss Bingley had killed her in a dispute over him – and

Patrick sensed that was what all this was about – then he would die himself. He scooped Lydia into his arms and carried her back to dry land, still unsure if she was breathing. He laid her on the bench and leaned over her, frantically searching for a pulse.

'What happened?' Darcy asked, panting as he joined Patrick. 'We heard a commotion.'

'She fell,' Miss Bingley said from her prone position. 'I tried to help her.'

Patrick sent her a scathing glance as he felt for a pulse. It was there. Faint, but it was there.

'Send for Sanford,' Darcy barked to a footman who had followed them out.

Patrick tried to recall what action was taken when he saw someone fall into a lake in America. Clear the airways, he thought, opening Lydia's mouth and checking it for obstructions. There were none. He pinched her nose, and breathed into her mouth, repeating the process with increasing desperation until she finally coughed and water spewed from her mouth. Patrick was dimly aware of her sisters anxiously standing close by and of Miss Bingley alternately keening and then protesting a little too loudly that she had been trying to save her.

After what seemed like an eternity, Lydia's eyes blinked open.

'Welcome back,' he said softly. 'You gave us quite a fright. Can you move?'

She wiggled her fingers and nodded, her teeth chattering. Patrick removed his coat and wrapped her in it. Considering it safe to move her, he swept her into his arms.

'This is starting to become a habit,' he said, carrying her back to the house with the rest of the party following in their wake.

* * *

Several hours later, Lizzy returned to the drawing room. Will and Mr Shannon were standing in front of the fireplace, glasses of whisky in hand, and turned to look at her expectantly.

'How is she?' they asked together.

'Sleeping,' Lizzy replied, feeling drained and exhausted. 'Dominic gave her something to make her sleep.'

'She was lucky,' Dominic Sanford said, walking into the room in Lizzy's wake. 'Another minute or two and it might have ended very differently. As it is, she ought to be fine after a good night's sleep, physically at least. It might take longer for the nightmares to subside.'

'Poor Jane,' Lizzy said, throwing herself into a chair. 'And poor Mr Bingley. I have never seen anyone half so shocked.'

'There is no question, I suppose, that she tried to deliberately drown Lydia?' Will asked.

'None whatsoever,' Lizzy replied. 'Mr Shannon saw her holding Lydia's head under the water and Lydia herself has confirmed it.'

'What I don't understand,' Mr Shannon said, 'is why?'

'Unbeknown to me,' Will replied, 'she'd harboured expectations of becoming my wife. I gave her no encouragement, but Bingley and I spent a lot of time in one another's company before our marriages. Caroline Bingley kept house for her brother and so we were often thrown together.' Will shrugged. 'With the benefit of hindsight I suppose I ought to have suspected something when she persuaded me that her brother's interest in Lizzy's sister was unsuitable.'

'We think she had noticed Will's partiality for me,' Lizzy explained.

'When I married Lizzy, Caroline Bingley and Wickham formed an alliance to try and cause trouble for us,' Will added, grinding his jaw.

'And now it seems she is fixated on you, Mr Shannon,' Lizzy added. 'Lydia told me she sought her out in the garden specifically to warn her away from you.'

'Me! I haven't encouraged Miss Bingley.'

Lizzy shrugged. 'No encouragement is necessary. Her mind is fragile, she hates my family and... well, she will have to be kept confined now, I suppose. She is a danger to herself and everyone she comes into contact with.'

'Bingley has asked if Jane can stay here until he has made arrangements for Caroline. I have never seen him nearly so overset. Naturally, I agreed.' Will shook his head. 'He has already left for Campton Park and taken his sister with him. He plans to take her straight to London and consult with the doctors who treated her previously.' He looked tired and severe as he scrubbed a hand down his face. 'Whatever decisions are made regarding her future, I think it safe to assume we shall not see Caroline Bingley in Derbyshire again.'

'I am very glad to hear it,' Lizzy said with feeling.

'I ought to take my leave,' Patrick said, putting aside his glass. 'May I call tomorrow afternoon and see how Mrs Wickham is faring?'

'I think you have earned the right, Mr Shannon,' Lizzy replied with a warm smile, 'seeing that you saved her life.'

21

When she woke the following day, Lydia could see through a gap in the drapes that the sun was high in the sky. Lizzy and Jane were both sitting beside her bed and looked as though they had been there for a considerable amount of time.

'How do you feel?' they asked together.

'Better, I think.'

'Oh, Lydia!' Jane cried, looking genuinely distressed. 'I am so very sorry about Caroline. Whatever made her do such a wicked thing?'

'She had her sights set on Mr Shannon,' Lydia rasped, shuddering as she recalled the burning in her lungs, the dizziness as blackness closed in. Her struggles had become weaker and her lungs filled with water as she felt her life slipping away. 'She thought I stood in her way.'

'She isn't rational,' Lizzy said, patting Lydia's hand. 'Mr Bingley has taken her to London, and the Hursts have gone with him. We shall not see Caroline in Derbyshire again.'

Lydia sighed. 'She really did intend to kill me and is getting away lightly.'

'Mr Shannon rescued you,' Lizzy said.

'I remember that much.' She blinked back tears. 'But it is all rather hazy.'

'It will save you nightmares if you don't remember anything at all,' Jane said, mopping her eyes with her handkerchief.

'This must be very hard for you and Mr Bingley,' Lydia said, reaching for Jane's hand. Even that small effort exhausted her. 'But you could not have foreseen what she intended.'

'Would you like some breakfast?' Lizzy asked.

'Yes. Something that will be soft on my throat. And then I shall get up.'

'Are you sure?' Jane asked. 'You've suffered a terrible ordeal.'

'Absolutely sure. And I would like a bath as well, if it's no trouble.'

Lizzy smiled. 'None whatsoever.'

Lydia lingered in her bath and slowly came alive again as she thought about her narrow escape. She had been given a second chance to live and would not squander it. She saw everything with crystal clarity now and would not waste another second on regrets. A 'disappointment' she might be, but she would no longer permit that knowledge to hold her back. She had thought of an increasing number of incidents when she had been kind to her sisters. She had also rescued Maisie without making a conscious decision to act. She had done so instinctively because it was the right thing to do. If she could throw herself in the path of a spooked horse, she could most certainly find the courage to offer herself to Patrick as his mistress.

And she knew exactly how to go about it.

Mid-afternoon, after she had seen Patrick ride up to the house, she descended the stairs slowly and entered the drawing room, where Lizzy and Mr Darcy, Jane and Patrick were gathered. Everyone expressed their pleasure at seeing her up and about again. Patrick said little, but then he didn't need to. His gaze lingered upon her pink muslin gown and she knew they understood one another perfectly.

After refreshments had been taken, Patrick asked if she felt strong enough to walk in the grounds with him. Lydia accepted and was glad when instead of heading in the direction of the lake, Patrick steered her towards the rose garden. They meandered without speaking, a tense expectancy making it hard for Lydia to think of a suitable topic. Their walk took them to the bench they had occupied once before and when

Patrick stopped walking, Lydia seated herself. Patrick took the space beside her and claimed her hand.

'I was right about pink,' he said. 'It is exactly the right colour for you. Ought I to take it as an act of defiance?'

'Certainly you should. I refuse to allow Miss Bingley to have the final word.'

He caressed her with his eyes. 'I wasn't referring to Miss Bingley.'

'I suppose I ought to be grateful to her in some respects. Coming so close to death tends to clarify one's thoughts.'

'You no longer consider yourself to be a disappointment?'

'Oh, I shall always be that.' Lydia waved her free hand nonchalantly. 'The difference now is that I will not permit it to hold me back.'

An enticing smile illuminated his features. 'I am very glad to hear you say so.'

'I have decided that life is too short to allow for procrastination.'

'I agree, but—'

'And so I shall speak my mind.' She swallowed and somehow found the courage to meet his gaze. 'We are attracted to one another?'

He nodded. 'Most certainly.'

'We excite one another's passions?' Lydia added, her cheeks flaming.

'That is certainly true,' he agreed, playing with the fingers of the hand he held. 'But it begs the question, what is to be done about it?'

'Precisely. And so I have a proposition for you,' Lydia said primly.

Patrick looked discouragingly alarmed. 'You intend to proposition me?'

She tossed her head to disguise her embarrassment. 'Evidently there is nothing wrong with your hearing.'

He chuckled. 'What is your proposition?'

'Well... that I become your mistress.'

He abruptly dropped her hand. 'My what?'

'Is that all you have to say?' she asked, miffed.

'Thank you for your offer but I must respectfully decline.'

'Oh.' Her cheeks burned with additional mortification. 'I obviously misunderstood the situation. Please excuse me. I thought it would be an ideal solution, but you had best forget I spoke.'

Lydia tried to stand but a strong arm snaked its way around her waist and pulled her back down again. 'Why the dickens would I want you for a mistress, sweet Lydia?'

'Do I need to spell it out?' *Really, the man is insufferable!* 'We neither of us want to marry, we have needs and I know what is expected of—'

'I respect and admire you too much to toy with your sensibilities.' One large hand gently framed her jaw as he ran the pad of his thumb across her lips. 'In short, although I haven't known you for long, I already know that I love you with a passion that will not be denied.'

'Love!' Lydia's mouth fell open. 'You? Love? Me?'

'Yes, you, my sweet.' He chuckled, presumably in response to her incredulous expression. She considered she was perfectly entitled to feel incredulity. Surely he didn't imagine that she had... well, imagined he was in love with her? 'And I want you very much indeed. Not as my mistress, but as my wife.'

'You... your wife.' She shook her head, convinced she must have misheard him. 'But you don't want to marry. You are adamantly opposed to the institution.'

'Because I had not met a woman worth changing my mind for.' He fixed her with an intent look. 'When I saw Miss Bingley trying to drown you, I thought my own life would come to an end if you didn't survive. That was when I knew for certain.'

Lydia could see sincerity in his eyes and knew he believed what he said. But surely it was too soon for him to be sure? He was still caught up in the drama of the previous day and emotions were running high. 'I'm not sure what to say.'

His sensual smile did strange things to her insides. '"Yes" would be delightful.'

'But the risks... What if I make more mistakes and—'

'Hush, don't imagine I am another Wickham.' He raised her hand to his lips and kissed the back of it. 'I will love and cherish you and give you not the slightest reason to doubt my constancy.'

She blinked back her surprise. 'How did you know that was my main concern?'

Patrick snorted. 'Because I know how Wickham used to behave.'

Lydia fell into momentary contemplation. Dare she? It felt so right. She was sorely tempted, but what if she failed to live up to his expectations? There again, there were no guarantees in life and if she had learned nothing else since her foolhardy marriage to Wickham, at least she knew that happiness ought to be grasped with both hands before it slipped out of reach.

'Do you need time to consider?' he asked.

'No.' She smiled at the uncertainty in his eyes. 'No, I do not. I love you, Patrick, and never thought I would have the chance to tell you. Indeed, I had promised myself I never would for fear of frightening you away.' She wrapped her arms around his neck, her head swirling again, but this time with happiness. 'Yes, if you really want to take a chance on me, I will certainly marry you.'

With a whoop of delight, Patrick claimed her lips to seal the bargain.

* * *

Lizzy and Will watched the scene in the rose garden from the nursery window. Lizzy sighed when Mr Shannon took Lydia in his arms.

'You see,' she said. 'I told you so.'

'What will you do now, Mrs Darcy?' Will asked, standing close behind her and wrapping an arm around her waist. 'It looks as though Lydia is about to become Mrs Shannon, Mary is on the brink of marrying her curate and you will have no sisters' fates to worry over.'

'Oh, I shall not mind that,' she replied, turning to face her beloved husband and nodding in the direction of their children, all three of them asleep at the same time for once. 'I shall reserve my worries for Pemberley's next generation.'

ABOUT THE AUTHOR

Eliza Austin is the Regency romance pen name of prolific, bestselling author Wendy Soliman. Wendy has written historical romance, revenge thrillers and cosy crime.

Sign up to Eliza Austin's mailing list for news, competitions and updates on future books.

Follow Eliza on social media here:

facebook.com/wendy.soliman.author

x.com/wendyswriter

bookbub.com/authors/wendy-soliman

ALSO BY ELIZA AUSTIN

Pemberley Presents

Miss Bingley's Revenge

Lady Catherine's Demands

The Daring Miss Darcy

Kitty Bennet's Ruin

The Scandalous Lydia Wickham

You're cordially invited to

The
Scandal
Sheet

The home of swoon-worthy historical romance from the Regency to the Victorian era!

Warning: may contain spice 🌶

Sign up to the newsletter

https://bit.ly/thescandalsheet

Boldwood

Boldwood Books is an award-winning fiction publishing company seeking out the best stories from around the world.

Find out more at www.boldwoodbooks.com

Join our reader community for brilliant books, competitions and offers!

Follow us
@BoldwoodBooks
@TheBoldBookClub

Sign up to our weekly deals newsletter

https://bit.ly/BoldwoodBNewsletter

9 781836 033042